The Curiosity of Water Closets

A Novel by

Paula J. Knight

This is a work of fiction. Any similarities between the characters and any person or persons, living or dead, is purely coincidental.
Copyright © 2014 by Paula J. Knight

Wooly Whippet Publishing
All Rights Reserved

Dedicated to
Cecelia Bernadette McCarthy,
My maternal grandmother,
who showed me the true meaning of family.

CHAPTER **ONE**

Kayla Battaglia shook the cobwebs from her head while she turned the water on in the shower. It was going to be a long day in CAT scan since it was a twelve hour shift on what should have been her day off. When she heard the sirens less than an hour ago, she knew her phone would be ringing and she would be called in to work. She had rolled over in bed, covering her head as if it would all go away. It didn't. She showered quickly, pulled on her scrubs and headed out the door for another fun day at Youngstown Regional Hospital.

By the time she pulled into the parking lot, the x-ray department slots were nearly full and she could see the red flashing lights of several ambulances emanating from the direction of the emergency room. Whatever had happened must have been a whopper from the look of things. Just don't let it be children, she really hated it when bad things happened to children.

Kayla punched the time clock and headed for her department. Everyone was in the report room getting ready to hear the gory details of their impending patients. She took her seat in the corner and pulled out her small spiral notebook that kept her organized and began jotting down notes as the report began. MVA involving 3 cars and a semi on Rt. 22; head injuries; fractures; one DOA; three rooms in use for x-rays and scanning. She felt the need to call for a huddle with everyone's hands interlocked yelling "1,2,3 CAT!" At a mere five foot three inches with a head full of curly blonde hair, reminiscent of a young Shirley Temple, she knew a day like this would require a lot of assistance from the orderlies and PCT's as well, to move these patients around in a quick, yet orderly, manner. Yes, this job was definitely a team effort.

The day flew by as she ran back and forth from the CAT scan room, to the office and back to the CAT. There were multiple injuries, some life threatening, so she moved gently but quickly with each scan. Thank goodness Ron Marshall and Jimmy Rayland, two of the ER orderlies, were sent over today! It made it so much easier to transfer the patients from the scanner to the gurney. Kayla was a bit vertically challenged and usually wound up climbing up into the bed with the patient and literally crawling across them while transferring. Her cracking knees were her testimonial to that. Ron and Jimmy made very quick work of transfers as she had expected. At the end of the day, they had transferred eight patients sixteen different times. Thank goodness none of them were children.

When the shift was over, Ron asked her if she wanted to go out for a bite to eat, but she declined, requesting a rain check. Kayla was just too tired to go anywhere, and she didn't really want Ron to think that she was interested in him. Ron was a decent enough fellow, moderately attractive, even with his thick black glasses, but Kayla genuinely had no interest in dating. She had a full life with her job, local theater troupe and church activities. At thirty-two, she knew her window of opportunity was slowly closing, but she had no intention of getting involved with someone simply because she was desperate for a child of her own. Maybe one day she would be inseminated at a sperm bank and get it over with...after she got her Master's Degree.

Kayla carefully checked her external environment and shone her pocket flashlight into the back seat before unlocking the door of her VW Bug. She had an irrational fear of being attacked in the parking lot which had created her ritualistic behavior after work. She, personally, had never been nor known anyone who had been a victim of such an attack. Perhaps she had been watching IDTV too much lately. Once she felt secure she called her best friend, Erika Livingston, to ask if she wanted to get some pizza and beer.

Erika was a big girl, five foot eight with curves in all the right places. She was loud and obnoxious, the polar opposite of Kayla and perhaps that's why they got along so well. Sometimes it is true that opposites attract. Erika's dark, medium length tresses were always astray, giving her a devil may care look. And Erika wasn't afraid to go after what she wanted nor ashamed of her methodology. Something Kayla would never be able to accomplish.

"Hey Kayla, what's up, girlfriend?"

"Hey Erika, what are you doing for supper tonight?"

"Supper, it's after seven o'clock, K. I've already have supper. Right now I'm getting ready for dessert."

"Watching NCIS again are you? I promise you, Tony is not coming out of that screen so that you can have your way with him! Get real!"

"Very funny. As a matter of fact, I have a huge slice of peanut butter pie with RediWhip on it. Why not come over and have a piece with me?"

"And you wonder why every fad diet you try doesn't work. I can't imagine that any of them list peanut butter pie with RediWhip on their list of permissible foods! I'll pass. I'm tired anyway, so I'm going to head home. See you at work tomorrow?"

"Yes, I'm on the graveyard shift, though. So we will be like ships passing in the night."

Kayla continued her drive home, pulling into her attached garage twenty minutes later. She reset the alarm once she was safely in the kitchen, her little terrier, Spinner, bouncing off the walls at the sight of his mistress. She dropped her purse on the counter, let him outside and opened the refrigerator to find some dinner for the two of them.

Spinner returned and waited patiently while his dinner was prepared, wagging his tail incessantly. When his bowl was placed on the floor, he dove in and chowed down, making quick work of the meal. Kayla rummaged around until she found some sustenance for herself, a pepperoni Hot Pocket, then moved into the den and turned on the television. She absolutely hated the rerun season, there was nothing worth watching. She rummaged around through her video library and selected her favorite movie, "The Thirteenth Warrior", and plugged it into the machine. She could think of worse ways to spend the evening than watching Antonio Banderas riding a beautiful Arabian horse and showing those Norsemen what he was made of. When the movie finished Kayla let Spinner out in the yard for his last evening constitutional, and then joined him in her huge queen size bed.

When the alarm went off, Kayla saw that she had a text message on her cell phone. She opened the text and was happy to see that her boss was giving her the day off since she had gone in yesterday to help with the big accident. Spinner didn't move causing Kayla to cover her head and roll over, making a concerted effort to go back to sleep. Sweet sleep, however, never returned. She got up, showered and started her exciting day, cleaning the house.

Around noon, there was a knock at the door, causing Spinner to go into orbit, barking and racing and jumping on the couch to look out the window, nearly pulling down the sheers. Kayla coaxed him into his crate so that she could answer it. A large envelope was shoved in her direction by the postman. She grimaced, then obliged him and signed for the registered letter, having no idea what it was. As she went back inside with it, the phone rang, causing her to lose her focus. She put the letter down on top of the television while she went for the phone call.

"Hello."

"Oh, um, hi Kayla, I was worried about you when you didn't come to work today. Are you sick?"

"No, no Ron, I'm fine. I got today off because I came in for twelve hours yesterday. Nothing to worry about."

"That's good. I just wanted to make sure you were okay. Will you be here tomorrow?"

"Yes, I am scheduled tomorrow. Thanks for calling. Bye."

Kayla hung up the phone feeling a bit creeped out. How did he get her phone number? It was listed in the phonebook, so she supposed it was easily available. Perhaps she should get an unlisted number. You never knew what kind of kooks were out there. She rarely even used her land line. The only person that called her regularly was Erika, so why did her number need to be listed? She picked up the phone and called the phone company to request a new number and to have it unlisted. She didn't even know why she kept that line anymore. Her cell phone was her primary one anyway. Oh well, she would try the unlisted one for a while, perhaps cancelling the land line sometime soon.

Spinner was whimpering in his crate causing Kayla to be distracted yet again from the letter she had received. She opened the door and he came bounding out, heading for the dog door in the laundry room. It was a beautiful day so she joined him in the yard, throwing tennis balls until he was exhausted. When she saw that it was one o'clock she rushed back inside to watch her soap operas. It was a rare day that she could sit on the couch and enjoy them rather than tape them and watch them after work. Grabbing a diet coke and a bag of pretzels, she settled in for the next three hours. Yes, her life was very exciting.

CHAPTER **TWO**

The next few days were extremely hectic for Kayla, between working twelve hour shifts, meetings with her church group and grabbing a bite to eat on the run with Erika. She made futile attempts to avoid Ron at work. She didn't really know why, but she just didn't want to get involved with him or anyone else for that matter. She had been alone so long that she had no interest in having to cater to another person. Her life was predictable and quiet, and she liked it that way.

When the weekend rolled around Kayla remembered that she had promised Erika that they would have a 'girls' day out', which would include shopping, dinner and a movie. She had left the movie selection to Erika while she chose a small Italian restaurant for the meal. They entered the mall just after two in the afternoon, surprised at how empty the place was.

"Hell, it's a ghost town in here today. I don't know how the place stays open."

"Well, with all the jobs being shipped out and the steel mill closing, I'm not surprised, Erika. No one has any money to spend on anything other than the bare necessities."

"I know, it's a shame, really. The Ohio Valley is a dying metropolis. Thank goodness we work in the medical profession. There will always be sick people no matter where we go."

"So sad, but true. Do you ever get tired of the same old routine, though? I would love to go back to school so I could move onward and upward."

"Nah, I don't mind being a lab technician. I can work out my frustrations without anyone knowing it. Stabbing people with needles is good for me!"

"You are one sadistic woman, Erika. I think you were a vampire in your previous life."

"I do have to admit there are some men whose blood I would like to suck, among other things!"

"Gawd, you have a dirty mind!"

Erika nodded, checking out the eye candy who had just sold them their tickets. They turned into the theater and settled into their seats for the newest version of 007.

Two and a half hours later they emerged, the lights of the hallway blinding them.

"That Daniel Craig is one hot Bond, eh, Kayla?"

"It was a good movie, but I still prefer Sean Connery. I just melt when I hear that brogue!"

"You always were a sucker for a kilt. I just don't see it. A man in a skirt is just not my style."

Kayla shrugged. She knew Erika would never understand that she believed that she had lived in Europe a previous life. It was the only explanation for her fondness for kilts, bagpipes, and rolling green hills.

As they were driving back to Kayla's house for an evening of ice cream and girl talk, she suddenly remembered the registered letter that she had gotten four or five days ago. She mentioned to Erika, who unexpectedly went ballistic.

"WHAT? You got a registered letter and you don't even know who it's from? You didn't open it right away? What is the matter with you, girl?"

"It's probably some junk mail or something. I never get registered letters."

"You wouldn't have to sign for junk mail, Kayla! Maybe it's a subpoena or something you need to respond to within a certain time. Maybe you have to do a deposition for a patient. You need to find that ASAP!"

"Okay, Erika. Settle down. You can help me locate it when we get to the house. I'll let the dog out and you can start snooping, er, looking for it."

They had a good laugh as they pulled the car into the garage. She jumped out to unlock the door, Erika hot on her heels. Spinner was happy to have company and was barking incessantly on his way out to the yard. Erika went right for the living room, turning cushions and pillows upside down searching for the mysterious piece of mail. After an hour of searching, the two friends decided to put a movie in the DVD player while they looked.

"Is this damned Antonio Banderas all you've got?" Erika asked as she ejected the recently watched film. When she picked up the case for it, an envelope tumbled from the top of the television set to the floor. "I think I've found what we are looking for. Open it!"

She handed the envelope to Kayla, but not before noticing "Wickett & Wickett, Barristers at Large, London, United Kingdom" in the upper left corner. Kayla went to her desk, extracted a letter opener and slid it delicately across the top of the envelope. She began reading all the legal prose while Erika watched impatiently.

"Well? What is it? Talk to me!"

"Um, I'm not really sure, Erika. It's something about a great-aunt's will. I don't remember any great-aunt."

"Let me see that! You know I watch Judge Joni every single day!"

Kayla handed the papers to Erika and watched her friend perusing them.

"Think, Kayla. Did any of your grandparents have a sister who lived in Europe, specifically Wales? Did you ever hear any stories about that part of the world?"

Kayla sat down and thought for a moment. The only grandparent she really remembered was her maternal grandmother whose parents had come over on a boat from Ireland. She fondly remembered the trip that she, her mother and grandmother had made to New York City where they took a boat out to Ellis Island to see the books of immigrants. She had run her little fingers across the page where her great-grandparents' names were listed. If she remembered correctly, she had been six or seven at the time. A smile slowly crept across her face. Yes, she had loved her Mamaw better than anyone else in the whole wide world. And she was quite sure that the feeling was mutual.

"Well? Are you coming up with anything?"

"I didn't know my paternal grandparents, and my father's heritage was primarily Italian. His grandparents had immigrated in the late 1800's. As far as I know, mom's parents were both of Irish heritage. Her father was born in England somewhere, but his mother was American. I have no siblings, Mom had no siblings. I think I need to get on that genealogy website and do some research. And I should probably get out the box of Mom's things that I haven't touched since she died. Maybe there is something in there."

"So let me get this straight," Erika said, not taking her eyes off the letter. "Some law office in London, as in London, England, wants to fly you over there for free to attend a reading of your great-aunt's will, even though you don't even remember having a great aunt. And you are worrying about looking up the family history? What is wrong with you? Why aren't you packing your suitcase right now? Get on that computer immediately and send an email to this address and tell them to send you the plane ticket!"

"That is too impulsive for me. I need to make sure this isn't some kind of scam."

"Scam, schmam. A free flight to London? Call and make the arrangements, then take a vacation from work. I'm sure you have a gazillion vacation days coming. You NEVER call off!"

"Well, I'll send them an email with some of my questions and I'll check my vacation days when I go in to work on Monday. But I really don't think this is real. Why wouldn't I remember her?"

"Good lord, girl, then get out that box of things your mother has packed away. Don't just sit there! Now!"

Kayla strode back the hallway to what was once her parents' bedroom and pulled two boxes out of the closet. She carried the first one to the kitchen and placed it on the dining room table, quickly followed by the second one. She and Erika sat down at the table, each one pulling a box in front of them to go through. They formed separate piles, one of photographs, one of paper goods and one of all other items.

Erika started going through the paper goods while Kayla focused on the photos. Nearly an hour after they had begun their excavation, Kayla laid out two photos.

"I think this is my Mamaw when she was in her twenties and I think other woman is her sister, according to the notes Mom wrote on the back, 'Cecelia and Rebecca McGowan, 1923'. My grandmother was Cecelia McGowan Williams. Hand me that letter, I think it said I needed to go to the reading of the estate of Rebecca McGowan."

"Yea, that's what it said, Rebecca McGowan."

"Hmmmm, I wonder if she ever married, because that is her maiden name."

Erika handed the letter to Kayla while she continued looking through the other papers from the box. There were several letters from London and Wales that were addressed to both Kayla's mother and grandmother. When she glanced down at the signature, it appeared to say 'Becca'. These were letters from the alleged great-aunt! As much as she wanted to snoop, Erika laid them aside until she had her friend's undivided attention.

"I think there are some letters here, too, Kayla, from Aunt Rebecca. Hurry up! What do they say?"

"Let me see those. Basically just talking about her life as a military nurse during WWI, then talking about hospital nursing in London. Oh, here's one where she says she has decided to retire and move out of the city to an estate outside of Cardiff, Wales. It sure sounds like we've hit the jackpot, haven't we?"

"We might not have, but maybe you did. Say you will go, Kayla! When is the reading of the will scheduled again?"

"Monday, March 20th. Heck, that's a little over a week away! I don't know if I can do it. I've never even flown before! But fortunately, I do have a passport because I went to Canada to see "Phantom of the Opera" last year. Thank goodness for that bus trip!"

"I never even would have thought of that! Geesh! Now get on the computer and email them for your plane ticket. You may just have a wonderful surprise coming!"

Kayla retrieved the laptop from her desk and brought it over to the kitchen table. She turned it on and continued looking through one of the boxes while she waited for it to start up. A million questions were going through her head, but she knew no one would be answering her very soon. Once the screen appeared, she opened up her email and hit the 'compose' button.

"What should I say, Erika? I have no idea."

"Just type what I say...Dear sirs, I received a registered letter regarding the reading of my great-aunt's will and I would like to be present. Please send flight information to me at yada, yada, yada. I look forward to meeting you. Thank you very much, yada, yada, yada..."

"So eloquent! Should I capitalize the yadas?"

They had a good laugh as Kayla sent the note off into cyberspace. It would be interesting to see what would transpire, she supposed. But deep inside, she was scared to death. Going to a foreign country alone wasn't exactly on her bucket list.

Over the next twenty-four hours Kayla began packing a carry-on suitcase by following Erika's advice and packing list. She figured she would not be gone more than a day or two, so that would suffice. By late Sunday evening she was exhausted just thinking about it. She fell into bed, visions of Tower Bridge dancing in her head.

When she checked her email before work in the morning, there was no reply from the law office, so she headed in to work, hoping the day would go fast. Fortunately for Kayla, the doctors must have been running a special on CAT scans, as they had over a dozen patients on the calendar to scan. She was relieved for two reasons, though. One, she didn't have time to make small talk with Ron, and second, the day flew by. As her timecard clicked on the way out the door, Kayla's cell phone was vibrating. It was a text from Erika asking about the plane ticket. 'Not yet,' she typed quickly as she pulled out of the parking lot.

As soon as Kayla got Spinner out into the yard, she fired up her laptop. Changing clothes quickly, she returned to her desk. She ran through her email until she came across one from the law office which she opened promptly.

'Miss Battaglia, thank you so much for your quick response to our notification of intent. Attached you will find your flight and hotel information. We have arranged for you to take an overnight flight out of Pittsburgh, Pennsylvania on Saturday, March 18th and arrive in London on Sunday morning, March 19th. You will depart on the following Wednesday, March 22nd at 9 a.m. These expenses are fully paid as indicated in your aunt's will. All information you will need is included in the attachment. Please let us know if we can be of any further service. Catherine Adamson, Legal Secretary, Wickett and Wickett, Barristers At Large.'

Kayla stared at the email for a moment, and then clicked on the attachment. There were three pages of information, including all her flight details, car service to and from Heathrow, hotel information and tube map. Her only expenses would be her food and any other non-related purchases. She could hardly believe that in less than a week she would be in jolly old England! She sent a text message to Erika to call on her lunch break.

She had just gotten settled into her robe and slippers when her cell phone demanded to be answered.

"I just got your text! You are going to London in less than a week! I can hardly believe it!"

"YOU can hardly believe it? I'm in shock here."

"Oh my gawd, this is SO exciting! I wish I could go with you. We would have one helluva good time!"

"I wish you could go, too. I'm more than a little bit nervous. But they made all the arrangements and a car service is picking me up. I wanted to ask for a favor, though. Do you think you could possibly take me to the airport and retrieve me when I get back? I really don't want to leave my car up there for four days."

"Of course I will take you. Do you think I'd want to miss any details of this adventure? Just tell me what time your flights are. Did you already clear it with your boss?"

"Not yet. I'll do that tomorrow. I checked my vacation days and I have twenty-three right now, so there shouldn't be a problem except that it is short notice. But we have plenty of staff and I can do some trades if I have to."

"Great! Well, I have to get back to the lab. I have two days off in a row after tomorrow so we'll get together then. I'll talk to you tomorrow."

"Bye Erika. Talk to you soon."

When she hung up the phone, the reality was starting to set in. Kayla couldn't believe she was going to Europe, on a plane, alone. It boggled her mind.

CHAPTER **THREE**

    The next few days Kayla felt caught up in a whirlwind. She had no problem securing her days off to go to London. She used three of her vacation days and traded with another staff for the other two. She didn't mind working weekends for people since she had no social life. Let others go to weddings and dances and weekends away. She was always happy to get that time and a half bonus. She also asked her doctor for a few Xanax in case the flight upset her. He was happy to oblige so she picked up the prescription and dropped it off at the pharmacy.

    After work on Friday she and Erika were going out to dinner and a movie, and then having a slumber party of sorts so her friend could help her finish packing for the trip. It was getting real now, and Kayla was caught up in Erika's enthusiasm. Maybe she did need to get away somewhere that she could be inconspicuous. Of course, she didn't realize that a Yankee always stood out in the crowd in London by the confused looks on their face and their inappropriate dress.

    After a quick Chinese buffet the girls caught the latest "Fast and Furious" installment before heading back to Kayla's house.

    "I'd do Vin Diesel anytime, anywhere."

    "Erika, you are nuts. You can't just sleep with every man that comes down the pike."

    "Why not? Men do it all the time. Why would women be any different? We control our own destinies, our own bodies. If we want to have sex for pleasure, what is wrong with that? And, hey, Vin isn't just every man that comes down the pike!"

    "You are just plain crazy!"

    "Maybe you need to loosen up some, Kayla. Look in the mirror, girl, you are very pretty. You have such a cute little body but you cover it with those frumpy scrubs and out of date clothes. Perhaps a shopping spree is in order for you in London. Sure, I get plenty of dates, but if I looked like you, hubba hubba! I would be completely out of control."

"C'mon Erika. You are attractive, and funny, the guys are always looking at you! And you know damn well you rarely spend a Saturday night home alone in your apartment."

"They are looking at my boobs, yes, my boobs, not my face. And that works remarkably well for me. You have to use what you've got. And my girls never let me down. But I'm not looking for a long term relationship or marriage. That's your thing. You should try uncovering your girls once in a while. Let them air out a bit from those flannel nighties! Don't you ever get tired of being alone on Saturday night?"

"Not really. I'm okay with being alone. I do what I want. If it's curling up on the couch in my footie pajamas, or my flannel nightie, with Spinner and a good book, it's fine."

"You're not getting any younger, Kayla. You always said you wanted to get married and have two kids and live in the little white house with a picket fence somewhere out in the country. That's not going to happen if you stay shut in your brick ranch house in the city. Your biological clock is ticking."

"I have pretty much given up on that goal. Just getting through this world in one piece is now the priority."

"How often have you preached to me, 'never give up on your dreams'? What else are you working for? Hell, you could have your own personal James Bond waiting for you in Jolly Old England, you know! That's why he never got married, he never met you!"

"You are completely bonkers, Erika. If James Bond never got married they would have to stop making movies with those sexy heroines, you know, like Pussy Galore!"

They pulled into the driveway and Spinner was bouncing off the bay window waiting for them. Kayla hurried into the house and ran Spinner out the back door as Erika grabbed her overnight pack and carried it to the spare bedroom. When she returned to the living room, she saw Kayla's suitcase neatly arranged on the coffee table with the letter zipped into the inside pocket.

"Good gawd! How many outfits are you packing, girl? You are only going to be gone for 4 days!"

"I was worried about the weather, so I thought I'd dress in layers. And what do you wear for the reading of a will? I didn't want to be too informal."

"It's not a black tie affair. Just a nice pant suit will work. And make sure you dress comfortably for the plane, it is about a seven hour flight overnight. And by comfortably, I mean sweat pants. You will be sleeping most of the time."

"But I don't want to look to frumpy when the car service picks me up."

"Hell, they are getting paid to get you from Point A to Point B. They don't care what you look like. And try not to go to sleep when you get to the hotel. It will really screw with your jet lag. Get into the activity as if you are on their time. If it's morning, go get breakfast and then do something touristy. Walk around and familiarize yourself with the area since you will be there for a few days."

"How do you know all this stuff?"

"I told you I used to travel like a maniac and stay at youth hostels and stuff when I was in my late teens, early twenties. Of course, I spent most of that time chasing men and drinking a lot, so I don't remember too much about the scenery. But I will make it back to Europe someday."

"You will, Erika. I have never known you to not accomplish anything. I remember in high school you were the big overachiever."

"Ha, and you were the brainiac of your class. Valedictorian, right?"

"Yes, and you were the most likely to succeed, weren't you? Well, look at us now. Stuck in dead end jobs at the local hospital."

"Well, it's a living. And with the job situation around here, we should be thankful that we are gainfully employed."

"I suppose you're right, Erika. Working in the health care industry we will always have a job. Anyway, back to the chore at hand. I have two pairs of jeans, a pair of sweat pants, black slacks, two sweaters, two T-shirts and my underwear. What else might I need?"

"Make sure you have a good pair of walking shoes. London is a great city to power walk. It feels so safe and secure. And there is so much you can't see from the seat of a tour bus."

"I probably won't have much time for walking, do you think? I'll be in a law office for a day or so and then back home."

"When you get off the plane, check into your hotel and take off. You will love the city! Then go to a nearby pub and order fish and chips for dinner before crashing in your hotel room for the night. You will be ready to roll in the morning for the reading of the will. Of course, then I expect you to text me and tell me everything!"

"I'll have to check those international rates. You might have to wait until you pick me up at the airport to find out anything!"

"Okay, Miss Frugality, I suppose you are right. But I will be expecting you to spill your guts the minute you get in the car, so be ready!"

Once they were satisfied with the packing, the two friends put on their pajamas and talked well into the night. Kayla always enjoyed Erika's tales of her sexual escapades, although she, herself, could not even imagine a fraction of them. They fell asleep dreaming of finding Mr. Right instead of Mr. Right Now.

CHAPTER **FOUR**

Saturday morning announced itself with a blazing orange-yellow glow siphoning itself through the blinds. The warmth of it caused Kayla to raise the back of her hand to her forehead, blocking the brightness that was irritating her eyes. For a moment she had forgotten where she was, caught up in a dream where a dapper Englishman in a grey pinstripe suit and top hat was sweeping off her feet. But when she turned on her side, she realized that the heavy breathing she had heard was just her best friend, Erika, asleep in the spare bedroom across the hall.

It was hard to believe that today was the day. So many firsts were in store for Kayla. Her first flight, first time out across the Atlantic, first time attending the reading of a will. Her parents' wills were cut and dried, When her father had died, he left everything to her mother. When her mother died she had been the recipient of all that remained. She hadn't even had to attend a reading. The lawyers handled all that. How she wished Erika could go with her, but that was just not possible. This was something that Kayla would have to handle on her own.

She headed into the kitchen and put on a pot of coffee, then settled in at the dining room table with her packing list. She certainly didn't want to be stuck in a foreign country without something important, like her toothbrush! Who knew what kind of toothbrushes they sold in England, being that very few people kept their teeth very long there! Or perhaps it was simply a tale often told, like those of all the uneducated hillbillies from West Virginia, many of whom were her friends. And none of whom were uneducated hillbillies! Exaggeration was definitely a human trait. Dogs never did that, they judged things exactly as they were, she thought, patting sweet Spinner on the head. Yes, she certainly preferred the company of dogs to the company of humans. They were always honest, nothing to hide, no reason to deny their feelings.

Kayla heard water trickling in the shower, a sure sign that Erika had arisen from her comatose state. She poured herself another cup of coffee and finished checking the items off her packing list. Just as she was down to the last item on the list, Erika made her entrance, her curly black locks throwing water droplets about the room.

"Put a towel over that, Erika, geesh! Can't you see I'm working here?"

"Working or re-working? You've been over that list about a thousand times. You should have the damned thing memorized by now!"

"Just making sure I didn't forget anything. See, the red check mark is the first check, the yellow one is the second one and the third one, well, is green, indicating that I am ready to go."

"I never figured you for and OCD type of person, but I'm having second thoughts. Now where's the coffee? I need it bad!"

"You're no guest in this house, dearie, get it yourself"

Erika went to the cabinet and pulled out a large mug, her usual, and filled it as the hazelnut aroma filled her nostrils. She topped it off with some French Vanilla creamer and joined Kayla at the table.

"So, are you ready to head to jolly old England?"

"I think so. But I am so nervous. I still can't fathom going to England alone. It boggles the mind!"

"You'll be alright. Just remember everything I told you. And try to have fun. Don't be worrying about stupid crap the whole time. Just listen to the lawyers, follow their direction and trust yourself. I always go with my gut on things. You have got to learn that, Kayla, seriously."

"I'm going to try. But you had better be ready to reply when I text you about stuff. I don't care if it's the middle of the night! What is the time difference? Six hours? I'll try to keep that in mind."

"Don't worry about the time. I'll be nuts until you get back anyway. So what is on the agenda this morning? Do you need a last minute run to the store for anything?"

"No, I think I'm good. Why don't we just hang out here for a while, then we can take Spinner and his things to your house, go to lunch and then head for the airport?"

"That sounds like a plan to me. Where are we eating lunch?"

"You pick this time. My mind is jumbled up and all I can think about is that long plane ride."

"We'll pick you up some magazines and a book to entertain you. The plane does have movies, you know. This *is* the 21st century, you know!"

Once the car was packed and 'the list' checked another half a dozen times, the two friends piled into Erika's car, Spinner happily tagging along this time. They sped over to Erika's house and got the dog situated, then moved on to lunch.

Kayla had chosen King's restaurant for lunch, primarily because of its famous apple pie with cinnamon ice cream. She doubted they would have that delicacy in England, so she thought she would have it now. It hadn't even crossed her mind what she would have for the main course.

"Kay, hey, Kay....what are you having? Are you lost in space?"

"Oh, um, I'm not sure, maybe the grilled ham and cheese sandwich? I'm not really all that hungry."

"Well you'd better eat up because they will barely offer you a crumpet on the overnight flight to London. A little nasty turkey sandwich, some Coke and a cookie that is hard as a rock."

Kayla shook her head. Erika was such an experienced traveler, she wished so badly that she could take her along. Maybe one day they would take a big trip together. That would be grand!

After placing their orders, they began discussing strategies for making the flight easier. Kayla reassured Erika that she had her tablet for gaming, her Kindle for reading and her peanut shell pillow for comfort. She still couldn't imagine sitting on an airplane full of complete strangers for over seven hours. But that would be her reality in a very short time.

Once the dessert dishes were cleared Kayla looked at her watch.

"We'd better head out since I hear it takes about three hours to clear security for international flights. I don't want to miss my plane."

"That's a bunch of BS, Kayla. It doesn't take that long. They just want to scare you."

"Well, they've done a good job of it, I am a nervous wreck. What happens if I am late or miss my plane? Then what?"

"You won't be late. We'll pull up, hand your suitcase to the man outside, then you'll go in and find the Lufthansa counter, check in, go through security and take the tram to the gate. Just follow the crowd. Keep calm and enjoy the ride."

"I really hate going without you Erika. I would feel so much more secure if you were coming along."

"I sure as hell wish I was coming along, but we both know that can't happen right now. One of us has to go to work to pay for our fun! Maybe the next time, huh?"

"Definitely next time," Kayla said, wringing her hands in her lap.

Erika pulled the Mazda up to the curb outside the departure terminal beneath the sign that said 'International Flights'. She turned on her flashers, popped the trunk and looked at Kayla.

"Get a five dollar bill out to tip the fellow who takes your suitcase. I can't stay but a moment because the damned airport cops time you."

Kayla looked around for the airport cops but didn't immediately spot them. She did as she was told and put the five in her coat pocket. She stepped out of the car as Erika did the same. They walked to the back of the vehicle and pulled out her suitcase and carry-on. The two friends shared a warm hug before Erika moved back towards the driver's seat.

"Now I expect you to misbehave and I want to hear some wild tales when you get home, girl! Let me know when you arrive safely in London. Have a great time and keep me posted."

"I'll can't call much, but I'll text you every day. Damn, I wish you were coming!"

With that Erika pulled away and Kayla was alone, standing on the brink of one of her life's biggest adventures. Could she do this on her own? What was she thinking? Would the plane be hijacked? Then what?

Kayla's train of thought came to an abrupt halt when the gentleman in a blue and red uniform approached her.

"May I take your bag ma'am? Which flight are you boarding?"

"Oh, yes," she muttered as she handed him her bag and the tip. "Lufthansa Flight 5672 to London."

"Very good. Your bag will be tagged for Heathrow. Have a good trip."

Kayla threw her carry-on over her shoulder and headed into the terminal. She analyzed the huge electronic flight board to locate her flight and gate. In big green letters next to it the words 'on time' appeared. Well, that was one relief, her flight was going as planned. She looked for and found the Lufthansa kiosk at the far left end of the terminal. The line was minimal and that also made her feel better. Maybe Erika was right. She should just relax and enjoy the ride.

Once she had checked in and obtained her boarding pass, Kayla followed the signs to the escalator that would take her down to the security check. The line was much longer than Erika had led her to believe, so she was glad that she arrived when she did. She was surrounded by a variety of characters and spent most of her time people watching during the long wait.

Two rows ahead of her was a man she would have nominated for father of the year. He had one toddler on his shoulders and two in a dual stroller buggy, all the while tugging two wheeled suitcases with his other hand. He spent time entertaining all three of them while his significant other was busily manipulating her smart phone. This man genuinely enjoyed his children, smiling the entire time while performing his balancing act.

Just in front of her there were two young men carrying cases which appeared to be holding their skis and ski poles. They each had a backpack slung over one shoulder and a small duffle on their forearm. From their conversation Kayla discovered that they were going to the Alps on spring break for skiing and womanizing. She smiled at the thought. She had never gone anywhere on her spring breaks from school. It must be so very exciting for them.

She smiled thinking how much her mother would have enjoyed this adventure. Kayla was never quite able to understand why she didn't have the wanderlust that she had seen in her mom. She had been content to stay at home for over thirty years of her life. And look at her now! Mother would have been proud!

Kayla arrived at the gate just as they were calling for priority boarding. She had been petrified that she would miss the plane. Her fears were unfounded however, as it was a very large plane and there were many priority passengers, followed by those with handicaps and then families with small children. She even had time to sit down and send one last text message to Erika. A huge sigh of relief escaped from her lips when the group that included her row was called.

A short jaunt down the ramp and Kayla entered the doorway of the plane. It was a 767, much larger than she had ever imagined. The friendly flight attendant double checked her boarding pass and assisted her to her seat. Thank goodness for Erika, who had chosen a window seat in the escape aisle, which provided a great deal more leg room than the others. And since she was a medical professional, she fit the profile for those who could sit in that particular section.

The jet was amazing to her, with its high tech toys and comfort with easy access to anything she might need. A digital video monitor with a touch screen was embedded in the seat in front of her. Headphones plugged into a jack that was hidden in the arm of her seat. As she was trying to find the volume adjustment, one of the flight attendants suddenly appeared on the screen. Following the usual safety precautions, read in English, French, and German, instructions were given on how to use the audio and video controls for the monitor. It would be switched off during takeoff, then resumed once they reached cruising altitude. Takeoff? She was suddenly nervous about the prospect.

Kayla adjusted her seatbelt and closed her eyes as the huge aircraft taxi'd down the runway. When the engines roared to propel the behemoth forward, she felt her stomach twist up in knots and nearly felt the need to reach for the little waxy bag that was in front of her. The feeling eased, however, as the wheels left the earth with a short, sweet kiss. She leaned back into the deep leather seat as the plane ascended into the clouds. This was going to be something she would never forget.

CHAPTER **FIVE**

The first few hours of the flight, Kayla kept her eyes glued out the window at the clouds, her mind imagining what her aunt's estate was composed of. Could it be a cottage or country cabin? Just where was it located in Wales? How would she get from London to Wales? By train? By car? Would she go alone? How could she find her way around by herself?

Her thoughts were disrupted by the steward who was asking what she would like for her dinner. After reciting the selections, he waited patiently for her to collect her thoughts. She chose the turkey sub with chips and a cookie which she would wash down with her usual, a Diet Coke. Although she knew it was a really bad beverage choice, it was one of those addictions she just couldn't kick. She was proud that she had reduced her intake of the stuff from one six pack per day to just two cans per day. But she couldn't give it up altogether. One day of abstinence turned her into a crazy person. It just wasn't worth it.

The food was delivered quite quickly and Kayla consumed it just as fast. She hadn't realized how famished she was. She was too busy worrying and thinking about what she would find when she landed in London. Her tray was disposed of and she pulled out her Kindle to get involved in a book. But within minutes, her eyelids had fallen and she was in a deep sleep. So deep that even the sound of a crying infant could not invade her thoughts.

    Kayla startled awake to the sound of the gentleman behind her coughing as if he would throw a lung at any moment. The tech in her immediately thought, COPD not adjusting well to the elevation and diminished air pressure of the plane. She silently laughed at herself for conjuring up such an image. You can never get away from your work, no matter how hard you try, can you? She glanced at her watch. Two o'clock in the morning home time, which would make it eight in the morning in London. What time was the plane arriving, eleven? She would soon reach her first destination. Again her stomach gave a little lurch. Better to sleep than let her nerves get to her.

    Try as she might Kayla could not get back to sleep. She reached for the Kindle, which had fallen on the floor during her nap and opened up the new Anne Rice she had just recently downloaded. Perhaps that would keep her attention. And for the next few hours, it did just that.

    "Good morning everyone," the pilot's voice boomed overhead. "We will be arriving at Heathrow Airport in approximately fifty minutes. The weather is lovely in London, currently eight degrees centigrade with partly cloudy skies. Later today it is to get up to fifteen with scattered light rain. We will notify you when you need to prepare for landing. Thank you for flying Lufthansa."

    Damn, Kayla thought. What was that method of converting Celcius temperatures to Farenheit? Temperature minus two plus thirty-two? No, no. Temperature times two plus thirty-two. It was going to be a lot of work to figure out what to wear every day. But she was pretty sure there was an app for that on her iPhone. Once she was able to turn it back on she should have no trouble with that. But did she pack the right clothes? Travel could be so frustrating at times.

In no time the flight attendant was on the little video screen informing the passengers to prepare for landing. All tray tables and seat backs were to be put in their secure upright position. Turn off and stow any portable electronic devices. Make sure your carry-on bag is completely under the seat in front of you and that your seatbelt is properly fastened.

It really hit Kayla hard at this point. She was in a foreign country, alone, with no idea what was going to happen next. Although it was frightening, it was stimulating as well. Her nerves were on edge and not necessarily in a bad way. Maybe this was a new beginning for her, a new life, a new attitude. Only time would tell, but in some ways Kayla was settling into the idea of inheriting her great-aunt's estate. Who knew where that would lead?

The nose of the plane tilted downward as it descended toward runway at Heathrow. As they cleared the clouds, Kayla could see beautiful rolling hills with stone fences and large houses in the distance. The sun was shining and there was no indication of rain on the ground. She felt the jerk as the wheels met the pavement and the plane shuddered slightly as it leveled out. It slowed to taxi around a corner and head toward the terminal. Kayla was amazed at the number of planes she saw as they approached. She had read that Heathrow was one of the busiest terminals in the world, and she could certainly see that it was the truth. She had never seen that many airlines represented at home, on the few visits she had made to the airport over the years. She suddenly worried that she might not be able to find her way out!

As the plane came to a standstill, it seemed that a tsunami of people leapt to their feet and were lurching forward. Since she was in the window seat, Kayla decided to let those that were in a hurry to go ahead and disembark while she sat back for a few minutes. When they got to her row, however, an elderly gentleman with wavy silver hair who had been seated in the row across from hers stepped back and motioned for her to go ahead of him. She gingerly jumped up and grabbed her carry-on and headed towards the front of the plane and into the unknown.

Kayla followed the hurrying masses down the walkway and into the chaos that was Heathrow. She had never seen such a crowded airport in her life, albeit she had only seen two airports in her life, the large Pittsburgh International and the smaller Akron/Canton. She was quite intimidated by the maze in front of her. She decided to follow the disembarking crowd and quickly saw the "Customs" sign with arrows pointing towards a row of glass enclosed desks. She headed in that direction, remaining oblivious to the poking elbows and crush of humanity as she stepped onto the lift. The line moved quickly and she soon found herself answering a laundry list of questions. She must have answered correctly as she was then pointed in the direction of a waterfall of escalators with the sign "Luggage Claim" hanging above them.

It turned out that there were three levels of escalators to be ridden to arrive at the ground floor where the baggage claim resided. When she was nearly to the bottom she looked up and saw several gentlemen in black suits wearing driving caps, all holding up signs with a variety of names listed. Just as she turned to follow the arrows towards the Lufthansa baggage claim, her eye caught a glimpse of her own name. "Battaglia" was written in bold black letters on a white board being held up by a fortyish gentleman in said black suit and plaid cap. Just to his left was her large piece of luggage, peacefully sitting in repose.

"I'm Kayla Battaglia," she stated as she approached the gentleman.

He nodded and, without a word, picked up her suitcase and gestured her towards an exit door. They walked out onto the sidewalk, the cool breeze feeling of impending rain, not very unusual for spring in London.

Kayla saw that his name was Ray, as indicated on a company badge which matched the magnetic sign on the black Mercedes limousine that she was directed towards. Ray popped the trunk and placed her suitcase inside, then quickly opened the back door on the passenger side for Kayla to climb in. Once she was safely seated inside, Ray strolled around the back of the vehicle and slid into the driver's seat.

Although it was a bit disconcerting to be on the side opposite to what she had grown accustomed to, Katie felt that Ray would certainly get her to her destination safe and sound. There was just something about him that made her feel comfortable. She leaned back against the seat trying to fight off the sleep that was nagging at her. What time was it anyway? It felt so odd.

She glanced out the window at the rolling countryside and few farmhouses dotting the canvas. How peaceful it all seemed compared to the wild few weeks she had just experienced! But as they got closer to the city, the serenity began to diminish and the congestion started to build. She smiled as she watched the row houses roll by, their clay rooftops with twin chimneys reaching towards the sky bringing back fanciful childhood memories of Dick Van Dyke quickstepping across them with his sweep handle as a partner, crooning to Julie Andrews in "Mary Poppins."

Her mind was taken back to her childhood diary, which she had diligently kept since she was in the sixth grade. In it were all her secret wishes and desires, including a long list of places she would visit someday, many of which were inspired by her Disney addiction. Through books, film and animation she had seen a great deal of the world, and she had vowed to experience it in person. But as

an adult, she had given up many of her dreams to care for her aging parents and she had no regrets that she had done so. But now that they were gone, what was holding her back? Fear? When we are young we are fearless, but as we age, being invincible changes.
Nonetheless, here she was, in London town, and she had to face her fears regardless of how powerful they were.

As they entered the city, Ray started talking to Kayla through the speaker system, noting that as they passed by the statue of a dragon they were in the city limits. The entire city was laced with the beasts to signify its boundaries. She listened intently as he described various sights and locations throughout. It was becoming real now. London certainly was as beautiful as she had imagined.

Suddenly, just over the horizon a huge ferris wheel came into view. It took Kayla's breath away as she was informed that it was called the London Eye and was put in place for the celebration of the year 2000 and only intended for five years' use. It was so popular, however, that it had been asked to remain and had since become one of the city's icons. As they crossed Westminster Bridge over the Thames, the immensity of the Eye became reality. Big Ben loomed off to her right as well and Kayla knew she wasn't in Ohio any more.

"You should go up on it, love. It gives you the greatest views of the city."

"I, I think I might, Ray. And thank you for all the information."

Within moments they pulled into the circular driveway of the Park Plaza Westminster. Ray hopped out of the driver's seat and moved to the rear of the vehicle, grabbing Kayla's luggage from the trunk. He then opened her door and assisted her exit. When she attempted to give him a tip he kindly refused.

"It's all well taken care of, ma'am. Enjoy the city then." With that he returned to his vehicle and slowly pulled away. The jet lag suddenly overwhelmed her and Kayla felt that she had lost her only friend in a city of millions. The heck with Erika's advice, she needed a nap!

Kayla opted to carry her own bags into the massive lobby even though several bellman offered assistance. There was a sense of security having her things in hand as they were the only familiarities she could grasp at that moment. She wheeled her suitcase up to the front desk and waited for her turn in line. An Indian gentleman gestured for her to come forward and she obliged.

"Welcome Madame, how may I help you today?"

"My name is Kayla Battaglia and I have a reservation. I just got in this morning but was told that I could get an early check-in."

"Of course, let me pull that up. One moment please. Oh, here it is. May I see a photo ID, please."

Kayla fumbled through her purse and found her passport, where she had stowed her driver's license during all the routine check-ins at the airport. She grasped the edge of the license and pulled it quickly out of the passport cover, not thinking that she could have just handed him the whole darned thing.

"Ms. Battaglia, you are booked for a three night stay through the law offices of Wickett and Wickett, is that correct?"

"Yes, three nights. Do you need a credit card or anything for extras?"

"No, not at all. All expenses are paid. Your room number is 517. The elevators are just down the hall to the right. Do you need more than one key?"

"I can't imagine why I would. No, just one will do."

"Would you like the bellman to handle your bags?"

"No, I've got them. Thank you so much."

With that she turned and started down the hall, feeling a bit nauseated and comatose. She wasn't sure which she needed more, food or sleep. Once she got into the room and settled a bit, she would let her body would choose.

    The trip to the fifth floor went quickly. It was the fastest elevator Kayla had ever ridden. When the door opened she was welcomed by the lovely scents of fresh flowers which seemed to be everywhere. She noticed on the wall plaque that her room was to the left so she headed in that direction. She was pleased that it was going to be on the side facing the Thames rather than the back of the hotel. These guys sure knew what they were doing! She fumbled with the key but managed to get it slid into the lock and was thrilled when the green light came on indicating she could enter. She always had trouble with those damned key cards. Why couldn't they use a normal key for room doors?

    Pushing the door open she could see a spacious room done in blues and beige. Immediately to the right was a huge mirror faced closet and to the left was the bathroom. She pulled her baggage in and moved into the bedroom area. A king size bed with piles of decorative pillows sat to one side. A large flat screen TV was attached to the wall, making more space on the top of the dresser. Near the window was a business desk with computer hookups and multiple electrical outlets. Several binders lay to one side with the hotel logo embossed in gold on the covers. She would get into those later. But for now, the OCD in her made her unpack and put everything in its place.

    Once she had the drawers organized Kayla begin to feel a surge of energy. Maybe Erika was right. She should get out and do the tourist thing. It seemed that many of the city's major attractions were within walking distance, so why not grab a bite to eat and take a stroll. She opted for a quick shower, brushed her teeth, tousled her hair and headed for the elevator. When she arrived in the lobby she stopped at the concierge desk to get some information.

The concierge at the desk was more than happy to give her a fistful of brochures, maps and ticket discounts to some of the nearby tourist attractions. He highly recommended that she start with a stroll over the bridge to investigate Big Ben and the Houses of Parliament, followed by a boat trip down the Thames, lunch, then ending the evening with a bang by riding the London Eye under the cloak of darkness to see the city lit up at night.

"Sounds like a great plan. I'm sure you've done this a time or two!"

The concierge laughed and pointed her in the right direction.

As she stepped out onto the sidewalk Kayla was glad that the clouds had dissipated and the sky was getting clearer by the minute. She headed straight towards Westminster Bridge and started across. The crowds were getting thicker now, and she stopped to watch a family with many children pose with the London Eye directly behind them. She felt a deep regret rise up in her chest. She was getting way too old to have children. A sigh escaped her lips as the sadness became more intense. Would she wind up like her dear great-aunt, with no one to leave a legacy to? At least no one she had actually met?

She returned her attention to Big Ben, which was much bigger than she had imagined. Taking her camera out of the bag, she stopped and leaned against the bridge railing, taking aim at the face. As she zoomed in for a closer shot, she was amazed by the mosaic of color that had not been apparent in any photo she had seen of the clock. She fired off shot after shot at different angles until she was satisfied with her work. One of the biggest advantages of digital photography was that you could view your images immediately, giving you the opportunity to discard the bad ones and keep the good ones, at least until seeing them on a bigger screen when doing edits. And these digital memory cards were astounding!

The fact that she could take over four thousand photos on one card (and hopefully one battery) was incredible!

As she moved down the bridge she was approached by two people dressed in clown suits. She had noticed that they were snapping photos for tourists, but she wanted none of that. First, she had a ridiculous fear of clowns and, second, she had a totally unwarranted fear of being alone in a foreign country by herself. When they approached her, Kayla waved them on, but they followed her a short distance, poking fun at her clothes, camera, etc. There was no way she was getting involved with that kind of people. She chose to ignore them and continue on.

Once she reached the other side of the bridge Kayla was standing near the base of Big Ben. She moved up close and pointed her camera skyward, taking some off the wall angles of the great landmark. She then turned and took some distant shots of the London Eye, which was reflecting in the water of the Thames. Checking her pictures out, she was sure she got some fabulous ones.

She turned the corner and strolled down past the Houses of Parliament, snapping away with her camera. She noted a few museums along the way but decided not to stop, it was so
refreshing to be outside. Buds were just beginning to form on the trees and birds were singing everywhere. She was amazed that in a city as large as London, there was still a peacefulness and sense of being in the countryside. She felt no tension as she walked along the great river. Yes, Erika was right. London was a great city for walking. She was glad that she had gone out for some fresh air. Now stomach was beginning to rumble, making strong demands. How long had it been since she'd eaten that sparse meal on the plane? Definitely too long!

She turned back towards the bridge and crossed it slowly, watching tourists from all walks of life take in the city of London. She knew it was a huge city and that she had just touched the hem of its skirt. Hopefully she would be able to experience a lot more during her short stay.

When she had completed her stroll across the bridge she veered to the left and walked down onto a cobblestone veranda strewn with picnic tables. She immediately noted the type of packaging most of the lunch garbage was in. She shook her head. Even the British knew what the Golden Arches represented. With no other food choice in sight, she ascended the steps of the London Aquarium and headed for McDonald's. She hoped they cooked the food the same here as at home. At least she would know what she was ordering!

Kayla took her time munching on her fish sandwich and fries. She was sure the fish and chips that the city was famous for was much more appetizing than the wallet sized pre-frozen version that she was stuffing in her mouth. She was still hungry when she was finished so she decided to walk towards the Eye and see what kind of street vendors were available. Perhaps a good ice cream cone could be found along the way. She strolled in and out of some shops which definitely were catering to the tourist crowd, resisting to make those knee-jerk purchases that she would regret when she got a chance to actually shop around. She did pick up some postcards and stuffed them in her purse, then strode over to a booth that had 'Thames River Cruises' emblazoned on the top in bright colors.

She stood in line for about fifteen minutes to acquire a ticket and, once she had it in hand, was directed to a white bench to wait until the next boat returned. There were about twenty people gathered in the vicinity of the bench and she correctly assumed they were going on the cruise as well. She sat back and took in the scene, especially checking out the women's shoes. It was such an interesting thing to see so many different shoes on women than on men. Fascinating, really. She was dressed in her flat Docksiders. The one thing that really kept her interest was the fact that no two women had the same shoes on. Anything from tennis shoes to fancy heels were the soup of the day and perfectly acceptable. Men, of course, wore such boring shoes, not veering far from tennis shoes, loafers and boots. And in the wild the men are the ones who have the bright plumage? Not so true with humans, she thought.

A loud horn startled her from her shoe fetish and the crowd began moving down the steps next to the white bench. The boat sidled up to the dock and the crew swiftly jumped off to secure the vessel with fat ropes wrapped tightly around silver bollard hooks. Once in place, the previous passengers unloaded in an orderly fashion and her group began to go aboard. Kayla opted to go up the steps to the uncovered top deck and headed to the front of the boat.

She wanted to see everything as well as be able to get photos that were not obstructed by people's heads or other body parts. She slid into her seat and started to get the camera equipment ready. She felt the camera bag vibrate slightly so she reached for her cell phone. Who would be calling her at this time of day? It was two in the afternoon in London which was just eight in the morning at home. Oh yea, Erika was probably just getting up. When she glanced down she saw that she had five texts so she pushed the icon on her phone. Yep, all from Erika.

"How is it? Tell me everything."

"I don't have enough data to tell you everything. Just that I got here in one piece and things are going smoothly. Right now I am going to cruise down the Thames. Wish you could join me."

"So do I!! Send pictures tonight! Have fun!"

"I will. I'll post some later if I get the chance. Have a good time at work."

She slid her finger across the phone and decided to turn it off while she was cruising. No need to have it going off causing her to lose a great photo opportunity. She could turn it back on when she returned to her room for the night.

Just as the boat pulled away from the dock, she slid it back into the side pocket of her camera bag and turned her full attention to the river.

The slight breeze blowing in her face helped Kayla stay awake. The rolling of the boat wasn't helping, though, rocking her like a baby. But she somehow managed to shake it off. The captain began describing the landmarks along the way as she snapped photo after photo. This river was the soul of the city, the reason it existed, she learned. There were more bridges across it than all three of the rivers in Pittsburgh combined. The captain spoke about each and every one of the bridges they passed under and their importance in the history of the city.

As they approached Tower Bridge Kayla was in awe. This was a sight she had seen many times over in books, magazines and on television. It was as beautiful as she had imagined. The intricate carvings and colorings of the bridge were awe-inspiring. And just to the left of it was the Tower of London. This surprised her because it wasn't really a tower at all. It was a fortress of sorts, with several smaller towers, but definitely not what she had pictured. As the captain
continued with his history lesson, she could barely imagine that the Crown Jewels were somewhere inside those buildings.

They went under a stone bridge which the captain said was London Bridge. This was the bridge that the children's song was about? It was nothing, really, but a plain stone bridge. But Kayla took a photo of the sign just for fun. Next she saw some large round columns standing along in the water next to the bridge. The captain explained that those columns dated back to when the Romans had taken over the city. Suddenly the enormity of this city's importance resonated in her head. We Americans are so smug, she thought, our history is nothing compared to what happened here. She snapped several photos of the Roman columns, knowing that they would be easily identified when she began working on her albums from this trip.

The cruise took about forty-five minutes and Kayla enjoyed the entire trip, especially the history that the captain was sharing with the tourists. He had probably said those same words hundreds, if not thousands, of times, but she could hear the pride in his voice that he was a Londoner.

When the boat returned to its dock near the Eye, she was feeling pretty tired. It was nearly four in the afternoon so she chose to return to her hotel room, take a shower, a nap, and then come back out to ride the Eye later that evening. Yep, that sounded like a good plan.

CHAPTER SIX

Once back in her room, Kayla pulled on some sweatpants and got a bit more comfortable, sliding into bed and pulling the comforter up close. She pulled out her e-reader so she could get further into the novel she had started on the plane. She glanced down at it, but something was distracting her. She turned her attention to the bedside stand where she noticed a white light blinking annoyingly on the telephone. Sitting up on the side of the bed, she pulled the phone closer to her. It was a message light. Now who would be leaving her a message at the hotel?

She had to squint a little to read the small typed directions on the phone for retrieving her messages. Following the directions, she pressed "7" and her room number for which she was rewarded with a hotel recording and a smooth male voice.

"Ms. Battaglia, this is Brent Dankworth from Wickett & Wickett Law Offices. Would like to make your acquaintance and perhaps show you around the town a bit tonight. Ring me back if you might be interested."

Kayla grabbed the pen and notepaper that was conveniently located next to the phone and jotted the number down. Perhaps it would be fun to have a relaxing evening with someone who knew their way around. Surely the man was just being friendly to a new client for his firm. Probably not a serial killer or anything. She shot a text off to Erika to get her opinion, but soon found herself engrossed once again in the novel. Maybe she should just stick to reading her book tonight.

Her phone beeped with a quick reply from Erika. Kayla was not surprised. Erika probably had that phone glued to her hand so she didn't miss anything. And, as usual, she got right to the point.

"Are you nuts? Of course you will go out with him this evening to see the town! Paint the town red, girl. NO ONE will know what goes on, except me! What happens in London stays in London. The town is your oyster, go crack that sucker open!!'

Crazy Erika! There was no doubt that she would say to go for it. That was her mantra for life. Don't pass up any chance to have a good time. But for once Kayla thought her friend was right. Why not go for it? What did she have to lose? She had never had a 'quickie' relationship before so it might be fun. No strings, no deep emotional ties. It might be one of the best things she could do for herself. It had been years since a man had even been slightly attracted to her, except for Ron from work. Maybe it was time to see if she's still got it.

She quickly shot a text back to Erika. 'Don't wait up, mom!'

The reply was simply a sinister smiley face.

Kayla picked up the note she had written then called the front desk to get instructions for making an outside call. She wasn't sure if she even had the ability to make the call on her own phone so she opted for the one in her room. Since she wasn't paying for the room, surely she could afford to cover the phone call.

After jotting the instructions down, Kayla lifted the receiver and started punching in the numbers. On the first ring she nearly hung up because all of a sudden butterflies started flapping in her stomach. It felt like she was asking a guy out on a date, which she had done several times with little or no success. Shake it off, girl, he called you, and it really isn't a date. She anxiously listened to the next few rings. His answering machine picked up and she felt a bit relieved. Maybe he had already made other plans.

Just before the little 'beep' to leave a message Kayla heard quite a racket in the background.

"Hello, hello, Ms. Battaglia are you there?"

"Yes, yes, I'm here. Hello."

"This is Brent from the law office. As I said in my earlier message I was wondering if you would like to see the town from a Londoner's point of view this evening."

"I think I would like that. I haven't traveled all that much by myself and am a little anxious about going out at night alone. I was planning on doing the London Eye because it is quite close to the hotel and perhaps dinner. What did you have in mind?"

"Perhaps a double decker bus ride, then the Eye followed by fish and chips and some clubbing?

"That sounds wonderful to me. What time should I be ready?"

"It's nearly five now, so can you meet me in the lobby at six-thirty? I'll make the bus tour reservations for 7:00 and the Eye for 8:30. Does that meet your approval?"

"Yes, that sounds fine. How will I recognize you in the lobby?"

"I have your photo so I'll recognize you. But I'll be wearing khaki pants and a button down, along with a black trench. And, Ms. Battaglia? Be sure to dress warm. These spring evenings can get a bit chilly."

"Thanks for the advice, um, Brent. And you can call me Kayla. See you then."

The phone clicked and the conversation had ended. Kayla smiled wondering what Brent Dankworth looked like. Probably super handsome, debonair and married!! And that accent! Nothing sexier than a British accent in her book! She set her alarm clock for six so she could take a short nap before the adventurous evening. Then she would shower and get dressed. Now came the big question. What should she wear?

Kayla jumped up when her alarm went off. For a moment she had forgotten where she was. It was a rare thing for her to wake up in a hotel room, no less one in London, England! Sitting up on the side of the bed she got her bearings, headed into the bathroom and turned on the shower, still not sure if the nap had made her feel better or worse. She quickly bathed and dried her curly blonde hair, stepping into the cool of the room. She grabbed the black slacks and sweater, which she initially was going to wear to the reading tomorrow, but she would figure something else out. The black slacks could still be worn in the morning. Checking her look in the mirror she approved. She flipped the lights off, grabbed her purse and headed for the elevator. It was six twenty-five in the evening.

Kayla stepped off the elevator and began to peruse the room. Brent was easy enough to spot, tall and slim with dark wavy hair. His black trench coat was hanging open to reveal khakis and a bone colored sweater. He had protruding cheek bones and a square chin, along with bright white teeth, probably from overusing chemical enhancers. His eyes narrowed as he started toward her and she felt her knees starting to knock. Dammit! It's just a social call, for goodness sake.

"Ms. Battaglia, I presume?"

"It's Kayla, and yes, that's me."

He took her hand and planted a soft kiss on the back and slowly released it. She felt a burning sensation where his lips had lingered.

"You look smashing! So let's get started, shall we?"

Kayla nodded and lifted her hand to place it in the crook of his elbow that was offered. They headed out through the revolving glass door into the crisp darkness of night. She caught her breath as the cold hit her, or was it the fact that she was out with a man for the first time in many years?

The pair turned right and set out to the area Kayla had explored earlier that housed the London Eye. When they were nearing the huge structure, she began rooting through her purse for her wallet.

"That isn't necessary Ms., er, Kayla. The firm is covering your expenses while you are here." He held up two paper tickets, handing one to her. "The line is pretty short this evening so we shouldn't have to wait long."

They stood near the white bench that Kayla had sat on while waiting for the Thames cruise earlier that day. As Brent had expected the line moved quickly and they started up the gangplank to the boarding area.

The Eye was just lighting up for the evening! It looked much taller and more massive in the dark than it had in the daylight. It created an eerie reflection against the dark waters of the Thames. For a moment she had her doubts that she would be able to handle being on the top of it. She had ridden many ferris wheels in her life, but nothing could even come close to the enormity of the London Eye. And she also noticed that it didn't stop moving when you boarded it. That scared the daylights out of her!

Brent noticed her hesitation and wrapped his arm behind her back as if to let her know that it was okay and that he was there. She hadn't been held by a man for, well, she had forgotten how long it had been, but it felt good. She didn't attempt to remove his hand from her lower back. He was explaining that each car held up to twenty-five people and that they were very stable. There was no reason to fear. The Eye carried hundreds of thousands of visitors and safely returned them to Mother Earth every single day. Why would today be any different? His smooth voice eased some of her fears.

Before she knew it, Kayla was being gently directed inside one of the huge pods and shuffled to the back where the view of the city would be unobstructed by any of the other passengers in the car with them. The lights of the city were moving further and further away as the Eye lifted into the sky. Brent had released his grip on her back and was pointing out a variety of landmarks as indicated by their lighting. He told her that on a very clear day you could see Windsor Castle which was nearly twenty-six miles away from London. He then showed her the lights of Buckingham Palace, which was merely a few blocks' walk from the Thames.

Kayla found herself engrossed in the views of London by night. It was a huge city which was brimming with life, even on a Sunday evening. It reminded her of the photos she had seen of New York City. What was it, the city that never sleeps? Brent's descriptions just added to her fascination. The history of this place continued to amaze her.

As they started their descent from the peaks of the London Eye, Brent asked what she would prefer for dinner, a pub or a restaurant. She thought a few moments and then told him to choose since he was the native and new the best spots around. He smiled broadly and nodded.

"I was hoping you'd say that."

The pod ahead of them was exiting and a voice boomed over the speakers instructing them how to dismount from the huge car while moving. They followed the other passengers to the exit door and the group seemed to move as one, stepping onto the platform and turning towards the exit ramp. It was a lot easier than Kayla had imagined it would be. She grinned at the thought of her fears. They were totally unfounded and ridiculous. Erika was right, she needed to let go of some of that.

Brent led her past the aquarium and up to the Westminster Bridge. He stepped off the curb and hailed a black cab, opening the door and ushering Kayla inside.

"The Jugged Hare my good man."

The taxi driver nodded and headed over the bridge. The passengers discussed the ride on the Eye and other points of interest in the city.

"If only I had more time here. I would love to see the castles and the parks and, of course, Harrod's."

"Tomorrow morning we will have the reading of the will, then you will take a train to Cardiff so that you can see the property. You will spend Monday night somewhere near the estate with whoever accompanies you. You will go back to the house in the morning, catching the late train back to London Tuesday afternoon. If I am in town I would love to show you around a bit more before you return to the states."

"So who would be accompanying me?"

"I'm not sure. Someone from the firm. Usually it is an executive secretary or legal secretary in case you have any questions about the will and its terms."

The taxi came to an abrupt halt in front of a brownstone tavern with the words "The Jugged Hare" written in silver cursive letters on the front door's oval glass. A fanciful rabbit was leaping across the words, a top hat between his ears. Brent paid the driver and exited the taxi, meeting Kayla as she started out the door, taking her hand and helping her up the curb. It had been a long time since anyone assisted her with anything. Maybe chivalry was not dead after all.

A young blonde hostess showed them to their seats and placed menus on the table. Brent ordered himself a beer and Kayla chose a pear cider. They perused the menus for a few moments and when the waitress returned they both ordered the standard fish and chips. There was a strained silence between them which was making Kayla uncomfortable. She decided to break the ice.

"So what is in my great aunt's will, may I ask? Did I inherit a moth-eaten fur coat and some pawn shop baubles?"

"Of course I don't know the entire contents of the will, Kayla, but I assure you it is much more substantial than a fox shawl. Included are some land, a home and other substantial items. You will know its entirety in the morning."

"And there are no other heirs or claims against it?" She remembered what Erika had told her to ask.

"Not to our knowledge. She passed away nearly three years ago and we have done the required public postings and attempts at notification. I believe it was your mother who was to inherit the entire estate initially, but since she is deceased and you are her only child, then the estate passes to you. It's as simple as that."

"I doubt that there is anything simple about this entire thing. It is probably some major quagmire about to swallow me whole." "What you choose to do with your inheritance is up to you. I'm sure you could sell it without any difficulty. It is close enough to a major port, within easy reach of London and walking distance from the coast. Do you have any idea what you will do?"

"No, not at all. First I need to know exactly what is involved. Are there any major liens against the estate? Do I owe anyone because of it?"

"Again, all of that will be explained in the morning. Better to enjoy a pleasant evening out tonight and be relaxed when you come into the office tomorrow. I think the estate will exceed your expectations. On the other hand, how are you finding London? Is it what you expected?"

The waitress arrived with their meals and they continued making small talk. Although Kayla was enjoying Brent's company, especially his smooth accent, there was something about him that was making her uncomfortable. His eyes were so dark, perhaps affected by the lighting. But she just kept thinking about the phrase 'the eyes are the doorway to the soul' and noticed that his were not translucent but opaque, hiding his soul, maybe? She just shook it off even though all her inner vibes were quivering. She was tired and a little scared to be this far from home. That was all it was, she was sure of it.

After dinner Brent paid the check while Kayla stopped in the powder room before setting out into the night. He hailed a cab and helped Kayla in, then gave the driver their destination. When it wasn't her hotel, Kayla cringed, wondering just what he was up to. But when they finished weaving through the streets away from the Thames, she was ashamed of herself. Before them stood the magnificence that was Buckingham Palace, well lit for all to see. They tumbled out of the taxi and onto the cobblestone pathways littered with statuary and fountains of every imaginable size and shape. The huge statue of Queen Victoria was centrally located among the artistry, a monarch overlooking their realm.

"Most tourists come during the day to see the palace as well as the changing of the guard. But they miss the glorious display that can only be seen after dusk. Isn't it magnificent?"

"Yes, yes, it is breathtaking, Brent. I could not have imagined it would be like this. Although I would like to see the changing of the guard someday, I would probably never have come here after dark. Thank you for bringing me here."

"I'm sure you will be making many trips to Britain in the near future. You can decide what you want to see each time and make it happen. Although the estate is in Wales, you are best off flying into Heathrow and taking the train over anyway. So plan an extra day or two in London before you head home."

"That is excellent advice, although I'm not sure how many trips I will be making to Britain. My head is still swimming with everything that is happening. I don't know what I will do at this point."

"Our firm will give you the facts and advise you in any way you need, I can assure you. And I guarantee you will want to come back again and again."

Brent bent his elbow and gestured for Kayla to entwine her arm in his and she obliged. They strolled along the sidewalks towards the Thames and he continued to describe the surroundings, from the parks to the Horse Guard and on to the river walk.

Kayla was pleased when they got to the river as she was able to identify her location by finding Big Ben to her right. They weren't far from her hotel when she went into panic mode. What if he wanted to come up to her room? What should she do? Should she be polite and ask him up for a cup of tea or coffee? She had made sure to follow Erika's advice and check his left ring finger for evidence of a commitment and found none. Although she was well aware that that wasn't necessarily any guarantee of his relationship status. Hell, she had no idea about dating protocol anymore. Too bad she couldn't text Erika right away. Of course, she knew what her advice would be!

They strolled across the bridge and halted outside the hotel doors. Brent held the door open for Kayla to get inside out of the cool night. Once inside he thanked her for the enjoyable evening and reminded her that the company car would be there to pick her up at 8:30am sharp. He bent forward and kissed her on the cheek.

"See you tomorrow, then?"

"Um, yes, see you tomorrow. And Brent, thank you for a lovely time tonight."

"You are so very welcome. A lovely time for a lovely lady is just what I planned."

With that, he turned and strode into the night, fading into the surreal darkness.

Kayla stared for what seemed forever but certainly was only a matter of minutes. Her knees had finally stopped shaking and the burn on her cheek from his kiss was beginning to fade. What a silly woman she was, thinking he would want to go upstairs with her! She was completely nuts! She looked at her watch and was trying to figure out the time frame. It was ten o'clock at night in London so it was, what, four in the afternoon at home? Yes, that was right.

She stepped onto the elevator and rode up to her floor. After fumbling with the key for a few moments she entered her room and began changing into her nightclothes. Once settled into bed she would text Erika. Again, there was that darned blinking light on the phone. Now who was calling her? She followed the directions and was greeted by Brent's smooth voice.

"Thank you again for the lovely evening, Kayla. I certainly hope we can do it again before you leave for the states. Good night."

Kayla felt the heat radiating up her neck and face. She also felt something else, a yearning in her belly that she hadn't felt in a very long time. It unsettled her somewhat knowing that she might actually want to be with a man. It had been so long since she had put that all behind her. But now it was staring her right in the face.

'You are horny' was the reply that came back after her initial text to Erika.

'Do you really think so? That is so early 20's."

"No it isn't! A woman can be horny whenever she wants to, just like a man can. And if I had been without sex as long as you have, I would have to be institutionalized!"

"Well, he didn't exactly indicate that he wanted to come upstairs, you know."

"He is being professional. He can't get involved with you until your business with the firm is finalized. But he DID say he wanted to see you again so that is a good sign. See maybe you are going to meet someone on this trip! Told ya!"

"Yea, right. Anyway, I am exhausted from the flight and busy day. I have to get up early to go to the reading. I'll text you after it's done, okay?"

"I'm taking that as a promise. And take a picture of this guy so I can see him, too!"

Kayla shook her head. "Sure, I'll just whip out my phone and say cheese! Good night Erika."

"Night K. Have a good one."

CHAPTER **SEVEN**

Kayla had a hard time sleeping, perhaps due to jet lag, perhaps due to her anticipation of what was to come or perhaps a combination of both. She tossed and turned, checking the clock nearly every hour, fearing she would not hear the alarm and miss her ride to the law office. By four o'clock she gave up trying and pulled out her e-reader. Immersing herself into the distant world of a book had always been her way of escaping.

By six she was so anxious that she decided to get her shower over with and then grab some kind of breakfast before she had to go. The hotel had a full English breakfast available from six-thirty until nine, so she knew she had plenty of time to get downstairs for that. She stepped into the bathtub but was completely befuddled by the faucet. The damned thing looked like a stick shift for a manual automobile! There was no indication of temperature or shower or anything that looked even slightly familiar. She stood back and started manipulating the stick. First she was scalding hot, then with a slight rotation she was freezing cold. What the heck? A few more millimeters to the left and the temperature was at least tolerable. She made quick work of bathing.

  After blow drying her hair, Kayla stepped out into the bedroom and began dressing in the clothing she had laid out the night before. Her black slacks and a sweater layered over a lightweight T-shirt. She slipped into her shoes, grabbed her key and took the lift down to the lobby where she was given directions to the dining room. She found a table by the window so she could look out at the Thames while having breakfast. Very quickly a young woman brought her a cup of tea and pointed out items on the menu. It wasn't exactly what Americans had for breakfast. Eggs, yes, but baked beans and tomatoes? That was very odd indeed. Kayla chose toast and a yogurt to go along with her tea. That was probably all her nerves could handle anyway.

  She ate her breakfast leisurely, watching all the people walking on the sidewalks outside and the boats going back and forth on the river. She was trying to settle herself down for the upcoming reading, but every relaxation technique she knew was terribly inefficient. It was going to be nerve-wracking until it was read and then nerve-wracking again when she had to make some decisions. She decided just to let the nervousness run its course and try not to show it on the outside. Checking her watch, she realized that her ride would be arriving in about twenty minutes, so she hurried back up to her room to freshen up before leaving.

The ride to the law office was short and sweet. She exited the limousine and stood for a few moments in front of the tall brownstone building nestled between two modern steel and glass structures. One thing that fascinated Kayla was how London was a vast contrast of the new and the old. Many of the buildings were destroyed in a fire long ago but the city continued to build and renew. Perhaps that's what she needed to do, rebuild her life.

She entered the building and read the placard that identified the location of all the offices inside. There was an information desk directly in the center of the lobby and she walked over to it, verifying her destination with the woman seated there. She was half an hour early and wondered if she should wait in the lobby or go ahead upstairs. A brief phone call gave her the information she needed. Yes, they were ready for her upstairs. She nodded her thanks to the receptionist and strode to the elevator.

The elevator was old and slow, but seemed to fit so well with the exterior of the building. She was actually surprised that there was an elevator at all, expecting to have to walk up several flights of stairs, which probably would have done her good. The lift strained and then stopped at the fourth floor, the doors opening to reveal a warm bank of offices, built of old wood and brass with soft yellow lighting. She stepped off the elevator and walked into the offices of Wickett and Wickett, Barristers and Real Estate Advisors.

The receptionist's desk was off to the right and the seat was empty. Kayla sat down in one of the cushy leather seats that were lined against the wall across from the desk. In a few minutes a fortyish woman with bleached blonde hair arrived and greeted her warmly.

"Ms. Battaglia, welcome to London. I'm Catherine Adamson. I sent you your paperwork for the trip. So nice to finally meet you."

"Thank you. Call me Kayla, please. It's lovely to meet you as well."

"How are you finding London?"

"It's a gorgeous city. I wish I had more time to explore."

"Yes, you are here a short time with a lot to do. Perhaps you will get back when you have more time to spend."

"I certainly hope so."

"The gentlemen are ready for you in the board room. Follow me, please."

The two women walked down the hallway and Catherine pulled open a large door with brass hinges and indicated that Kayla enter first. She obliged and walked into the huge room which had a massive oval table as its centerpiece with an entire wall of windows overlooking the Thames. Six men were seated at the table, with Brent sitting off to one side. There was one seat remaining with a stack of papers stacked neatly in front of it. The men stood to greet Kayla and she was overwhelmed with the courtesy of the group.

"Would anyone like some tea, coffee or a crumpet before starting?" Catherine indicated a small buffet of breakfast items at the far end of the room. Several of the men nodded, going to the table filling small plates and cups with steaming hot liquids before returning to their seats.

The receptionist took a seat at the far end of the table and took out a notebook, recorder and pen. Obviously she was going to be taking notes of the meeting. Kayla took her seat as well, waiting for the men to settle back into their seats. Her nerves were getting the best of her so she did some breathing exercises to calm herself. She wasn't sure if it was fear, anxiety or anticipation that was driving her right at that moment.

A very tall man in a grey pinstripe suit stood at the end of the table, garnering the attention of everyone present.

"Ms. Battaglia, I am Jacob Wickett, the third generation of barristers in this law firm. We are so sorry for the loss of your great-aunt, but we are also delighted to be the ones to deliver her last will and testament to you. As her only living relative you are named as the sole heir of her estate. My partner, Richard Chapman, shall read the will aloud and then we will give you time to ask any questions you may have. Once the will is read and all clarifications taken care of, we encourage you to take a trip to the estate to evaluate what you have inherited. We will be of complete service to you during your stay. One of our staff will accompany you to Wales if you desire. Is all of this alright with you?"

"Yes, of course. This is all so new to me. I would be grateful for any assistance."

"Then let's get to the meat of it, shall we?"

Kayla nodded as Mr. Wickett was seated. Another man rose to his feet and went to a podium near the table. He was carrying a very thick folder and began removing a large stack of papers and arranging them on the podium. He took a long drink of his beverage, then put his empty cup back on the table.

"Let's begin." He opened the seal on the folder and pulled out the contents, clearing his throat before reading the document. "I, Rebecca Catherine McGowan, being of sound mind and body, do declare this document to be my last will and testament. As of this date, 21st February 2002, I leave all my physical possessions and finances to my only blood relative, my niece, Cecelia McGowan Battaglia, of Steubenville, Ohio, USA. In the event that she should precede me in death, all of my physical possessions and finances shall go to her only child, Kayla Rebecca Battaglia, currently of Steubenville, Ohio, USA.

My estate consists of the following properties, items and accounts:

The property known as Anwylyd, or Beloved, consisting of 148 acres of land, a manor house, guest house and outbuildings located in Cowbridge, Wales. All taxes and liens have been paid through the year 2020. My estate also includes any and all of my belongings within the property as well as those contained in my safety deposit box located in Cardiff, Wales. Although the value of my financial accounts will differ from this date, all finances in my name, including stocks, bonds and other accounts, also located in Cardiff, Wales will also go to my beneficiary. Any life insurance policies from my work or other sources are left to my beneficiary via the company that holds them. All other accounts are held by the firm of Wickett and Wickett until such time that my sister or her daughter are able to sign for them, after which they are the sole property of my named heir.

These are my final wishes."

There was a hushed silence in the room as Kayla began to take in what had just been read. Why hadn't she known about all this? Had her mother kept it a secret her whole life? Had the sisters been estranged or separated for some reason? So many questions swirled in her mind. But her train of thought was interrupted when Mr. Wickett cleared his throat.

"Do you have any questions, Ms. Battaglia?"

Kayla couldn't even speak. She began to look at the documents in front of her. She felt her legs quivering against the seat of her chair. "I have so many questions that I can't even think right now. This is all so sudden."

"In that case, I believe you would like to see the property? I've made arrangements for Ms. Adamson to accompany you on the train this afternoon. We will have your things brought from the hotel and our car will take you to Victoria Station. It is approximately two and a half hours on the train, then an additional twenty minutes or so after you arrive in Cardiff. You will stop at the bank there to verify your accounts and check any safety deposit boxes before driving out to the house. There is time to have some lunch before you are off to the train station. Please feel free to step out for lunch now. Just be sure to return by one o'clock so you ladies can make your train."

The gentlemen all rose and left the room except for Brent, who was pacing nervously by the window.

"What do you think you will do now, Kayla? Do you want to move to Wales? Or perhaps you would consider selling the property."

"Oh lord, Brent, I have no idea what I will do! It hasn't even sunk in yet. I surely couldn't leave the United States to live in Wales! What would I do for a living? I wouldn't know anyone. It's mind-boggling at the moment. I think I'm going to go to lunch and let it all sink in."

"May I accompany you to lunch, then?"

"No, I'm sorry but I really need to be alone for a little while. Soon I'll be on a train trip with a perfect stranger going to a new city and a new country and a new, well, a new home perhaps. I need to clear my head a bit. I hope you understand."

"Certainly. Stop in my office before you leave for Wales, though. I want to ask you something."

"Uh, okay, I'll do that. Now where is a good place for lunch nearby?"

Brent gave her a few lunch options with directions just a few blocks from the office. Kayla stepped onto the elevator and pulled out her phone. A few quick strokes of her thumbs sent a long text flying across the pond to Erika. Why couldn't she be here right now?

Time flew by quickly as Kayla pushed her food around the plate, taking a small bite here and there. What was she thinking? She was in no mood to eat. She finished her cup of tea and hurried back to the office building where a shiny black limo waited outside, she supposed for the ride to the train station. Stepping off the elevator she looked at the directory and found Brent's office number, scurrying down the hall to his doorway. He looked up just as she entered the room.

"Hope your lunch was enjoyable. You have a long train ride with nothing to eat coming up. Ms. Adamson will be lovely company for you. She has a very bright personality."

"I bought a few snacks just in case. I need to meet her downstairs in the lobby soon. But you wanted to ask me something?"

"Oh, yes, I had nearly forgotten. Would you do me the honor of having dinner with me tomorrow evening when you return from Wales? I'd like to see you off before you return to the states on Wednesday."

"Yes, I would love it! I'll call you when I get back to the hotel tomorrow. Not sure what time that will be, though. How late is too late?"

"London is like New York, my dear, a city that never sleeps. See you tomorrow evening, then."

Kayla smiled and strode back down the hall to the elevators, feeling her phone vibrating a mile a minute as she stood in the elevator. She would get to that once settled on the train. She was enjoying making her friend wait for the gory details for once. Generally it was the other way around. The elevator doors opened and Ms. Adamson and a valet were waiting for her in the lobby. She slid into the backseat of the limo and they drove away.

CHAPTER **EIGHT**

Victoria Station was a massive stone structure that had opened in 1862 and served as one of the main lines of transportation for Londoners. Not only did it host trains, but the London Tube, buses and other methods of movement were housed here as well. It was a hubbub of activity and covered with various shops and services throughout.

The valet removed their luggage from the trunk of the car and then Ms. Adamson took over. A native of the city, she was quite familiar with all things Victoria and moved briskly towards the entrance, Kayla hot on her heels. Once inside, they stopped briefly in front of a large kiosk which showed the departures and arrivals. Catherine motioned for Kayla to follow her and she obeyed. They were soon going through the ticket terminal mounting the National Rail train to Cardiff. Baggage was quickly stowed and the ladies settled into a booth resembling a dinette, Catherine riding backwards, as Kayla would surely have a severe case of motion sickness if it were the other way around.

Kayla was amazed at the quality of the train. The seats were well padded and comfortable, and one could lay it back as if on an airplane to rest. There was a table for card playing, reading or laptops, whatever you desired, with wifi included. What hadn't they thought of? If only the US would utilize trains as well!

"So what are your thoughts about your great-aunt's estate, Ms. Battaglia?"

"Oh, I have no idea. And please call me Kayla. It is just so much to absorb, I don't really think it has set in. I was not even aware I had a great-aunt until you contacted me. Then I looked into mom's old photos and boxes of letters and found quite a few pictures of them together and many letters from Great Aunt Rebecca. It was so strange that mother hadn't told me very much, if anything about her. I wonder if they had a falling out over the years."

"That's an interesting thought. Makes one wonder, doesn't it?" Catherine paused. "So, how are you finding London?"

"It's an amazing city. I'm sorry I don't have more time to spend there. I have to get home to my house, my dog and my job. Then I'll do some serious thinking about the estate here and how I want to move forward. It is very intimidating to be a property owner in another country. I don't think I could ever leave the US, though. It is my home. There is a lot to weigh. Not to mention how difficult it is probably going to be to make arrangements across the Atlantic."

"You know our firm also handles that kind of thing. You should look into it a bit tomorrow. I can tell you some of the services we offer. And I'm sure Mr. Dankworth will be able to fill in some of the holes. He has been with the firm for a long time."

"I really appreciate any and all information. I have no idea what I'm doing."

"It really is much simpler than you think, Kayla. Just let someone with experience guide you and listen to their advice. Perhaps get a lawyer at home, too, on a retainer, for any questions you might have. You surely can afford it now."

Kayla laid her head back on the seat and closed her eyes. She didn't want to talk about her personal business, especially with a total stranger. Sure, Catherine worked for the law firm and seemed to be a lovely woman, but she was still a stranger. She wanted to talk to Erika. ERIKA! Oh no! She hadn't checked her texts for over an hour. She pulled out her phone and opened the text folder. No surprise that she had over twenty from Erika alone.

She read all the texts from Erika before sending any replies. Why answer something more than once? After perusing all the messages Kayla composed another long one. 'On the train heading for Wales. The train is marvelous. The trip is short, about 2 hours. No idea how much money is in the bank or what is in those 'other accounts'. Going to the bank first thing and would have a better idea then. Talk soon.' She hit the send button but had a second thought. 'Wish u were here.' Then she hit send once again.

When Kayla looked across the table she saw that Catherine was napping so she decided to join those ranks. Leaning back in the seat, she watched the world go by until she could no longer keep her eyelids from crashing down across her upper cheeks. She didn't realize how truly exhausted she was. The rhythm of the rails lulled her into a deep sleep.

Kayla jerked forward as the train came to a semi-screeching halt. She saw that Catherine was reading a book across from her. Looking at her watch she quickly realized that they were stopping for a reason. They had reached their destination. What a fast trip that was! As Kayla was fishing around in her purse, Catherine told her that there was no need for her passport in Wales, as it was a part of the United Kingdom. Kayla breathed a sigh of relief. She was so tired of having to show some kind of papers every time she turned around. It was like she was in Nazi Germany or something. 'Ve vant to see your papers!'

They gathered their things and stepped off the train, heading for the exit signs at the end of the walkway. When they emerged to the outside, a beige sedan was a few steps from the exit with a gentleman in a tweed suit holding up a sign that said "Wickett and Wickett".

"There's our ride, Kayla, on time as always."

Catherine gave the driver a smile as he took her suitcase and placed it in the trunk. She climbed into the back seat quickly followed by Kayla.

"We'll only be just a few minutes to the bank, so don't get too comfortable. And there you will have to have your papers with you for identification and so forth. I will wait in the car with Wilford while you take care of your personal business in there. We might even walk over to the pub and have a snack since this might take a while. The bank is expecting you, though, so you shouldn't have to wait long. Just ring me on your cell when you are done and then we can head out to Anwylyd."

"So you won't be accompanying me to the bank, Catherine?"

"No, it's not necessary. This is private, none of my affair. I'm just here to assist you."

Kayla nodded and turned towards the window, taking in the sights of Cardiff. What a strange turn of events that had occurred over the past few weeks! She could hardly believe all this was happening to her. Would she ever return to her quiet life in Ohio?

The sedan pulled up in front of a tall narrow stone building emblazoned with the letters CSF in gold on a red background. Cardiff Savings Foundation was located on the corner of a narrow cobblestone street facing the waterfront. Kayla exited the vehicle which then pulled away, turning left down another narrow lane.

She walked up the steps admiring the handiwork of the stoneworkers who had originally built the bank. The façade was covered with Celtic knots of all sorts carved into the stone. Grabbing the brass handle, Kayla pulled the heavy door open and went inside, noting that no expense was spared in the remodeling of the interior. She walked up to the counter and addressed a young teller who was busily filing her thumbnail.

"Excuse me, but I need to see someone about my great aunt's estate. I believe they are expecting me."

The teller jotted Kayla's name on a piece of paper and then directed Kayla to take a seat. She disappeared through a doorway behind her station while Kayla eyed it warily. Moments later the teller appeared, followed by a dark haired man in a suit with a well-trimmed beard.

"Ms. Battaglia, I'm Mr. Harrold, bank vice-president. We have been looking forward to meeting you."

Kayla stood and shook his outstretched hand.

"Please follow me to my office so we can discuss Rebecca's legacy."

The pair walked down a narrow corridor to an office on the far left of the building. Mr. Harrold's massive desk and leather chair filled the majority of the room, with two leather chairs in front of it for customers, Kayla assumed. He stepped around the desk and seated himself in his chair, indicating that Kayla follow suit. She lowered herself into the buttery leather and pulled the heavy chair closer to his desk. She could see that he had a several large folders and a set of keys sitting directly in the center of his blotter. Her great aunt's name was typed in bold face letters on the tabs of the folders.

"We have been quite honored to serve your great aunt's needs all these years and we certainly hope to be able to continue the family legacy. We are at your service to assist with any of your financial needs or questions during this difficult time."

"Okay, Mr. Harrold, I get all that, but I need to know just what my financial status is before I can ask someone to assist me with it. I am not a greedy person, but I do want to know what is coming to me and how best to manage it. I am well aware of the real estate, but not so aware of her financial situation. Is there a huge debt? Is the real estate in poor condition? What is in the safety deposit box?"

"There, there, Ms. Battaglia, you certainly have no huge debt. Quite the contrary, I assure you. Rebecca was a very frugal person and, although she maintained the manor house and property, which was a gift to her, she lived quite simply. She amassed a small fortune over the years and you stand to inherit all of it."

He fumbled with the folders and pulled out a financial statement, handing it to Kayla. She noticed that her hand was trembling when she took it from him. As she perused the statement, she realized that she had no idea what the conversion rate was from pounds to US dollars. Pulling out her iPhone, she found an app for currency conversion, quickly typing in the numbers on the statement. She hesitated and then put her phone down on the desk.

"Really, Mr. Harrold, instead of me fumbling around with this, why don't you just give me the bottom line? I am plugging in numbers but it isn't making much sense to me."

He turned the paper sideways and pushed up his eyeglasses. Taking a yellow highlighter he began to go over each line. Kayla listened intently as he went over each item. At the bottom of the page there was a total worth of six hundred seventy eight thousand pounds sterling. Now what was the conversion rate again?

Kayla drew in a deep shocked breath. Over one and a half million US dollars? How had her great aunt acquired such a fortune? It boggled her mind! She could barely wrap her mind around that amount of money! Her thoughts were disrupted when Mr. Harrold pulled out a small key.

"Her safety deposit box is downstairs. The value of its contents has not been evaluated for quite some time. I'll have someone take you down to look at it. You might want to have some of the jewelry appraised. I would imagine its value has increased quite a bit over the years. After you get a chance to look the box over, I'd like to meet with you to discuss some of your investment options."

Kayla shook her head, still taking in the reality of it all. Everything was like a bizarre dream that she found difficult to digest. Shortly the teller joined them in the office. Mr. Harrold instructed her to take Kayla down to the safety deposit area to view her aunt's belongings. The girl nodded and motioned for Kayla to follow her. They rose to their feet as she obliged the young woman.

They walked down a short hallway and entered a small room with an overstuffed leather chair, small table and two folding chairs. The teller entered another room to the right and Kayla followed suit. Three of the four walls were covered with drawers, each displaying two keyholes. The teller inserted her key into one of the larger drawers and Kayla inserted the key she had been given. They pulled the drawer out together and placed it in the center of the table. Kayla's key was needed again to open the top of the drawer. The teller handed her a notepad and pen and headed out of the room.

"Let us know if we can be of any service. I know this is a difficult time for you."

With that, she disappeared down the hallway, leaving Kayla alone with the box on the table. Kayla assumed that the paper and pen were to make a written record of what was in the box. She popped open the lid and began writing. By the time she had finished, it had been forty minutes. She was amazed at the variety of things Rebecca had seen fit to keep in there. Various photographs, certificates, military awards and jewelry, lots of jewelry. From the photos she had seen of her, it hadn't struck Kayla that Rebecca was the kind of woman who wore fancy jewelry, but perhaps she had been wrong. She had a gnawing feeling that there was a whole lot more to this woman than she had first believed.

She closed the box, removing a few pieces of jewelry and photographs for herself, and returned it to its resting place in the wall. When she returned to the lobby,

Mr. Harrold was seated at his desk and motioned for her to join him. Kayla told him that she wished to withdraw a small amount of the money but the rest would remain with the bank and she would continue to maintain the safety deposit box as well.

"Once I see the estate and make some decisions, I will let you know what I am going to do next. Until then, things will remain as they are."

They finished their business, exchanged a few pleasantries and then Kayla stepped outside into the cool, brisk air. Catherine was in the car, listening to the latest British pop sensations when Kayla joined her.

"On to Anwylyd, I suppose. Do you know how to get there?"

"We have a good GPS and map. I don't think we'll have any problem. Ask any local, I think they can tell us where it is."

Catherine chuckled, nodded to the driver, and down the road they went, Kayla full of anticipation to see just what her great aunt's life was all about.

CHAPTER NINE

Within thirty minutes Kayla saw a large stone fence rolling along the hills and the massive brownstone house off in the distance. As they pulled between the two large stone columns, she saw the inscription "Anwylyd - 1942" carved on a worn metal plate just inside the entrance. The road into the complex was a dirt and gravel mix, tossing stones and dust into the air behind the car. The disrepair made the drive hazardous at best, with huge ruts carved from many winter's ice and snow. Thank goodness she didn't have a tendency to get carsick, or she surely would

have lost her lunch then and there! They pulled up in front of the massive stone structure that was the manor house, and Kayla's mind was going in a million different directions as she stepped out of the car.
Kayla had no idea where in the world Cowbridge, Wales was, but she, herself was there now, standing in front of her great-aunt's estate.

There was a large manor house, a smaller guest house and an oval barn, all made of white limestone, gracing the 148+ acres. Each was in some state of disrepair, mostly due to the lack of attention during the past few years. It was evident by the layout of various paths that stately gardens had stood proud prior to being overgrown.

The typed description that she held in her hand noted that there were two banqueting halls, 3 living rooms, a parlor, one master kitchen and two lesser ones, seven bedrooms, eleven staircases and nine bathrooms, some with their original 18th century toilets still in use. Fifteen stone fireplaces of varying sizes dotted the manor house as well.

What in the hell have I gotten myself into, she wondered as she grasped the cold brass doorknob. Catherine gathered close behind her as she stepped into a world decades away.
The foyer was grand, stone and marble flooring in patterns of waves, giving a hint of the movement of the sea. Eighteen foot ceilings were crowned with oak moulding and the chandelier was encircled with blue, white and beige tiles in a mosaic pattern nearly matching the flooring beneath her feet. A long hallway lay before them, and a boldly masculine oak staircase stood to the left. Sliding wooden doors on the right led to the parlor, which was dotted with white sheet covered furnishings leading to a massive stone and wood fireplace, which was enclosed in an intriquitely carved mantelpiece. Faded velvet drapes covered the triple window facing the front of the house, their tassels unraveled and covered with dust.

Kayla gently lifted the sheet from what she assumed to be a sofa and sat down on the edge of it, still trying to take in the massiveness of the house. She was just beginning to understand that all of this was now hers, and hers alone. Never in her wildest imagination could she have created such a scenario. Even with all the books she had read over her thirty plus years, she had never envisioned such a home. She sat quietly for a few minutes to gather her thoughts.

"Can you believe this place, Catherine? I am in shock."

"It is really something, Kayla. Your great aunt was living her dream life here, I'd imagine."

"Perhaps, but I wonder why she never married or had children. I would think it would have been very lonely here at times."

"She stayed here for over forty years, so there must have been something appealing to it." Catherine reached for a light switch and flipped it, stimulating a stained glass ceiling light, which illuminated the large room. "I believe the utilities were just recently resumed once we found the true heir to the estate. You will probably have some problems with plumbing and the like, as we will see shortly."

"Let's continue doing the walkthrough, then we'll figure out the arrangements for staying tonight. I doubt there are any groceries or necessities so we'll need to find a store to get a few things."

"I had thought that we would take a room in town, but we can certainly stay here. I saw a grocer on the way out not too far back down the main road. We can run there when we are done with our initial walk through."

"That sounds marvelous, Catherine. In the meantime, let's get to it." Kayla pulled out her camera and the schematic of the house and headed back the main hallway with Catherine in tow.

They spent the next two hours exploring the main house, never making it to the outbuildings. Kayla's camera was clicking away, recording the furnishings, stained glass windows, flooring and views. It was an exhausting experience so the two decided to head into town for dinner and a stop at the grocers. Kayla could not begin to wrap her mind around all that had happened in the last few weeks. She was totally spent.

The driver proceeded a bit more slowly back to the estate now that it was dark. The roads were too narrow and unfamiliar to drive haphazardly at night. There were virtually no street lights and it was pitch black. They had also forgotten to light any lamps in the house and it was eerily dark when they returned. It took a bit of creeping against the walls to find the light switches and the ladies were laughing hysterically while trying to locate one. Once the lights were on, things settled down.

Mr. Hughes carried in their bags and asked to be excused for the night. Kayla nodded, suggesting that he pick a room that actually had furniture in it and perhaps an attached bath. He gladly set off in search of accommodations for the night, leaving the women to talk woman talk. He was not getting any younger and driving these clients around, listening to their chatter, was beginning to work his nerves. Soon he would be able to retire and not leave his family for weeks at a time. The thought brought a wide grin to his face.

Kayla wandered around the huge kitchen trying to sort through all the ideas that were running through her head. Could she leave the States and live here? Was it really possible that she could run a bed and breakfast? She had toyed with the idea a few times, but it was just not financially possible so she had placed that dream on a back burner. But now, perhaps she could have a dream fulfilled. If she couldn't be a wife with a wonderful husband, two children, a little house and white picket fence, surely she could be an independent business woman!

"What time do we have to leave in the morning, Catherine?"

"Our train departs for London at 2:45pm, so we need to be at the station by 1:30 I would think. Leaving here at noon should give us plenty of time to grab lunch and get to the station on time. Why? What would you like to do tomorrow?"

"I'd like to get a look at the outbuildings and see what kind of repairs are needed to make this a working farm or bed and breakfast. I need to be realistic about it. If I decide to keep it, I would be taking a giant leap of faith, leaving my home country, my job, and my life behind to start anew. I have to be sure it is the right thing to do."

"I might be slightly out of line here, but what will your friends think? And your boyfriend? Would he agree to it?"

"Yes, you are out of line, we barely know each other and it is a business relationship. But I will tell you, no one will care if I stay or go except for my best friend. There is no boyfriend, no significant other, no one to tie me down there."

"Then maybe it would be good for you here, don't you think? But if not, I'm sure there is a buyer out there waiting for a place such as this."

"I don't know yet. I need to go home and gather my thoughts, figure out the logistics and finances and then I will make a decision. I'm going to use the desk in the library and do some figuring tonight. I'm physically tired, but my mind is racing. I need to write down what is going through my head and possibly people I might need to contact for advice. Feel free to find yourself a room and settle in. I will be up late tonight. And Catherine…"

"Yes, Kayla?"

"Thank you for all your help. You have been a godsend. I really appreciate your time and advice. See you in the morning."

With that Catherine headed upstairs and Kayla fixed herself a cup of tea before proceeding to the library. It already had become her favorite room in the house, its massive walls lined with shelf after shelf of books dating from the 1800's to the present time, most first editions. She picked up an old feather duster that had been lying in the corner of the room and shook it out, then gently proceeded to dust off the books, one shelf at a time. She wasn't able to get to the three top shelves, but knew she would attend to them when she returned. She pulled out "Don Quixote" and stroked its spine gently. It was one of her favorite books of all time. She herself had been battling windmills for oh, so long.

She removed the sheet from the large cherry desk and softly placed the book on the corner. One by one she opened the drawers, finding new and different treasures in each. Her great aunt was obviously fond of dogs, as she was, and many of the items in the desk featured a canine in some way. There was a long silver letter opener with an elegant greyhound handle, a leather notepad was embossed with foxhounds in a pack, as well as wax stamps featuring a paw with the letter "R" in the center. Maybe this is where she got her love of dogs, from her great aunt. She surely didn't get it from her mother, who had allowed her to have one mixed breed that followed her home from school in the fifth grade. No other dogs had been in her life until she was an adult and paying the bills.

Kayla pulled out a legal notepad and grabbed a pen from her purse and began jotting down notes so that she would not forget any of the things that had popped in her head during the day. It didn't have to be organized or make any sense just now, she would have a very long plane ride which would be perfect for doing that. She knew she had a lot to think about and decisions would have to be made.

An hour and a half passed and Kayla had finished scribbling down her ideas about the house and it's potential. She knew it was going to be a huge undertaking if she decided to keep the place. And what if she couldn't make it work. She would need to find a job locally. She would need to hire help. It would all be so difficult from 3000 miles away! Maybe she should just consider selling the place and get what she could for it. Of course, that was the 'safe' thing to do. Maybe it was time she took a chance on herself.

She realized that she was losing a battle with her exhaustion and decided to call it a night. Gathering her overnight bag and a one of the sleeping bags that had been wisely packed she headed for the large bathroom off the foyer.

"My god, I looked like a drowned raccoon!" Looking in the mirror, she saw the toll that both jet lag and exhaustion had taken on her. She quickly washed her face, slipped into her pajamas and headed back to the library. She didn't want to disturb the others sleeping upstairs, so she arranged the sleeping bag on the large leather sofa and slipped into a deep disturbed sleep. Although her body was shutting down, her mind would not stop. It was going to be a long night. She tossed and turned until the early hours of the morning, finally giving in to her exhaustion.

Kayla was awakened by the smell of bacon and rattling of pans in the kitchen. She bolted upright and slid to the floor, forgetting that she had slept on the sofa. She laughed quietly to herself and got up, then rolled the sleeping bag and tied it tightly. Trudging towards the staircase, she heard the distinct laughter of a man, something she had missed horribly since the death of her father. She smiled as she skipped up the steps to one of the larger bathrooms. She made quick work of a shower, dressed quickly and joined Catherine and the driver in the kitchen.

"Wow! What a surprise! I didn't know you could cook Catherine!"

"Oh, raising four children alone teaches one a lot of skills, young Kayla. I worked full time and raised my children after their father was killed in an accident at work. I can cook, sew, not too fond of cleaning though."

They sat down at the table and enjoyed eggs, bacon, toast and cinnamon buns. The clean-up went smoothly with everyone pitching in. Kayla helped carry the suitcases and sleeping bags out to the car, then grabbed her notepad and jacket.

"I'm going to have a look around at the outbuildings before we head out this morning. I want to get a feel for their possible futures."

"I think I'm going to stay back here and relax a bit, if you don't mind. I'm just not as young as I used to be I suppose." Catherine laughed as Kayla headed out the door.

As Kayla entered the nearest of the outbuildings she could see that it had been a kennel at some time. On one side there were metal runs with openings to the outside, although the external fencing had all been knocked down at some point. There was a wide hallway of large stones and then various rooms on the opposite side. The first room must have been the office, as it had a large desk and filing cabinets along one wall with a large picture window. The next few rooms had been used for storage most likely, with various hooks and fixtures on the walls. She jotted some notes down and then headed toward the more distant structure. There was a moderate wind this morning and the new grass was blowing in aqua waves across the field. No wonder Becca had done most of her décor as the sea.

Within minutes she was standing at the doorway of the stable. She opened the side door and went inside. It was quite dark and it took a few minutes for her eyes to adjust.

It was obvious that this had been one of Becca's delights, her showplace. There were four stalls on either side of the stone hallway, each one done in halfway up in cherry wood with black wrought iron rails on the top half. Each stall door was Dutch, so that the top half could be opened for the horses to look out. There was a concrete wash rack on the far end and an office across from that. Kayla was sure that it was a stellar stable in its time. She smiled, realizing that perhaps she had indeed gotten her fondness for animals from Great-Aunt Becca.

She glanced at her watch and realized that they would be leaving in about half an hour, so she put her notepad away and strolled towards the guest house. Perhaps, she thought, I could live here and start a new life. It might be just the thing she wanted, or just the thing she needed.

When she returned to the manor house, they piled into the car and said good bye to Anwylyd for the moment. But Kayla knew in her hear that she would return, and soon. There was just something about the place that she felt in her gut. She couldn't quite describe it, but she knew it was real.

They arrived at the train station with minutes to spare. Catherine and Kayla rushed through the turnstile and leapt onto the train just as it was beginning to pull out to head back to London. A nervous laugh escaped Kayla's lips as she settled into her seat. She was still amazed at all that had occurred in just a few weeks. She also knew she had a date tonight with the charming Brent Dankworth. Maybe, just maybe, she would let go of her inhibitions. She leaned her head back against the headrest and fell into an unknown oblivion.

CHAPTER **TEN**

Kayla was just beginning to stir as the train pulled into Victoria Station. Catherine had already gathered her things and had them neatly arranged on the seat next to her.

"Did you sleep well? You must have been exhausted."

"Well, Catherine, I'm not sure. I was in and out the whole trip. So much has happened and I think the jet lag and excitement all finally got to me. The anticipation of this trip and what was in the will had my mind in high gear for a week. So at least now I know what I am dealing with and getting some ideas of how to deal with it. So I suppose I was able to relax a bit. Now I need to go home and gather my thoughts and make some decisions. I have a lot to think about."

"Well, I really enjoyed meeting you and spending time at Anwylyd. It is a fabulous place, to be sure. I hope you decide to make it your home. Then we can spend some time together again."

"Thank you, Catherine. I don't know if I could have made this trip without your help. You have been a godsend. No wonder the company treasures you so much. It has been lovely meeting you. I'll let you know when I'm returning."

The two made their way off the train and out to their waiting car. The driver dropped Catherine off at the office and took Kayla back to her hotel. She hurried up to her room and got out her phone. There was a text from Brent stating he would pick her up at six for dinner. And she had SO much to send to Erika back home. She started with the photos and a bit of information. She jumped into the shower and let the steam clear her mind. Sliding into her robe, she planted herself in the big orange chair next to the window overlooking the Thames. Her only decision right at that moment was what she would wear tonight.

She suddenly remembered a sweet little black number in the window of the one of the hotel shoppes downstairs. She jumped into her sweats and ran downstairs. Fortunately the shoppe was still open and she was the only client in it. She tried the dress on, was shocked at the tag, but then remembered that she could certainly afford it. She flew back upstairs and slid it on.

As Kayla was putting on the finishing touches, her phone vibrated insistently. She picked it up. Although it was only 5:45, it was Brent, he was in the lobby. She texted that she would be right down, then spritzed herself lightly with French perfume and strode to the elevator, a new sense of pride in her step.

She saw him immediately when she stepped off the elevator. He had his back towards her and was chatting with the gentleman at the concierge desk. She tapped him on the shoulder and he whirled around, taking her into his arms and planting a kiss on her cheek.

"You look fabulous!"

"You don't look to bad yourself."

"Hopefully your trip to Wales went well. You certainly look refreshed."

"Yes, it was fast but fun. I have a lot of things to sort out when I get home, but I have been doing a lot of thought about everything."

"Going to sell the old place, are you? That is probably the best thing you can do. It would be pretty difficult to manage from across the pond."

"Well, I haven't quite made that decision yet, but it is one of the possibilities."

"Enough business talk. Let's focus on having a grand evening, shall we?"

"Absolutely!" She took his outstretched hand and he led her out the revolving door to a waiting limousine.

Within minutes they were pulling up in front of Le Pont de la Tour, one of the most outstanding French restaurants in London. The doorman swiftly swept them into the restaurant and soon they were seated at one of the best tables in the house, overlooking the Thames. The dusky sky made for spectacular reflections on the water. Kayla was quite impressed by both Brent's choice and his French fluency. Although she had taken four years of it in high school, most had been forgotten, but she was able to make out bits and pieces of the conversation.

"We will start with escargot and a delightful wine. What would you like as your entrée?"

"Let me peruse the menu a moment, and then I'll decide. This is just wonderful Brent. I am so happy that you chose a French restaurant. We don't have any near us at home. I have to drive quite a while for a good meal."

"I'm glad you like it. I always worry about choosing for visitors. You never know what cuisine they prefer. But I think you mentioned something about a French restaurant when we were driving through the city, so I thought you would like it."

"You have a great memory, Brent. I did mention that I would love to eat in Paris one day. This comes fairly close, I think."

Kayla smiled as the waiter filled their water glasses and opened the bottle of pinot noir, allowing the wine to breath before pouring. Brent sniffed and then tasted it, nodding his approval. It had been so long since she had been on a 'real' date that Kayla watched every little thing and memorized every moment. To be wooed by an attractive man in London was something that she could have only imagined in her previous life.

She made her dinner selection which she ordered in her own rough French when the waiter returned. Brent smiled at her attempt and nodded his approval. She was starting to relax now, thinking that maybe she might remember how to behave in public.

Soon the appetizer had arrived, smelling of garlic and the sea. Kayla realized that she had nearly forgotten what it was like to be at a nice restaurant eating something other than burgers and fries. If there was one thing Americans did not do well, it was eating.

Kayla was wrestling with the wet shell of the escargot, when her tiny fork escaped and made a break for freedom. It removed itself from a life at table level to take up residence on the plush carpet, just past the white linen tablecloth border, where it remained momentarily until she regained her composure. She started to lean over, but was stopped when she felt the intense heat of Brent's hand on her knee as he leaned into her, reaching for the fork. She felt his hand glide slowly upward, his pinky slipping beneath the fabric of her dress toward her inner thigh. A small sigh escaped her lips as he uprighted himself and laid the fork back on the tablecloth, then motioned for the waiter to bring another. It had been a very long time since a man had entered those waters.

The dinner conversation was light and festive and several people came over to greet Brent. He was obviously well regarded in London and introduced Kayla to each one, taking some time to tell her something about the person. Kayla was amazed and delighted that he was taking such an interest in her knowing that she would be gone tomorrow. Maybe there were still some good guys left out there after all.

"Do you like to dance, Kayla Battaglia?"

"Um, well, yes. It has been a while, but I do enjoy dancing. Why do you ask?"

"I'd like to take you to a nice club where we can have a few drinks and do some dancing before retiring for the night. Is there a genre that you prefer? Pop? Rock? Jazz?"

"I really like jazz but it has been a long time since I've been to a club. My life is usually working and sleeping."

"Then a jazz club it is! You will have plenty of time to sleep on the plane tomorrow. So why not live it up your last night in London?"

Brent quickly paid their cheque and led Kayla back out onto the street.

"It's a lovely night, why don't we walk a bit to get our dinner settled before we go clubbing."

"That sounds wonderful, Brent. I'm up for it."

The pair strolled arm in arm down the sidewalk next to the Thames, Brent pointing out various places in the city and some of the history, including the story of the devastating fire. Kayla found it very interesting how the old blended in with the new, architecture that was centuries old standing next to a 21st century state of the art complex. It boggled her mind to think of all that had happened here.

Brent stopped outside a club where the sound of horns trickled into the night air. He motioned for Kayla to go ahead of him through the entrance door. Inside was a blossoming crowd of jazz lovers and the band was just getting hot. They found a small corner table for two and ordered their drinks, enjoying the buzz. After a few sips they found their way on the dance floor.

Both Brent and Kayla could cut a rug, and they showed their immense talents, getting a hand from the standing crowd. Kayla was laughing and dancing as she had never before. Maybe the London scene was a good place for her. Or maybe it was just being away from the usual drudgery. Either way, she was having the time of her life. A slower song began and Brent took her into his arms. She looked into his eyes and hesitated. There was no spark, no smile, just a distant look. He was smiling with his lips, but his eyes showed little interest. She shook it off, believing that it was just her imagination.

As the song was winding down, Kayla felt his hands sliding down onto her hips. She felt a mixture of lust and caution blowing around in her head. Her thoughts were interrupted when Brent bent forward and kissed her on the neck.

"Let's get out of here."

She smiled as he led her from the dance floor to their table. He threw back the rest of his drink and left a generous tip. Once again they headed out into the night.

Brent hailed a cab this time and directed the driver to Kayla's hotel. By now her senses were on high alert. How she wished Erika was here now to tell her what to do. But she was a big girl in the big city and needed to pull up her panties. Whatever happened next would be of her choosing, or so she believed. When they pulled up to the revolving door she was still unsure of where all this would lead. She was simply going to play it moment to moment. She had nearly forgotten all about this part of life.

They rushed through the lobby to the elevator, Brent's foot tapping impatiently as they waited for its arrival. When the door closed he pulled Kayla close and began kissing her softly on the mouth, then moving to her earlobe and down her neck. To Kayla, her skin was suddenly a living thing with a mind of its own and she was feeling a desire that hadn't been part of her life for at least ten years. Should she give in to the emotions that were threatening to take her over?

The elevator jolted to a stop and they spilled out into the hall, Brent not missing a beat with his kisses. Kayla fumbled in her purse for the room key, noticing her hand shaking as she slid it across the lock. Brent shoved the door open with his fist and kicked it shut with his foot, forcing Kayla to walk backwards into the room. She took a deep breath and pulled away from his grip.

"I need to go freshen up. I won't be but a minute."

She went into the bathroom and leaned on the sink. She heard Brent's voice in the bedroom, most likely making a phone call of some sort. She wiped her face with cold water and washed her hands. She knew that if he touched her again she would not be able to resist him. And why should she? Didn't Erika say what happens in London stays in London? She straightened up her blouse, unbuttoning one more of the top buttons, spritzed herself with perfume and rejoined Brent, who immediately resumed kissing her, more forcefully now.

Kayla leaned into him, taking in the smell of his sweat mixing with cologne. It was quite an aphrodisiac, sending her mind reeling once again. His hands moved quickly to unzip her dress and were roughly massaging her back, which she found even more stimulating. She now believed she had passed the point of no return. And so be it, they were both consenting adults. As she envisioned what would happen next, there was a knock at the door.

Brent pulled away and answered it, returning with an ice bucket containing a bottle of expensive champagne. He expertly popped the cork and poured two glasses, handing one to Kayla.

"To Kayla, to celebrate your first, but hopefully not last, trip to London!"

He raised his glass and took a long sip. Kayla followed suit. When he pulled her against him she could taste the sweet nectar on his lips and the growing urgency in his loins. She reached for his suit jacket and removed it, then began unfastening the buttons of his shirt. He slipped it off and hung it on the back of the desk chair, then got back to the business at hand. For a moment Kayla felt faint, as if she would collapse at any moment. But when he slid the straps of her little black dress over her shoulders, she released her inhibitions faster than dark silk could hit the floor.

Kayla was awakened by the sound of water running. She rolled over in bed and saw that Brent was not in the rumpled pile of linen. She laid back and listened again. He was in the shower. Grabbing her watch she saw that it was just four in the morning. Odd that he would be showering at that time of day.

She heard him quietly open the bathroom door and emerge completely dressed.

"I was hoping not to wake you, Kayla. I'm so sorry. I must go because I have an important court case today and need to finish my statements."

"No problem, Brent. I am just surprised you would be leaving in the middle of the night."

"Remember that London is like New York. I had a two hour power nap and now I have to get to work. I have enjoyed your company so much. I look forward to seeing you again. Will you return to London soon?"

"I have to make some decisions and get my affairs in order, but yes, I will most likely be back within a few months."

"If you decide to sell Anwylyd let me know. I can handle that for you. I'm sure you could easily make a small fortune on it."

"I don't know if I want to sell. I have to think long and hard about that. I might start my life over in Wales."

"That is silly, isn't it? You are now a million heiress. You can live anywhere in the world. Why would you choose Wales? The weather is horrible and there is nothing exciting there."

"Like I said, I just don't know. Don't you need to be going?"

"Yes, yes, I do. Keep in touch, will you? I put my business card on the desk there. Have a good trip back to the States."

"I will. I will probably sleep the whole flight. And, Brent?"

"Yes, Miss Battaglia?"
"Thanks for last night. I had a great time."
"Glad you did. Take care now."

With that, Brent was gone. Kayla rolled back over in bed, reviewing everything that happened over the last 48 hours. Never in her wildest dreams could she have imagined it. Never. She dropped back into a contented sleep.

The alarm clock sounded promptly at seven and Kayla hopped out of bed and into the shower. She quickly dressed in comfortable clothes and finished packing her things. She picked up Brent's business card and called the number, leaving a voicemail to wish him good luck with his trial and thank him again for his kindness during her visit. Then she slid it into her wallet. She hurried down to the lobby leaving her bags at the concierge desk while she had a quiet breakfast. Knowing the minimal fare that was offered onboard the plane, she placed a few snacks in her purse and then waited for the limousine to arrive.

Ten minutes later she found herself en route to Heathrow Airport and home. She had so many mixed emotions about going back it surprised her. Maybe she did belong in Wales. The house and all her ideas came flooding into her mind. She knew that the flight would not seem nearly as long with everything she had to think about. Once she was seated she checked her phone one last time before turning it off. No messages from Brent. She typed a quick note to Erika and shut it down. Perhaps a nap would do her good before opening up all her notes about Anwylyd. The plane taxi'd down the runway and left the rough surface of the earth as Kayla's eyelids went south.

CHAPTER ELEVEN
Rebecca

Rebecca Bernadette McGowan was the eldest of three children born to Patrick and Etta McGowan on a small family farm outside Cadiz, Ohio. She was the first one in the family to procure a post high school education when she attended nursing school. It was a matter of pride in the family as she had always been the favorite. Her degree only served to raise her up another notch on that pedestal.

Rebecca and her younger sister, Marguerite, were just two years apart in age and had a very close relationship. The youngest in the family, Joseph, was nearly ten years her junior because their mother had a series of miscarriages. Joseph was considered a miracle baby as their mother was nearly forty when he was born. They were a tight knit group and family was of utmost importance.

After finishing school Rebecca expressed interest in volunteering to help with the war effort and soon was enlisted in the army nurse corps. Although her parents were petrified to let her go, they were also very proud that she had chosen to help her country in some way. She left for Germany the day after Marguerite finished her classes to become a clerk at the courthouse. It was a bittersweet memory for both of them.

Rebecca, or Becca, as she preferred, found herself fitting easily into the routine at the army hospital. She was a creature of habit and found the ritualistic days refreshing after spending most of her young life in the chaos that was a family farm. Although she adored animals, she did not miss having to rise before the crack of dawn to trudge through three feet of snow, break ice on water buckets and assist with milking, fetching eggs, or finding wandering sheep. She arrived at work on time every time and enjoyed taking care of the men who were fighting for everything she believed in. Her dedication was rewarded as she moved up through the ranks.

After two years she was able to take a long leave over the holidays and spend some time back in Ohio with her family. She had forgotten how simple the life was and she enjoyed relaxing and reminiscing with friends and family, particularly Marguerite, who she had missed more than anyone. But she knew she would be happy to return to her predictable routine.

Margie continued to work at the courthouse and was full of stories about the locals and their indiscretions. Sure, she had been on a few dates with paralegals and police officers, but none of them were the man of her dreams. The two sisters spent a lot of time talking about their hopes, dreams and the men that held their interest. Neither had found Mr. Right and Rebecca herself was fairly sure that he didn't exist. She also had dated a number of men, mostly from the military ranks, but was not ready for any kind of serious commitment. She had so many things she still wanted to pursue. Although Margie didn't understand it, she respected her big sister. Margie just wanted to find a nice husband and settle down.

The two weeks flew by quickly and soon it was time for Becca to head back to Germany. She hated leaving her sister and vowed to continue to keep in touch weekly with letters and photographs through the deathly slow mail system. Margie agreed to do the same and took her sister to the airport. The said their goodbyes and Becca headed to the gate to meet her flight.

Several months after returning to Germany, Becca was given orders to leave immediately for London, where she would be assuming the role of Operating Room supervisor at the Army hospital there. She finished her work day and said her farewells to the team she had put together in Germany. She was given an engraved gold locket and other small gifts by her team. She was so very melancholy about leaving them behind. They had been her family for the last three years. She knew they were well trained and capable of handling any situation. She had done her job and done it well and she was looking forward to advancing her own career.

    Becca got her orders in the morning and boarded the military plane that would carry herself and several of the surgeons she had worked with over the past few years to their new assignment. She was delighted to find out that they had specifically requested that she join their team in London. It would be a great new experience for her, of that she was sure. She had always wanted to visit England, London in particular, and now it would be her temporary home. Although the city had been under attack several times recently, she was not afraid. Fear was just not something that ever entered her mind when it came to doing what she loved best. Taking care of people was the core of her being.

    After arriving in London and being briefed on their assignments, the staff was taken to special military housing which was adjacent to the hospital. Becca's apartment was small but neat, just the way she liked it. And she didn't have to share her accommodations this time. She had an apartment all to herself. She anxiously got to the job of unpacking and putting things in their place. Work would start early at 0600. She made a quick trip to the grocer and settled in for the night.

    Becca was up at 0500 ironing her uniform and cleaning her shoes, ready to start the day. She hurried across the lot to the hospital and quickly found the OR reception area. She introduced herself to the receptionist who asked her to sit in the waiting area for a few minutes until the current supervisor could meet with her. She felt very relaxed and had just picked up a magazine when the older woman arrived.

"Ms. McGowan, your reputation precedes you. I am Corporal Thelma Williams from Kansas City, MO. It's time for me to retire and you have been chosen to replace me here in London. Welcome!"

Becca immediately felt at ease with this woman. She was sure that they were kindred spirits of sorts, giving themselves to the cause and the career that they adored. She rose to her feet and they shook hands, each with a strong steady grip. The Corporal gestured to Becca to follow her and she obliged. They started down a long hallway which was adorned with the lettering "Operating Room", a place Becca was very familiar with.

"I'll be staying on for the next month before retiring to the country. I really am looking forward to it."

"I'll bet you are anxious to get home and settled once again."

"Rebecca, if I may call you Rebecca, this is my home. I have no intention to return to the States. I've bought a small house in the countryside in the southern part of England and plan to look out over the ocean while I sit on my deck with a glass of port in my hand. And my son has property in Wales as well. Believe me, you will come to love it here as I have. It will always be a part of you no matter where you may go. You will always return to England."

Becca nodded and continued to listen as the elder familiarized her with the ins and outs of the OR. She was relieved that the woman would be staying on for a while until she got her 'sea legs' so to speak in the hospital. Thelma actually was a breath of fresh air with her honesty and integrity. Becca believed that they were kindred spirits who would bond very strongly, even though they would only be together a short time. And Thelma felt the same. Becca reminded her of her younger self.

Within a week Becca was running the OR with an iron hand, keeping it organized and running smoothly. Thelma was very impressed with the younger nurse, her exceptional ability to manage people and handle emergency situations. It seemed that there was a bombing or attack every other day anymore that demanded their attention. They often would put in sixteen hour days putting soldiers or citizens back together. But that was a pace Becca was accustomed to and she felt as if she was right where she belonged. She felt needed and accepted here, something that had been lacking in Germany. And she was grateful for the common language. It made things much easier to deal with and patients much easier to triage.

Two weeks before Thelma was to retire, she invited Becca to spend the weekend at her cottage in Cornwall. They both deserved a decent rest and it was the most peaceful place on earth as far as Thelma was concerned. Becca reluctantly agreed, worried that there would be a major disaster at the hospital that she really should be close by to handle.

"You are only 3 hours away and can get back quickly if necessary. If they cannot wait that long, they can send a helicopter for you. You need a short holiday and you have earned it. You have trained your staff to handle any disaster. Just pack your bag and meet me at three o'clock Friday. We'll have a nice visit."

Becca knew Thelma was right. She needed this break from all the violence that was war. Maybe it would be good for her mind to be where men were not killing each other on a daily basis over some stupid sense of right or wrong. She smiled at Thelma.

"Thank you. I'll be ready." With that, she headed home from another long tedious day.

The next two days dragged as more and more wounded were being brought in from a bombing outside of London. The OR crew scrambled to make room for all of those that were coming in. Becca supervised the triage while organizing the surgical schedule. It was a brutal reality of war. When Friday afternoon edged closer and closer she doubted if she would be able to get away. She was a control freak of sorts and didn't want to leave 'her' OR in the hands of just anyone.

Dr. Robert Etchison stopped her in the hallway with two cups of coffee in his hands.

"I think you need to take that trip with Thelma this weekend, Becca. From what I have heard, the violence is going to escalate and we are going to be up to our elbows in bloody bandages very soon. Take this cup of coffee, sit down and breathe for a few minutes. Then finish up your shift and get the hell out of here. I don't want to see you again until early Monday morning."

"Is that an order, sir?"

"Indeed it is. Go get some rest and prepare for all bloody hell to break loose."

"Yes, sir!" Becca saluted the man and grinned as he headed down the hallway to yet another massive surgery.

When her shift was over, Becca checked in with her staff and gave them all the information they would need if they had to contact her in an emergency. They practically shoved her out the door and wished her well for the weekend. No, they wouldn't need her and could handle a few days without her. Yes, they would call if they felt compelled for any reason. She walked out the front door, hesitated on the step, and then joined Thelma in the car for the ride to Cornwall.

Becca was still a little anxious about being a passenger on what she considered the wrong side of the road. But Thelma seemed to be a pro at it, having lived in England for the past eight years. Those roundabouts in the villages were the worst, Becca just couldn't get the proper turning in her mind. After an hour of chatting and 'shadow braking', she leaned her head back on the seat and fell into a deep sleep, images of young men with bloody bandages racing through her head. She startled awake when one became too vivid, only to find that they were pulling into the driveway of a quaint brown cottage with a partially thatched roof. Yes, this was Thelma's Valhalla.

"Here we are sleepyhead! I hope your boyfriend is hard of hearing. You snore like a freight train!"

Becca shook her head. Although she was very fond of Thelma, her personal life was not for public view. She hadn't dated in years and had buried herself deep in her work. She convinced herself many years ago that she didn't have time for a relationship. She didn't need a man to complete her life. She had a very full and busy life without one. Husbands were for sissies.

Just as that thought was leaving her, she was distracted by an extremely handsome young man who was approaching the vehicle from the cottage.

"Mother! So glad you are home! Let me help you with your bags."

Mother? Thelma hadn't mentioned that she had a gorgeous son at home. Was she up to a little matchmaking? Well, Becca was having no part of it! She would be friendly enough, but she didn't have time for such nonsense. She was here to relax and rest up, that was all. She stepped out of the car and reached for her suitcase.

"I'll get that for you, Miss." He said with a welcoming smile.

"No, no, I've got it. You help your, um, mother, then."

"Oh, Becca, this is my son, Ian Williams. Ian, this is the young woman who is so unfortunate to be stepping into my shoes, Rebecca MacGowan."

He held out his hand. "Pleased to meet you Ms. MacGowan. Mother has had many great things to say about you."

"Really? She hasn't said anything about you. But lovely to meet you just the same."

"Come on in the house, I have tea brewing and have just started gathering wood for the fire tonight. Dinner will be fresh haddock and some vegetables from our own little garden. I also have several nice wines if you prefer. Come, come in."

Becca carefully maneuvered the cobblestone walkway and followed Thelma and Ian into the tiny house. It was a step back in time. A stone fireplace with logs piled high lined the south wall of the main living area which opened up to a small dining room then to the kitchen. The floors were stone with a multitude of colorful throw rugs strewn about. Large wooden beams were overhead and the rooms were painted a muted yellow.

Thelma sat her bags down in the living room and motioned for Becca to follow her. They went down a narrow hallway to a small bedroom on the left. It was a masculine room, decorated in warm earth tones and smelling of men's cologne. The scent caught Becca off guard, as she could barely recall being near a man wearing cologne. It was relaxing in its own way.

"I can't take your son's bedroom. Where will he sleep?"

"On the living room sofa. He falls asleep there anyway on a regular basis. It won't hurt him to sleep there for the two nights you are here."

"I can sleep on the sofa. I don't want to displace or inconvenience anyone."

"Oh pshaw, you are not displacing anyone. Ian insisted that you take his room and he even cleaned it up a bit for you. Now no more of that nonsense. The room across the hall is my bedroom and the one at the end of the hall is the bath. So go freshen up and get ready for dinner. He is quite the cook, my son. You will see. I hope you like eating well, because this weekend there will be no quick sandwiches. You are going to get a full English breakfast and roasts and Yorkshire pudding."

"I'm not used to eating like that."

"That's why it's a holiday dear, so you can eat like that once in a while. Come now, I have the entire weekend planned so we need to get started."

Thelma pulled the door shut as she left the room. Becca continued to take in the masculine presence. Yes, it felt lovely to be near a nice looking man. But she didn't have time for one in her life. A shame, really, he was quite nice. She unpacked her toiletries and went into the bathroom to wash up. As she dried her face, she actually was sad that she hadn't packed any makeup. The war was wearing her down and the bags under her eyes told the tale.

Becca joined them in the dining room where Thelma was seated at the table cutting noodles from rolled out dough. Thelma handed her a bag of onions, a sharp knife and a cutting board, indicating that she needed to chop, chop, as they say. She smiled and took the onions, slicing them in thin strips and placing them in a bowl. It was nice to perform a mindless task for a change. She was grateful for Thelma's insistence on this trip.

Ian took the onions from Becca and threw them into the pot on the stove. The smell of a home cooked meal made her ravenous, but she tried to hide her anticipation. She helped Thelma place the cut noodles on a drying rack that had been sitting on the kitchen counter. Once those chores were done they walked out onto the back porch of the cottage.

The view took Becca's breath away. Not thirty yards away was the sea in all its glory. The waves were pounding against the rocks with the reflection of the sun setting on the horizon. It was one of the most magnificent views she had ever seen. It wasn't that hard to imagine living the rest of your life there. Now she was beginning to understand why Thelma had chosen to stay in England. There was a stillness and peace where they stood.

The silence was shattered when Ian yelled 'dinner's ready' from the kitchen window. The ladies returned to the dining room where he had put on quite the spread. There were fresh salads at each setting and a small bowl of fruit. Biscuits were in a serving bowl next to creamery butter and a jar of honey. The fish was coated in a light coating of pale brown breading and smelled like heaven. Cooked tomatoes and kale were the accompaniments.

Becca's stomach was growling with anticipation as she sat down to eat. She barely participated in the dinner conversation because she was so engrossed in enjoying the meal. She was totally amazed that a man could cook this well. Her curiosity got to her and she turned to Ian.

"Now where did you learn to cook like this, sir?"

"Please don't call me sir. I am in the Royal Navy and spend a great deal of my time in the kitchen. Although we rarely serve something this glorious on the ship, there are many wonderful cooks in Her Majesty's commission at the current time and I have learned from the best. I take it you are enjoying it?"

"Oh yes, very much. It is all too much, really. But I am indulging myself this weekend as I fear there are many more horrors on the horizon. I needed to lighten up a bit, as your mother as said. Thank you for this meal. It is wonderful."

Becca helped clear the table and get the dishes cleaned up. She then joined Thelma back on the porch for a glass of wine. The sounds of the waves were so relaxing. This was a little piece of heaven in a chaotic world. Surely there were places like this back home. She would begin investigating immediately upon her discharge. No more farm for her. She knew she would need her own little oasis when she was no longer in the employ of the US Air Force.

She retired to bed a little after ten o'clock, unaware of the rough night ahead. Becca's mind was racing with a myriad of thoughts, but most of all with visions of Ian. What was wrong with her? She did not believe in love at first sight, if she believed in love at all. Physical attraction was what kept the species going. There was no magic to it. All of that was imagined by dreamers. What was she thinking? She tossed and turned until an exhausted sleep overtook her.

Saturday flew by as Thelma had a full itinerary for her guest. They drove down to Tintagel to see the ruins of what was rumored to be King Arthur's castle and ventured down to visit Merlin's cave. Stopping at little shops throughout the area, Becca selected a few small items to remember the trip by. Again the evening meal was sumptuous, prepared by the dashing Ian. For a short time, Becca had forgotten the ravages of the war. But she knew that soon she would be right back in it.

After spending most of the evening sitting on the back porch sipping a delectable local wine, Becca said her good nights and retired to Ian's bedroom. She stood for moment, taking in the scent of him, letting it envelope her as if it were her lover's arms. She climbed into his bed and pulled the covers up to her face, dozing off with his faint aroma tickling her nostrils.

She was awakened by the feeling that the bed had shifted, first listening to the howling winds coming off the ocean, then turning onto her back. She sat up abruptly when she saw him, sitting on the side of her bed in a dark navy robe, simply staring at her.

"What are you doing, Ian? You can't be in here!"

"But I am in here. This is my room, you know."

"Are you uncomfortable on the couch? I can surely move out there so you can have your bed back. Just give me a moment and I'll return your room to you. I told Thelma to let me sleep on the couch in the first place."

"I'm uncomfortable, yes, but not because of the couch. You are making me uncomfortable."

"In what way? What have I done?"

"Don't be coy, Becca. I saw the way you looked at me when we first met. And the hidden glances that have been continuously thrown my way. Don't deny that you are attracted to me. I'd merely like to help you, what was it? Oh yes, lighten up a bit."

"Any woman with a set of eyes would be attracted to you, Ian. I am a living breathing human being. And yes, you are very attractive."

He scooted closer to her and placed one hand where only one man had ventured before.

"I think you need to remove your hand, Ian. One word from me and your mother will come running, I'm sure. All I need to do is cry out."

"But you won't, will you? You want me as much as I want you, Rebecca. I'm heading back to war very soon, as are you. We could both be dead in a very short time. I think we would both regret missing out on this opportunity."

"I don't deny that I want you, Ian, but…"

He leaned forward, pressing his lips hungrily against hers. She turned her body to meet his, reaching for him as if he belonged to her. The aching she had felt in her core demanded to be relieved. And Ian Williams was the only cure. She pulled him further into her hungry arms.

When Becca awoke, the sun was just beginning to pierce the horizon. Memories of the previous night flooded her mind. Had it been a delicious dream of giving in to her desires, or had Ian actually come to her bed? He was not lying against her in contented sleep. But somehow the aching in her soul had transformed into a deep contentment.

Becca quickly showered, then returned to her room to pack her things for the return trip to London. She pulled herself together, carrying her bags to the living room. Thelma was in the kitchen cooking a pot of oats when Becca joined her.

"Did you sleep well, Becca? I know those beds in the apartments are like laying on a pile of bricks. At least you may have gotten a bit of rest here this weekend."

"Yes, yes, I had a marvelous sleep, Thelma, thank you. And where is Ian this morning?"

"I sent him into town to get a few things for us to take back to London with us. He'll be back soon. Would you like some oatmeal and biscuits?"

Becca nodded and joined Thelma at the table but had very little appetite. She pushed her oatmeal around the bowl, taking only a few bites. She ate half a biscuit and took the other outside to toss to the sea birds who had gathered on the rocks. She was overcome with emotion, unsure of whether it was guilt or rapture that enveloped her.

When Ian returned a few hours later, her heart was beating so rapidly Becca thought she might faint. He greeted her warmly, giving her a peck on the cheek before heading into the kitchen. Both she and Thelma joined him and pitched in to help with afternoon tea. They had a lovely lunch of mozzarella and tomato sandwiches followed by a marvelous crème brulee. Thelma hugged Ian and went out to start the car for the return trip to London.

"When do you return to duty, Ian?" Becca inquired.

"I had a two week furlough so I have to go back a week from today. Going to enjoy the solitude and sweetness of home for a little while longer. I may go up to my father's estate in Wales for a week, then it's back to the ship. May I be so bold as to call you if I am in London?"

"Yes, I would like that. Thelma has my number. And Ian, I really enjoyed my visit to Cornwall."

"So delighted that you did. I certainly enjoyed your visit to Cornwall as well. You must come back soon."

Thelma entered the kitchen as Becca was picking up her bags.

"I'll be back next Saturday, my son, so please be here when I return. We shall do something glorious before you ship out."

"Thanks mum, I am looking forward to it. So very nice meeting you Becca. I do hope we meet again one day."

Becca nodded as she closed the front door. She certainly hoped they would meet again and again. He was so dashing and had a special aura around him. There was just something indescribable about this man. Maybe it was fate that she had come along for the ride. Thelma put her foot on the gas pedal and they pulled away from the cottage. Becca sighed as Ian grew smaller and smaller until he was completely out of sight.

The conversation turned mostly to work and Thelma's impending retirement. It was a quick ride with good company and they were in London before dark. Thelma dropped Becca off at her apartment and told her she would see her in the morning. Becca knew it was going to be another long night thinking about her life, her future and the man who had filled her mind with such silliness.

The week flew by and a retirement party was held for Thelma on Friday. She tried to act surprised but it was difficult, knowing how send-offs were done in the past. In one way Becca was sad to see her new friend and mentor go. But on the other hand, she knew that now she alone would be commanding the ship without having to defer to someone else. Her main regret was that she would no longer hear stories and see photos of the dashing Ian. She walked Thelma to her car and they shared a long hug.

"Best of luck in your retirement, Thelma. You have a beautiful place to spend it."

"And best of luck to you, Becca. You will do a fine job I'm sure. But you need to be good to yourself, too. Take care now and please come visit anytime."

"I will. But don't let me make a habit of it, will you?"

Becca waved as Thelma drove off into the sunset, knowing that she would make time to visit in the coming months. The thought of never seeing Ian again gnawed at her whole being. She had to make sure that didn't happen.

The months flew by as the war pushed harder against Western Europe. Becca was putting in sixteen hour days with barely one off, sometimes sleeping at the hospital rather than the comfort of her own bed. It was a very difficult time for many, food was being rationed, there was limited fuel for personal use and much of London was under curfew due to bomb threats. She often thought of how safe people were back in Ohio. They could listen to the radio or read news stories of what was happening in Europe, but they could never imagine the reality of war on their own shores. At least not yet.

Becca tried to write letters to her sister regularly, to keep her up to date on the war effort and check on things at home. Marguerite answered her letters religiously, but they were boring and droll, who married whom, new neighbors, and new farm animals being born. She loved her sister dearly and keeping in contact with her kept her sane in a way. Becca wished Marguerite could find a nice fellow, get married and have a family of her own. But she was so busy helping with the farm, her job and their parents that she had little time for recreation. Becca felt guilty that she was not there to help, even though she sent a large portion of her pay back home for their expenses. She had very little that the military didn't cover, so why not? She surely didn't need it as much as they did.

Sitting in a corner of her favorite pub enjoying her usual, fish and chips, Becca was able to unwind for a brief moment. She was wondering where Ian was in the world and what he was doing. She smiled a private smile at the thought of him cooking dinner for her, his mother's apron tied appropriately around his muscular back. The vision was stirred something deep in her loins, making her fully aware of the nausea that had taken over as of late. Suddenly, her thoughts were shattered by a loud boom that shook the building, knocking the bottles and glasses to the tile floor in a deafening crash. She immediately dropped to her knees, covering her head under the table as tightly as she could. She waited for the next shoe to drop, but it didn't. An eerie silence lingered in the air for a moment, and then the cries started.

    Becca scrambled to her feet to respond to the cries. Several of the bar patrons were injured, but they were nothing compared to the barkeep. He was buried beneath some rubble and needed to be extricated as quickly as possible. She grabbed a few of the men who had nothing but scratches and enlisted them to lift the debris while she pulled the barkeep out. They made quick work of it and she grabbed the telephone, expecting to have a dial tone but there was none. After checking the other patrons, she ran out onto the street and stopped the first vehicle she saw, insisting that they take the barkeep and herself to the hospital. She assured the other patrons that she would send help as soon as she got him stabilized. They nodded their appreciation and began plastering their cuts with towels, napkins and anything else they could get their hands on.

    She had the driver wait while she rushed into the emergency room for a gurney and some help. Two orderlies assisted her with extracting the barkeep from the back seat of the car. She sent the driver on his way after thanking him profusely. Donning her scrubs from her locker, Becca prepared herself for what was going to be yet another difficult shift.

    "What the hell happened?" Dr. Etchison asked.

Becca described the events of just an hour ago and he agreed that he had heard a loud explosion from that part of the city. They both knew they were going to be bombarded with injured people from all walks of life, not just the military. They prepared the six OR suites quickly and Becca made sure that there were plenty of supplies on hand. Her staff joined her as the chaos began.

The radio in the break room was blaring with a combination of static and stories trying to piece together the events. From what various staff members were catching, a single fighter plane had dropped a bomb on several ships that were tethered in the Thames, sending the river over her banks and metal flying in every direction. The force of the blast rocked homes and businesses, breaking windows and wood. It was calculated that nearly four hundred persons had been affected, particularly the crews of the three vessels that had been the target. One was military, the other two civilian.

As the injured came pouring in, the hallways became the triage area. Becca rapidly assessed each patient on the gurneys, making notes and putting numbers on their chests as to the order in which they needed to be seen. She came upon a young man lying on his side facing the wall, his shirt burned into his skin and his leg matted with blood. She moved him up in priority based on his burns and the probably massive leg injury. As she stepped away from the gurney he rolled over on his back and mumbled.

"Becca..."

She was frozen in her tracks at the sound of his voice. Without turning around she knew it was Ian Williams. She gripped her clipboard close to her chest as she returned to him. He reached for her hand and she gave it, feeling the weakness in his pulse and grip. She motioned for an orderly to take him to the OR immediately. It was the first time in her life that she had let her emotions overcome protocol and she didn't care.

"I'll be right there with you in a few minutes. Just hold on, Ian, we will get your wounds taken care of."

"Mother, don't tell my mother."

"I have to let her know eventually. But I'll wait until you are safely out of surgery. Now go along with the orderly and I'll be there soon."

"Promise?"

"Yes, I promise."

Becca hurried through the rest of her triage, her heart in her throat, and moved to the OR suite, changing into new scrubs to attend the surgeons. Another case was just finishing up so she went to the prep room to see what was happening with Ian. The staff had soaked his back and were able to remove most of his melted shirt and they had cut the shredded pants off his injured leg. The burns appeared to be mostly second degree across his shoulders, neck and right jaw. He had a gaping wound down his right thigh but it had clean edges and should be easy to repair. He had been given a heavy sedative so he was not aware of her presence, but she was torn up inside. She had to maintain her professionalism and not let her feelings enter into the OR. She threw back a cup of coffee, took a deep breath, and scrubbed up, nearly scraping the skin off her hands, which were obviously shaking. She pulled herself together and strode mightily into the OR suite.

Ian's surgery went well, his leg was sewn back together and a few of the burn wounds were repaired. It would take a long time for them to heal, so he would spend the next few weeks prone on a bed that had been newly developed for burn patients. As soon as he went to the recovery room Becca slipped away and called Thelma. Her friend was beyond devastated and grateful that Becca was there for her son. She was on her way as soon as she hung up the phone. Becca returned to the OR to continue fighting the fight.

The next six hours dragged as patient after patient was receiving the best medical care that the facility could offer. Becca scrubbed in on more than half of the surgeries and the physicians were grateful to have such a skilled and caring nurse working with them. As the severity of the wounds began to trickle down, she took leave to check on Ian. When she arrived at his room, Thelma was at his bedside.

"He's a bit groggy, you know, but alert enough to know what is going on. He says you saved his life."

"Hardly. The surgeons did most of the work. I just helped."

"Now you and I both know that those guys couldn't do crap without us. You did the triage, didn't you? Then you moved him as quickly as possible to the top of the surgical list. Don't be modest. I know what you are capable of and I am grateful that you were nearby when this happened."

"There's my guardian angel," Ian said weakly. "Thank you."

"Now you just hush, sir. I did my job. And today, you were part of my job. And how are you feeling?"

"Tired, so tired."

"That is probably from the pain medication they gave you. Burns can be very painful so we want to keep that pain under control. You realize you will have to lay like that for a while, until the burns start to heal."

He nodded and dozed off, probably a result of exhaustion and medication. The women quietly stepped into the hallway.

"Becca, what do you think of the burns on his neck muscle tying into his back. I think it is more damaged than anyone imagined."

"I'll have to take a better look at it Thelma, but for now I think we need to let him rest. Where are you staying tonight?"

"I hadn't thought of that. I suppose I'll be up here for a while. What about you? When is the last time you had something to eat?"

"I, I don't remember. Lunch at around eleven, I suppose, just before the explosion. Why don't you stay at my apartment with me. You can stay as long as you need to. There is no reason for you to spend money to be with your son. You are a welcome guest. And I can pick your brain about some of these injuries."

"I would be delighted to stay with you, Becca. That is so generous of you. At least we know we get along. Who knows who I would be stuck with at a hostel, which is probably all I could afford just now."

"Here is the key to my place. I have a feeling I'll be staying here all night and probably most of tomorrow. Just make yourself at home."

"I will probably go and freshen up, but I don't want him to wake up and me not be there, especially for the first few days, so I will most likely be living here too. I'll see you later on."

The next few days went as Becca had predicted. There was no rest for the wicked, and the OR was in constant motion. She and Thelma met up in Ian's room several times a day and Becca finally took the time to look at the neck wound that had concerned her friend. Yes, it was more severe than previously believed and probably beyond repair at this point. The damage was so bad that it would probably be nearly impossible for him to turn his head for the rest of his life. And the scarring from the burns would be life changing. She was saddened at the thought that this handsome man who she vehemently denied she loved, might no longer be the belle of the ball, in control of his own life and destiny.

Several weeks later Thelma declared that she was going to take Ian back to the States to be seen at the renowned Cleveland Clinic where they were doing a great deal of research on muscle control, stimulation, and reconstruction. Although the thought of it pained Becca, she knew that if she were a mother she would do anything in her power to protect and care for her own child. If Thelma believed there was hope, then perhaps there was. It would be several more weeks before he would be able to travel, but he was in agreement to at least try his mother's suggestions. So the two woman busied themselves making arrangements for Thelma and Ian to travel to Ohio for treatment.

Less than a week later they got the call. Ian had been accepted into the program for muscle regeneration following traumatic burn injury. It was an experimental clinical trial but it seemed to be their only hope for his full recovery. Becca knew it was what was best for Ian. She sent them on their way to Cleveland with her best wishes for a successful treatment. She knew she would miss him desperately until he returned from his treatment. But she would wait for him no matter how long it would take. She was in love with Ian Williams and there was no room for any other man in her life. Sadly, she had no way of knowing that she had sent him directly into the arms of another woman.

CHAPTER **TWELVE**

Kayla awoke several times during the overnight flight, her mind working overtime with all of the choices she had to make. Just when she felt she was sure of a decision, doubt would raise its ugly head. Should she keep the manor house or should she sell. If she sold it the odds of her ever returning to London were quite low. She would probably never see Brent again. Did she have feelings for him or was that just a one night stand? Did he have feelings for her or just use her for sex? Her mind was reeling. Too much to think about. She desperately needed to discuss it all with Erika. Soon, very soon, she would get the chance.

The 767 taxi'd down the runway of Pittsburgh International Airport around four in the afternoon as scheduled. Erika would be happy to get out of the cramped quarters of the airplane. Fortunately, other than her own demons, it had been a quiet night. She had feared it would be a disaster as she was seated very close to the same gentleman with three small children she had travelled with before. But she had to admit, this guy should get the 'father of the year' award. He was well equipped with games, toys, snacks and blankies for his crew. It made her heart ache. If only she could find a wonderful man who loved children to marry. That would make her life complete.

Those thoughts were disrupted as the stewardess began reciting the debarking instructions over the intercom. Kayla waited a few moments for the exiting push to diminish, then stood up to get her bag from the overhead compartment. She smiled when the father with his hands full reached up and handed it to her. If only…

She stepped onto the people mover just as the doors were closing and headed for the baggage claim area. She had one suitcase to retrieve and then she would head outside to look for Erika at the pick-up zone. She was slightly surprised to find Erika waiting at the foot of the escalator.

"Tell me everything and I mean everything! Don't leave out one little detail. I am dying here!"

"Geesh, give me a minute to get my land legs back, will ya? I have been sitting for nearly seven hours on a plane, have a five hour time change and I'm starving! Let's get my suitcase to the car and then I'll tell you the story. I have tons of photos to show you, too. Can we stop and eat on the way home please?"

"Yea, yea, sure. Your stomach is more important than your best friend. I know where I rank now."

They strode down to the baggage claim where Kayla's suitcase was just coming down the ramp. Erika quickly grabbed it and headed for the escalator, from where the people mover would sweep them to the parking lot in no time flat. Her car was just outside the door to the right and Kayla was not surprised. Erika would drive around a parking lot for an hour just trying to get the best parking spot. It was one of her weird but lovable quirks.

Erika revved the car up as the pulled out of the parking lot. Kayla began at the beginning, starting with her flight across the big pond. Erika listened intently to every detail. Questions, she had so many questions and Kayla responded as best she could to each one. By the time they pulled into the restaurant for dinner the exhaustion was catching up with her. Kayla knew once she had satiated her hunger, she was going to fall into a deep sleep for days. Too bad she had to go back to work tomorrow. She wasn't anxious to cash in her reality check.

Kayla pulled out her camera after they had placed their orders to show Erika around London, and then, of course, Anwylyd. She found herself feeling drawn to it so strongly,
a tear escaped and rushed down her cheek. That was it, she knew she could not sell it, even though it would probably guarantee that she would never have to work again if she did. Somehow, she knew that keeping the estate was the right decision.

They continued chatting during lunch, but all Kayla wanted to do was sleep. She tried her best to answer most of Erika's questions, but really wasn't in the mood for an interrogation. She would tell more tomorrow. They finished eating and returned to Erika's car. For some reason, Erika sat eerily still and made no move to start the engine.

"What, what is it? Is there something wrong?"

"Yes, there is something wrong. You know what I am dying to know. When we were in the restaurant I was being polite, but now we are alone in my car, so did you do it with the lawyer?"

"What? Geesh, Erika, why not get right to the point?"

"I am getting right to the point. Did you do it?"

"Yes, yes we did it. More than once too. I got over myself. Are you happy now?"

"I am a little bit happy. But I will be happier when you tell all! But I'll give you a chance to rest up. Slumber party at your house tomorrow night. I'll bring the pizza. And you will tell me every gory detail. Deal?"

"Yes, it's a deal. Now let's get my dog so I can go home and sleep."

The drove out of the parking lot, Erika wearing her biggest snarky smile.

Spinner was delighted to see his owner. He nearly broke the window of the screen door trying to get to Kayla. And she was glad to see him, her true and loyal companion. It was a touching scene as they got reacquainted. Erika ran in the house to get his bag and returned shortly. She took the happy pair back to Kayla's house and dropped them off, vowing to 'get it all out of her' tomorrow. Kayla waved as Erika pulled out of the driveway, then went into her house, turned the heat up, took a hot shower and fell into bed. Her canine companion was under the covers in no time flat.

Kayla slept like the dead and was shocked to find that it was nine a.m. when she woke up. She had slept a solid eleven hours! Well, she needed the morning to unwind and readjust before returning to work. She set herself to the chore of unpacking and doing laundry when she noticed that her message light on the house phone was blinking. That was unusual. Most of the people who called her used her cell.

She pushed the button to retrieve the message and was pleased that it was Brent. He had called to make sure she had a pleasant flight and had made it home safely, adding how much he had enjoyed their few days together and was hoping to see her again soon. He left his email address, probably forgetting that he had given her his business card, or perhaps thinking she may have lost or misplaced it. He finished his message sweetly telling her he missed her. Kayla started to blush at the memory of their time together. Now she was be sure that she would see him again, and soon.

She hadn't returned to the laundry room for very long when she heard the grinding of brakes in the driveway. Erika wasn't going to be put off very long when it came to the intimate
details of her nights with Brent. She pulled on some jeans and a sweatshirt and met Erika at the door with a cup of steaming coffee. Two creams, one Splenda, just the way she liked it.

Erika made herself at home at the kitchen table and began to munch on an apple that was leaning precariously over the edge of Kayla's favorite bowl, one that her grandmother had left her. Kayla had stolen many a piece of candy or fruit from that very bowl and her elders were sure would ruin her appetite for dinner. But, in fact, it never did. It always made her even hungrier. As a child she rarely missed a meal, as evidenced by the chubby cheeks in her hideous grade school photos.

"So let's get down to it, girl. What happened? And I mean everything!"

Kayla relayed the story of their first meeting, dinner, the night out in London and the first intimate encounter. She briefly talked about the trip to Wales with Catherine Adamson and how much she loved the place. She didn't tell her friend the entire worth of the estate, not yet. She herself was still having a difficult time believing it. Then she proceeded with their last night in London.

"He was taking a shower and getting ready to leave you at four in the morning without waking you? What a scumbag!"

"What? He is not a scumbag. I think he is really attractive and kind. He treated me like a queen when I was there. I don't expect him to put his job on the backburner for me. Maybe I was just a few nights' stand. So what? I had a great time and it was good for me and my teetering self-esteem. But I do have to say I miss him."

"He probably forgot who you are already."

"No, I don't think so. I had a sweet message on my answering machine from him this morning. Do you want to hear it?"

"Well, hell yes I want to hear it? What are you thinking?"

Kayla proceeded to play the message to Erika, who was looking very pensive during the whole thing.

"He isn't sincere, Kayla. I'm telling you, there is something about this guy I don't like."

"You don't even know him, Erika. Really! How can you figure that out just from listening to his voice?

"Trust me. I am an expert on sleazy men. He is one of them."

Kayla shook her head and went into the bedroom to retrieve her computer. She uploaded all of her photos while Erika played with the dog in the back yard. Once they were done she called the exhausted pair back into the house. She put a pan of frozen lasagna in the oven while she and Erika looked at the photos, one at a time.

Erika had to admit that the estate was impressive, even though it had stood empty for a few years. It still had its visual appeal as well as its historic relevance. Kayla had done some internet investigation and had printed it out for

Erika to see. The place had potential, that was for sure. Maybe it would make someone a great bed and breakfast or hotel. She must have said it out loud because Kayla was just staring at her with her mouth gaped open.

"For someone? What about for me?"

"You aren't really thinking about moving to Wales are you? That is just nuts. Going thousands of miles away from everything you know? How can you afford such a thing? Sell the
place and then you will be pretty well set here. You can fix up this house and live a pretty comfy life."

"Yes, I am definitely thinking of moving to Wales. I felt so at home at Anylwyd, like it was the place I belonged my whole life. I don't think I can sell it, Erika. I need to be there. And, not that it's any of your business, but I was left with a bit of money and jewelry as well."

"Whatever it is, it will be pissed down the toilet by the time you fix that old place up."

"I think there is enough to fix it up and live for quite a while. I'm planning on going back in July. Why don't you take your vacation days and come with me?"

"You are really serious about this, aren't you?" Erika stared at Kayla. "Hmmm...I'll have to see how many days I have coming. Maybe I can take three off added to the front of my regular two weeks. How are you going to swing it? You just took several of your days?"

"I'm quitting, Erika. I'm planning to move to Wales permanently."

Kayla stared blankly at her friend. For once in her life, she was speechless. How could Erika have changed so much in such a short time? Moving to Wales? The thought was inconcievable!

They spent the next hour in spastic planning, all of Kayla's ideas coming forth to fan the flames. They decided to meet back at the house after her shift to continue their discussion. At 10:30 Kayla was home with their midnight snack. By the time they had eaten the pizza, consumed a bottle of moscato and eaten half a gallon of ice cream, Erika was one hundred percent on board.

"Maybe I should move there too! I'm sure there are jobs in the medical field, maybe even with some incentives. What do you think?"

"I'd love it. We could run the B&B together and work at the local hospital. I have been looking into it and they have all kinds of flexible schedules. The B&B would be busiest during the spring and summer months, and we could work more in the fall in winter at our boring professions. Still have a lot of investigating to do, but I am very serious about this."

They finally fell asleep, Kayla in the recliner with her laptop stuffed into one side of the chair and Erika on the couch. Neither was prepared for the phone call that came at three a.m.

Kayla flew out of the recliner when the phone rang, a knee-jerk reaction from when her parents were ill. She fumbled with the receiver as her mind began to grasp that she was no longer sleeping.

"He-, hello," she managed to blurt out, suddenly coming alive.

"Did I wake you?"

She recognized his smooth voice immediately and unconsciously smoothed out her nightgown.

"I have to be honest, Brent, yes, but that's alright. I wasn't sleeping well anyway."

"I miss you. When are you coming back to London? Soon, I hope."

"I am trying to figure out a schedule now. That's what I spent most of last evening doing. I think I am going to quit my job."

"Now why would you do that? You have worked there for a long time haven't you?"

"Yes, I have. I think it is time for a change."

"Once you sell Anwylyd you should be very comfortable financially. I suppose you can do whatever you wish. But the rest of your aunt's fortune won't sustain you forever. You are
only thirty-two. You will need at least three million to retire now. And a good investment advisor."

"Um, I don't really know if I will sell Anwylyd. I feel really attached to it, as I told you before."

"The old place needs to be bulldozed and rebuilt. Are you sure you are up for that?"

"I don't really think that's the case. Have you actually been inside the manor house? Or any of the buildings, for that matter? And do you realize what time it is here?"

"Remember that I have worked in this business for a long time, love. I know what it takes to restore an old crusty like that place. You would spend half your fortune on it. And for what? Family values? You didn't even know your great-aunt, you said so yourself."

"Just what are you getting at, Brent?"

"Nothing, just wondering when you are coming back so we can spend some quality time together and not be rushed. I have to get off to a meeting myself. Think about what I've said, though. I have only your best interests in mind. I'll call soon."

Before she could reply Kayla heard the 'click' of his receiver being returned to the cradle. By this point Erika was awake, quietly listening to her friend's side of the conversation.

"What the hell was that all about?"

"Oh, it was nothing. Brett just wanted to find out when I am coming back so we can spend some unrushed time together. That's all."

"Didn't sound like that was all. He was trying to pressure you into something. I could see your shoulders tightening up. I'm telling you, don't trust him, Kayla. You will be heartbroken."

Kayla shook her head and settled back into the recliner. "Don't worry your little head about me, Erika. Now go back to sleep."

Morning came quickly now, and the two jumped up at the sound of the alarm clock. Kayla had to work dayshift and Erika was on afternoon turn. Kayla let Spinner out and fixed his breakfast then jumped into the shower. Erika drank a cup of coffee and waited for Kayla to join her. They exchanged a few pleasantries before Kayla left for work.

"See you this afternoon, Erika," she yelled as she ran out the door.

Erika rolled back onto the couch for another few hours of relaxation.

Kayla punched in with seconds to spare and headed for her department. She had a totally different attitude today. No one was going to bother her. It was a grand feeling knowing that she could just say 'take this job and shove it' if she wanted to. Now that the estate was settled, finances were not going to be a problem for quite a while. It gave her a freedom that she had never felt before.

Of course she was overwhelmed by her co-workers with questions and comments about her trip. She was well prepared with her plethora of pictures and other souvenirs she had picked up along the way. Everyone oohed and ahhed as she described Anwylyd and the surrounding area. She smiled knowing that she had done something very few in her acquaintance had done, visit a foreign country that wasn't attached to US borders. She had a new spring in her step.

"So Kayla, I am planning a European vacation someday. How about we have dinner one night and you can tell me where to go."

Kayla stopped in her tracks. That voice always made the hairs stand up on the back of her neck. Since she would soon be resigning, she no longer had any reason to be particularly nice to Ron. He had borderline sexually harassed her for years although she had made it perfectly clear
that she had no interest in him whatsoever. She had tolerated him for professional reasons only. She slowly turned to face him.

"I don't care where you go as long as it is away from me. Please just leave me alone or I will file a restraining order against you. Do you understand?"

The faces of her co-workers reflected a combination of shock and pleasure. One of the girls she had worked with for over ten years, Savannah, leaned over and whispered in her ear.
"Who are you and what have you done with meek, mild Kayla."
"I locked her in a broom closet and she will never get out again."
Ron backed away and exited the room not saying a word, the eyes of all the other techs following him out the door and down the hall. Kayla felt like a huge burden had been lifted from her shoulders. She was no longer the wall flower with no hope. It was a glorious revelation!

She continued chatting with her co-workers as the first patient was brought into the department. The rest of the day flew by smoothly and she was ready to get out of that musty old hospital. There were other fish to fry now and none of them were coming out of the Ohio River. Passing Erika at the time clock she indicated that she would call her later on. Plans needed to be made and timelines established. She was now in control of her life. She would give her boss a thirty day notice on June first, and spend the month of July packing and getting ready for a one month trip to Wales.

    The next two months flew by as Kayla and Erika worked on travel plans and ideas for the bed and breakfast at Anwylyd. Their excitement rubbed off on friends and everyone else when they would relay their ideas to them. Kayla had no one to report to and Erika never had, even though she had a great deal of family living far away who were all estranged. Things were falling into place for the adventure to begin in August and they were well-prepared.

    Their mutual friend, Christy, drove them to the airport on Friday morning for their overnight flight to London. She dropped them off at the 'departing flights' doorway and told them not to do anything she wouldn't do. Knowing Christy, that pretty much gave them carte' blanch to do whatever they wanted. There wasn't much Christy hadn't tried.

    They handed off their luggage outside and hurried to the self-check kiosk to get their boarding passes. Grabbing a cold drink and some magazines at the little shop outside of security, the reality of what was happening became clear. This was a new start, a new life opportunity, and they planned to make the most of it. It wasn't long before the 767 was leaving the earth and winging its way to jolly old England.

    The women chatted continuously until exhaustion overtook them. When Erika woke up she checked her video screen to see what their time frame was. Three more hours until they would arrive in London. She glanced over at Kayla, noticing the content look on her face, one she hadn't seen in many years. This was good, very good. She unbuckled her seat belt and quietly made her way to the rest room as her beverage consumption had been quite liberal during the first half of the flight. She surely didn't want to be the one who slowed their arrival.

She returned to her seat and noticed that Kayla was suddenly restless. Kayla's eyes flew open and she was breathing heavily.

"What's wrong, girl, you scared the life out of me?"

"I was having a weird dream, not a nightmare really, but just that someone was pushing me off the side of a boat or something. Strange."

"Not a nightmare? I'd like to see what you think IS a nightmare, geesh!"

They laughed a moment and then resumed chatting about the landing and their plans for the day.

"Once we get into London we'll get something to eat and see a few sites. We aren't going to Anwylyd until tomorrow, so you decide what you want to do, Erika."

"I have to find somewhere to hide out while you and lover boy do the humpty dance."

Kayla blushed. "No you don't. We can go to his place. You can stay at the hotel. That is, if he wants to do the humpty dance with me again. Maybe I wasn't all that exciting."

"He keeps calling you, girl. I think he wants to do it. Don't know how sincere or if it's going anywhere, but I'm sure he wants another lap dance."

CHAPTER **THIRTEEN**

The captain's voice boomed overhead. "We will be arriving in London in thirty minutes, which will be ten in the morning. The weather is looking beautiful. The sun is shining and it's a balmy sixty-four. Thank you for traveling with us tonight and we look forward to having you join us again in the near future."

The friends smiled and Kayla giggled nervously. She could not believe what had happened in the past six months. She was still in a state of disbelief. She wondered what Aunt Becca and her mother would think of all this.

They disembarked quickly and made their way to the baggage claim area. Kayla was pulling up the hotel information on her iPhone when she felt a hand on her lower back. She turned around to see none other than Brent Dankworth, smiling like the Cheshire cat. She whirled around to face him.

"Your chariot has arrived, ladies!" He spouted, kissing Kayla on the cheek.

She turned to Erika and made the introductions, Brent giving the same kiss on the cheek to her friend. Before Erika could make a smart remark, their luggage came through the rubber flaps on the conveyor belt. They grabbed their bags and threw them on the cart that he had brought over to them, then headed outside. The air was refreshing after being inside an airplane for over seven hours. Kayla took a deep breath and addressed Brent.

"Which way do we go, sir?"

"Stay right here and I'll get the car. Be right back, love."

Erika rolled her eyes as he strolled across the four lanes of traffic into the parking garage.

"What?"

"Please. How rude is he? He kissed you on the cheek and did the same to me. If he considered you an intimate partner, he would have greeted you differently than a total stranger. And he wouldn't make eye contact either. All he did was stare at my cleavage. Did you not see any of this? Were you not in the same room?"

"Erika, give him a chance, will you? He is meeting a new person for the first time who is the best friend of his love interest. I'm sure he is sizing you up just the same way you are sizing him up." She couldn't believe she had used the term 'love interest'. That definitely was not the way she had ever described herself.

"He's a scumbag, I'm telling you. Think with your head, Kayla."

"What? You don't think I'm good enough for some hot shot London lawyer?"

"No, I don't think he is good enough for you. But I'll shut up about it for now. You have been warned by someone who knows about these things."

Before Kayla could reply, Brent pulled up in his shiny black BMW, honking the horn twice as if they wouldn't know it was him. The pulled their wheeled bags to the back of the vehicle as he jumped out to assist. The trunk popped open and he lifted their suitcases into the trunk. He held the front passenger door open and Kayla slid in. Erika helped herself into the backseat. Again, it was strange to be on the opposite side of the car. Everything just seemed out of balance.

Although the traffic was brutal, Brent managed it with the ease of a true big city resident. He knew shortcuts and back streets and they arrived at the hotel within an hour. He pulled into the circular drive and handed the busboy a bill and the young man made haste getting the bags onto a dolly and into the building. Brent stayed very close to Kayla as she went to the desk to check-in. Erika lagged behind, analyzing the whole scene and wondering what was going to happen next.

Kayla grabbed the keys and had a short conversation with Brent. He kissed her gently on the lips, waved to Erika as he headed through the revolving door and drove away. The two ladies stepped into the elevator, which was tightly packed with a large Pakistani group, and rode up the eight floors in silence.

Erika followed Kayla down the hall and into their room. Once the door closed she stared at her friend.

"So what is the plan Kayla?"

"I told you it's up to you since you haven't been to London in a while. Whatever you want to do is fine with me."

"I want to go against my own advice and sleep the rest of the day but I know that isn't a very good way to spend my limited time here. So what do you suggest?"

Kayla went into the bathroom and closed the door. "I'm going to freshen up a bit, maybe even take a shower, then I think we should take a nice long walk, maybe ride the London Eye and then get a light meal. Brent wants to take us out to dinner tonight."

"Us? You mean both of us? I thought maybe the two of you might have a date or something. I don't like being the third wheel. It feels strange."

"Well, now you know how I have felt many times over the years. You and I would go out, you would hook up with someone, but I was driving and would hang out waiting to see if you were going home with me or with some strange man."

"I never intended for you to feel that way. I can't help it that I like men. I'm sorry."

"I just always hoped you would meet and stay with one guy once in a while. What is the longest you have dated the same person without straying? One, two weeks?"

"Now that's not fair. I dated Jack Helson for ten whole days! I probably could have married him. But I just can't put all my eggs in one basket."

"Pretty soon you won't have any eggs, Erika. We aren't getting any younger. I don't know about you, but I would love to get married and have a family. My biological clock is ticking very loudly these days."

"Well, just don't get too involved with this guy. Get your life together, get settled and then I believe things will fall into place. Fate has not been good to us, my friend, so maybe it is our turn."

"This is the only time I am going to say this. We have been friends for a long time, but I am asking you not to interfere in my life. I have never judged you nor interfered with what you have chosen to do. So please give me the same courtesy. Okay? No more 'scumbag' talk about Brent. Promise?"

"Yea, yea, I promise. No more talk about the scumbag. I'll find some other word to use. Now get the hell out of that bathroom before my bladder bursts! It's my turn."

The two friends stepped out of the hotel room and onto the street overlooking the Thames River. The sun was shining and a light breeze was caressing the trees as they crossed Westminster Bridge. It was a beautiful day to explore London on foot and they chose to take full advantage of it. Soon the found themselves feeding birds in St. James' Park just in front of Buckingham Palace.

The plethora of bird species in the park was overwhelming and the squirrels that followed them amused and delighted the visitors. The little fellows came extremely close to beg for any morsel that might be available, climbing up on the fence railings to get a better look.

Turning toward the palace, they were just in time to see the horse guard passing on the street. It was a glorious sight to see and the cameras continued snapping away. Of course they both posed in front of all the statuary at the palace as well as in front of the gates. Erika even sidled up to one of the guards in full regalia, pretending to plant a kiss on his ivory cheek. No one was as cheeky as Erika that was for sure.

Several of the small souvenir stores, as long as the official palace shop provided the opportunity to pick up a few 'London' items for friends back home. Neither wanted to buy anything too large or bulky that would require shipping. Nor did they want to carry any extra weight in their bags that were nearly full of clothes and shoes. Those things could wait for another time.

They stopped at a small pub on the way back to the hotel for a light lunch, splitting a fish and chips meal between them. The walk had done a world of good and both ladies were feeling much better than when they had arrived. Jet lag had been avoided for the moment anyway.

"I want to grab a newspaper to take up to the room, Kayla."

Erika stopped at a street vendor who had magazines, papers and books just outside of the hotel. She grabbed two different papers and slid them into her purse, thinking she could read them tonight after dinner. She was not looking forward to the threesome dinner, but felt that she needed to be there to protect her friend somehow. Although she had made a promise not to say it out loud, that guy was a scumbag to the nth degree.

"I'm going to take a short nap before dinner. I'll set my alarm for six so I can be ready by seven thirty."

"I think I'm going to do the same. The walk was refreshing, but the jet lag is getting to me. I think a nap would do me good. It won't take me too long to get ready. Sounds like a good plan. Nighty night Erika."

When Erika opened her eyes she saw that Kayla was dressed in a shimmery silver dress, black hose and heels. She rolled onto her side then into a seated position and summarized her friend.

"Maybe I should just stay here and let you two lovebirds go out on the town."

"Nothing doing, sister. You are coming with me so you can see how nice Brent truly is."

"Alright, alright. Just let me get awake here and then we can go suffer through it."

They met Brent in the lobby and he was right on time, his shiny BMW purring just outside the revolving door. The trio hopped in and he gunned the engine once before putting it into drive, causing Erika to do yet another eye roll. What a scumbag, she thought to herself.
The sleek vehicle pulled up in front of an Italian restaurant in the very expensive part of town and was met by a valet in a tuxedo. He assisted the ladies from the car and then slid into the drivers' seat, running his hands over the smooth leather steering wheel before driving away. They were quickly greeted by the maitre' d who was furiously shaking hands with Brent.

"So wonderful to see you, sir. I have your table ready for you. My staff will assist you with your coats."

Kayla was smiling smugly at Erika with that 'I told you so' look. Erika countered with her best 'he's a scumbag' glare, but Kayla just ignored it. She was very impressed with the entire experience.

Once they were seated it seemed that food and drink were appearing in rapid fire succession. Kayla was barely able to finish one course when the other magically appeared. Brent kept their wine glasses full, making small talk about London, his job, and Anwylyd. Erika found it very odd that he kept mentioning the estate even though he had never seen it himself. She stored that observation in the back of her mind.

Just before dessert was to be served, Erika found that the wine had taken its toll on her bladder. She asked

Kayla if she wanted to join her in the ladies room, but Kayla declined. Erika asked Brent to direct her to the restroom as she didn't see any indication of its location.

"Kayla tells me you have been to Europe, including London, several times. Do you not know how to find a bathroom?"

"Of course I know how to find a bathroom! But you seem awfully familiar with this restaurant and, considering that familiarity, I thought you might be kind enough to keep me from wandering aimlessly."

"The sign is quite obvious, Erika. The square one over there that says 'WC'. You know, water closet. From your extensive travel I assumed you would have no problem locating that."

"Who the hell calls a bathroom a water closet these days? I was here decades ago. I must have forgotten that little tidbit."

"Yes, of course. We are all getting older, aren't we? Our memories just aren't what they used to be."

Erika glared at him. "If you will excuse me, then."

Erika strode away from the table as the couple continued their conversation. Within minutes, however, Kayla's cell phone began to vibrate.

"Excuse me, Brent. I need to check this if you don't mind."

She reached for her phone and saw that it was a message from Erika.

'Can you come in here?'
'For goodness sake, what's wrong?'
'Just come here, please.'

Kayla turned to Brent. "Please excuse me, I need to go to the WC myself. I'll be back in a moment."

Kayla rose from her chair and headed for the rest room, having no idea what she might find there. Fortunately, there were no other patrons in the room at the time. She whispered Erika's name.

"I'm in stall number two, now get in here!"

Kayla opened the door to find Erika standing on top of the toilet facing the wall.

"What the hell are you doing?"

"I don't know. That's where you come in. How the hell do you flush this thing? There is no handle, no button, no automatic eye, and the damned tank is on the wall. Stupid British!"

"Duh. See that chain hanging down with the wooden knob on it? Just pull it. For a woman of the world, you sure are dumb."

"Well, if they would come into the twenty-first century I wouldn't be having this problem. How can you like it here? I don't understand it. Even back home we have modern amenities! And how is the conversation with lover boy going?"

Kayla shook her head and stepped out of the stall. The two washed their hands and headed back to the table, where Brent was engaged in a conversation with a beautiful blonde in a very tight red number. He told her he would call her about 'it' tomorrow and she nodded, shaking her booty as she walked away.

Kayla did not feel comfortable questioning him about it so she sat back down and looked at the dessert tray in the center of the table. Before Kayla could kick her under the table, Erika opened her mouth.

"Just who was that, Brent? Why didn't you introduce us?"

Brent eyed Erika warily.

"She is a colleague of mine and we are working on a big case. She just wanted to bring me up to speed on her end of it. Not that it's any of your business."

Erika harrumphed and dug into her crème brulee without saying another word. There was an awkward silence as they finished the last course. Kayla was shifting uncomfortably in her chair by the time she had taken the last bite of her cake. She was hoping she would not have to choose between her best friend and her love interest for company. It might be a tougher decision than she had anticipated.

When the ticket arrived, Brent grabbed for it, but Erika was faster.

"Dinner's on me tonight, my friends. Celebrating my vacation of sorts. You can leave the tip if you'd like."

"I'm not accustomed to ladies paying the bill for a dinner I have invited them too. But I think you want to flex your liberated American woman muscles a bit, eh, Erika, so have at it. The tip it will be then."

Kayla remained silent during the interchange and allowed it to play itself out. She had seen Erika in this type of power struggle many times during their friendship and she was not about to start intervening now. The issue was between them, she was not involved and had finally learned to stay that way.

They quickly left the restaurant and the car was waiting just outside. Brent generously tipped the valet and they were soon back out on the street. A quick drive around London to see it lit up was pleasant until they pulled into the hotel drive.

"It was nice to meet you, Erika, but Kayla and I have some private business to discuss. If you please, you may take your leave now. I'm sure I'll be seeing you again soon."

"Just be nice to my friend, sir, or you won't like the consequences." She turned to Kayla, "If you need me for anything, I'm just a text away."

Kayla sneered at Erika. "Don't wait up." Then the shiny black panther pulled away.

Erika slipped through the revolving door without turning back. She had a bad feeling about the whole situation, but couldn't put her finger on it. Sure, Kayla was a grown woman who could make her own decisions, but would her naivete put her in harm's way? It was a lesson we all have to learn, sometimes with devastating results.

She read the newspaper and listened to the late night BBC News, trying to wait up for Kayla to return, but jet lag finally overpowered her and Erika fell into a deep sleep. When she was awakened by thin lines of bright yellow light in her eyes, she saw that Kayla was fast asleep in the other bed, her dress thrown haphazardly over the back of the settee. Erika breathed a sigh of relief to know that Kayla was safe and sound, for the time being anyway.

Erika jumped into the shower and headed downstairs for breakfast. She ate very little of the full English breakfast. Who the hell serves baked beans for breakfast anyway? She stuck with some yogurt, juice and fruit, then gathered a plate of the same to take up to the room for Kayla when she got up.

Much to her surprise, Kayla was up and dressed, methodically packing her suitcase for the trip to Wales.

"Hey sleepyhead. I was trying to let you get some rest. Brought you breakfast."

"Thanks, I really need that. The dinner last night didn't sit well for some reason. Probably my nerves."

"So, how did it go? Everything okay with Brent?"

"Oh yes. We went to a piano bar for a few drinks, then back to The Luna Simone for, um, you know, some romance. I sat out on his patio and watched the stars for a while, then he brought me back, fearing that you would send out Scotland Yard to find me if I weren't back at a reasonable hour."

"The Luna Simone Hotel? That's odd." She let it go at that.

The two laughed, although Erika had to admit that she had actually looked up the contact information for Scotland Yard, just in case. One can never be too careful when travelling abroad, you know. She threw her own suitcase on the bed and crammed her things into it just tight enough so it would close. In the meantime, Kayla called a cab to take them to Victoria Station to get the train to Wales. She just wasn't up to the tube this morning.

Within minutes of the train pulling out of the station, the two friends were fast asleep. The soothing rhythm of the train could lulling them into submission.

CHAPTER **FOURTEEN**

Kayla startled when a child a few rows away began crying hysterically. She had been having an odd dream about Brent, but could not remember the majority of it. As she struggled to recall the theme, she realized that they were nearly to Cardiff where they would disembark. She gently took hold of Erika's shoulder and shook it.

"Wha, what the hell are you doing?"

"We are almost at the end of the line and you need to wake up so you can make yourself presentable. You never know who you might meet in Cardiff. Get that hair shaken out and put some lipstick on, girl. We are in Wales."

The train slowly drifted to a halt and the doors began to open. They grabbed their purses and suitcases and stood in the line of exiting passengers. A lovely gentleman assisted them as they stepped down onto the platform. Chivalry isn't dead, Erika thought, at least not here. A smile arose from her stern lips, unnoticed by Kayla, who was busily perusing the car rental signs.

"I don't know if I can drive here or not, but I have to try. It's either you or me, and I don't know if your road rage would get us in deep trouble. I don't fancy the idea of being on an episode of 'Locked Up Abroad'. So you will be the navigator and I'll do the driving. It might be a slow pace, but I'll get us there."

"Road rage? What are you talking about? I'm a great driver!"

"Erika, I don't know who you think you are talking to! I have ridden with you for nearly twenty years. I don't want to be jailed in a foreign country, even if it is a friendly foreign country. Just let me do the driving for now. Okay?"

"Yea, okay, but I still think you are overreacting. I'm a great driver."

The blue convertible Mini-Cooper was near the front of the garage and they found it easily. Stuffing their bags into the back proved challenging, but effective. Kayla did an equipment check to make sure she could locate and operate all the bells and whistles before she put it in gear. It sure felt strange being on the 'wrong' side of the car. Soon she was on the 'wrong side' of the road, heading out of the city of Cardiff to Anwylyd.

Erika did not press Kayla about her relationship with Brent. Instead she chatted about the news of the day and the weather. There was a fine line when a friend is in a relationship you think is toxic. She decided to avoid that topic completely unless Kayla brought it up herself. That was the safest plan of attack. Keep the conversation light.

When Erika thought there would be no end to the bone jarring ride, Kayla slowed down and stopped, just outside two looming stone pillars. The metal sign was barely hanging on to the stone, held only by one stubborn metal bolt. "Anwylyd, 1942" stood out in bold black letters standing out from the bronze metal. She heard Kayla take a deep breath as they started down the dirt road.

Erika could not believe what was looming before her. She imagined a time gone by when this had been akin to Tara in "Gone With The Wind". She could understand why Kayla was so taken with the place. It was utterly fabulous! And with a little, no, a lot, of elbow grease, it could be returned to its previous glory.

"Holy crap, Kayla! This place is amazing! I can't wait to start exploring! How big is it again? I mean, acres and stuff. And are there a few menfolk who work as staff? Hmmm? I can't wait to explore some of them!"

"Yes, it is amazing and huge, but there aren't any menfolk working as staff. There is no one working as staff. You are looking at the staff. Me, and now you. We have to look it over and see what needs to be done and if it is worth the time and money involved. No one had mentioned that it was a 'fixer-upper' when I went to the reading of the will. But there is something special about this place. I can't put my finger on it. I feel so deeply drawn to it. I need to be here."

She pulled around the circular driveway to the main door and parked close to the house. It was a little bit eerie being here without the driver and Catherine. But she really wasn't afraid, just being cautious. Back home in Ohio she would never go into a house like this without some kind of protection, but she didn't feel threatened here. She couldn't explain it, but she somehow felt very safe inside those walls.

Glancing at the sky, Kayla noticed that it was just turning a deep orange with darkening grey clouds on the horizon this late afternoon. It would probably rain tonight. It seemed to always rain in the United Kingdom.

She pulled out her keys and unlocked the double locks. She felt for the first light switch inside the huge oak foyer and flipped it, Erika hot on her heels. They both stood in silence for a moment taking in the immensity of the place. Kayla turned around and locked the door, then headed for the kitchen. That was the room that she liked best. It had such a feel of joy and love. She could imagine all the wonderful times that were had cooking in that kitchen and preparing to entertain friends.

"Wow! This is one mother of a house, Kayla! Can you imagine just one person living here? That would be kind of creepy, don't you think?"

"I don't know if Aunt Rebecca lived alone, took in boarders or what. I still have so much to learn about her. I'm guessing some of the town folk knew her so I hope to get to know some of them in order to know her better. I think I would have liked her."

"So, what's on the agenda this afternoon boss lady? And where is the bathroom."

Kayla laughed at her friend. "Which one? There are plenty of bathrooms, er, water closets in this house. You can have one of your very own. But for now you can use the one just off the kitchen, over there to the left. It's a little powder room, but so convenient when one is cooking in this kitchen. Do you want some tea? I feel the need for tea."

"Sure, I'll have some. Be right back."

Kayla opened the cupboard next to the stove and took out the copper tea kettle they had used when she had first visited the place. She would have to rearrange a lot of the cupboards due to the fact that she was vertically challenged. Frequently used items would be put at eye level or below and rarely used ones above. One thing was for sure, there was no shortage of storage space in this massive room. She wondered how someone had enough material things to fill the place. She surely didn't. She was coming from a three bedroom/two bath ranch house to this mansion. It might be fun to go shopping without financial restrictions for once.

Erika joined her at the kitchen island where they slowly sipped their tea and discussed a few ideas on how to tackle Anwylyd in one month's time. At that point Kayla would make some major decisions and Erika would have to go back to the States. Kayla pulled out two yellow legal pads, handing one to Erika along with pens and some highlighters.

"I think what we should do initially is address the most urgent repair needs, then minor repairs, then the cosmetics. So I am going to send you upstairs and I will start here in the kitchen. Write down anything and everything you see that needs worked on in, say, two or three bedrooms and baths and I will do at least the kitchen, dining room and study today. We will tackle a few rooms a day and each evening sit down and prioritize. In a few days we will go into town with our lists and try to find some workmen to do the jobs. Oh, and, Erika, there is no internet here at the moment, so you will have to depend on your phone for contact to the outside world, and don't forget how expensive it is if you go over your data limit."

Erika gave her an evil look, grabbed the notebook and headed for the staircase. A smile slid back across her lips, however, when she arrived at the first landing. This place was beautiful and she had always wanted to try her hand at interior decorating. Maybe she would get the chance after all. She skipped up to the second floor and entered the first room on the right.

This must have been Aunt Rebecca's bedroom because there were photos of her in military garb on the distant wall and a modest full size sleigh bed centered against the wall. Beautifully carved bedside stands flanked each side of the bed with a matching armoire and dresser completing the set. There was an elegantly carved dressing table with a rose covered gathered skirt which released fine dust particles when she brushed against it. On it sat a faded photograph in a gilded frame of two women, a dapper young man between them, their genuine smiles revealing their closeness.

The room had a definite floral theme with a multitude of rose varieties adorning the linens and curtains. The wallpaper had raised flocked flowers of pinks and mauves scattered about in a random pattern. It was odd how they clashed with the uniformed woman in the photos. She imagined that very few people got to see Rebecca's softer side. This room was her sanctuary from all that she had seen in the war.

Meanwhile downstairs Kayla was making her own observations. Indeed Aunt Rebecca liked the finer things, especially beautifully carved furnishings. The formal dining room consisted of a table for eight, a sideboard and china cabinet. There was nary a nick on any of the items and she imagined that they would bring a hefty sum if sold at an antique auction. The red velvet seats were barely worn and there were no visible stains on them. Pink, red and yellow roses adorned the formal china and it appeared to be a complete set, none of them broken over time. She suddenly felt a sadness that Aunt Rebecca had had no husband or children and that her family was thousands of miles away. It hadn't yet dawned on her that perhaps she had wanted it that way. She continued down the hall to the library and was daunted by the task of cataloging all the books.

Within a few hours Erika descended from the upper level and met Kayla in the library, her legal pad covered with drawings and scribble.

"Are you sure you really want to tackle this old place? Remember that movie 'The Money Pit'? Well, I think you now have one of your own."

"That's one of the reasons I wanted you to come along and help with the evaluation part of this. Once I get an idea of what it is going to entail, I will have to decide if it is worth it and how much I need to do. If I want to sell it, I need to get it cleaned up enough to pass inspection. If I want to stay here, I need to do a whole lot more. If I want to make it into a bed and breakfast, I'd have to find out what is required to get that up and running. There is a lot to do and a lot of decisions to be made. For now I have worked up an appetite and think we deserve to go out to dinner and check out the town. What do you think about that?"

"I think it's a great idea. Let's get out of these dusty clothes and head into town. You are driving, of course!"

They climbed into the car and headed back out the bumpy road into town. Little did they know that almost everything closed at five o'clock and the only place to get a meal was at a little pub called The Red Bull Inn. Kayla urged the car forward as she turned around to find a parking spot nearby. Erika led the way into the dark room, her eyes taking a few moments to adjust. A few patrons were seated at the bar and only one table had occupants. They sat down at a table and read the menu on a blackboard next to the jukebox. Some of the menu items were unfamiliar to them but they didn't really want to ask. They could feel the eyes of the locals checking them out, but it wasn't in a negative way. Folks were probably curious about the two Yankee lasses in their midst.

When no one came to their table to take their order, Erika sidled up to the bar. She was told that there was no waitress, just the bartender and a cook in the back. Everyone always placed their order at the bar in pubs, didn't she know that? She laughed and acknowledged her ignorance as to the proper procedure, then went about ordering two fish and chips and two pear ciders. One man at the bar gave her a wink and she smiled sweetly back in his direction. Maybe she would like it here after all.

The barkeep called out to Erika and she picked up their order from the bar. When she pulled out her wallet to pay she was told that it was on the house tonight. It wasn't very often that they had such fine American women in their midst. He asked if they were staying long and she told him that they might be staying forever.

"That's what they all say," he chortled.

They were famished and the delicious meal disappeared quickly. Once they had thanked the barkeep once again, they headed back to Anwylyd for a well-deserved rest.

The next three days flew by as they continued the room by room assessment of the main house. On day four they tackled the outbuildings, including the guest house and stable. By the time they were finished there were large sheets of yellow legal paper plastered all over the kitchen counters, cabinets and table. Yes, there was indeed a great deal of work to be done.

Kayla sat at the table meticulously analyzing the lists and prioritizing the jobs while Erika began taking an inventory of everything in the house. She would take a photograph and write a note with the item number in a large notebook including any and all markings, such as manufacturer's names and the like. By the end of the week everything was becoming compartmentalized and organized, just the way Kayla liked it.

"So how far along are you, Erika, as far as the inventory is concerned?"

"Are you kidding me, Kayla? I have two, that's right, two rooms done. Your great aunt must have had a great fondness for nick-nacks, especially roses and dogs. For goodness sake, I have five pages just from the two corner cabinets in the dining room alone! This job is going to take forever! I sure hope you pay well!"

Kayla started to answer but her phone began to vibrate. She looked at the caller I.D. and saw that it was Brent. "I need to take this. Just give me a few minutes. Okay?"

"Sure, sure, it must be lover boy." Erika poured herself a cup of coffee and sat down at the table, perusing the ever growing priority lists. Kayla stepped out on the back porch to take her call.

Erika was totally engrossed in making her own list of the types of handy men that would be needed to do everything that needed to be done. Unless there was one helluva jack of all trades in this county, Kayla would be needing at least seven or eight different people to handle all of it – a concrete guy, a plumber, a drywall guy, an electrician, a painter, a tile guy. You name it, she needed it. Well, maybe not a painter, they could probably handle that themselves. Oh, and a stonemason, too, to fix some of the grout between the stones on the house itself. She relished the thought of being surrounded by a large group of shirtless Welsh men. She would serve them meat sandwiches and cold beverages and rub their muscles.

Erika's daydream was interrupted when Kayla returned to the kitchen, letting the screen door slam behind her, caught by an errant breeze. She had a Cheshire Cat smile across her face when she joined Erika at the table.

"We have been working so hard here that Brett thinks we need a holiday weekend in London. He's making the arrangements to get us there late this evening. How does that sound, Erika."

Erika gave her the old Ohio stink eye. "Um, it doesn't sound all that appealing to me, Kayla. Why don't you go on down to London and you two can paint the town red. In the meantime I'll stay here, keep working on the inventory and plan some interior decorating. When you come back we can start picking out paint swatches, wallpaper and think about some flooring."

"Really Erika? I can't just up and leave you here by yourself. You barely can drive on the wrong side of the road, you can't cook and you have no internet access. That wouldn't be fair really, would it?"

"Seriously, I am actually having a great time here doing all this. It has been very therapeutic not to have to worry about whether or not I have a date, if we'll do the wild thing, will he ever call again. And I have an interior decorator buried deep down inside me who is screaming to get out. I at least have a chance to do some sketches and present some ideas. It's very exciting. I think it will be good for me. Besides, you two need some alone time without me tagging along. And I promise I won't press you for details when you get back. Go ahead and let your hair down, girl. You deserve it."

Erika was surprised when Kayla rushed around the table and gave her a big hug. Kayla really wasn't the kind who showed physical affection. Perhaps this guy was better for her than she first thought. But that idea was fleeting. He was a scumbag through and through.

Kayla ran upstairs to what was, for now at least, her bedroom, Becca's bedroom just around the corner. She threw a few things in an overnight bag, jumped in the shower and raced back downstairs, just as a black limo pulled up in the circular drive. Erika walked out onto the massive porch to see her friend off. Kayla climbed into the back seat and continued waving until she was out of sight. Erika took a deep breath hoping that she did the right thing. She turned around and took in all that was Anwylyd. Deep in her heart she felt like she belonged here, too.

Erika returned to the lists on the dining room table and began working feverishly on each one. She took a separate notebook and made lists based on the type of work to be done. Then she pulled a dusty phonebook from beneath the telephone and began perusing the ads for construction workers. She doubted that any of them were still in business, since she noted that the book itself was nearly twelve years old. But with the multitude of listings, she was sure there were workers available, and with the local economy taking a nosedive, they would be happy to have work, and lots of it.

Just before sundown she decided to head back to the pub where they had eaten the night before, mostly so she didn't have to cook, but also because she wanted to ask about local workmen. If anyone knew who did a good job and who didn't, it would be a bartender. They listened to all the woes of everyone who sat on one of their stools. And the bartender had been so very friendly to them last night, she felt comfortable talking to him again.

She grabbed her purse and pulled the car keys off the hook near the door, leaving several lights ablaze so she could find her way around when she returned. Firing up the car, she drove very slowly up the long rutted driveway which reminded her that they also needed someone with a backhoe to fill in the damned thing!

Erika drove into town and parked a few hundred feet away from the pub. It must be supper time, she thought as she reached for the door. When she opened it, the place was standing room only. She worked her way to the crowd and found an empty stool at the far end of the bar directly in front of the air conditioning unit. Not exactly a comfortable seat, but a seat nonetheless. There was a band consisting of a few guitars, a banjo, a set of drums and a piano setting up on the postage stamp stage at the rear of the building. Perhaps that was the reason for the crowd, it was party night. After a few minutes she was approached by the bartender, who she could barely hear because of the drone of the people talking and laughing. But she was able to place her order using a few hand gestures and he nodded his understanding.

While she was waiting for her dinner she cracked open a few of the peanuts sitting in a bowl in front of her, crunching on them as she scribbled on a napkin. When her meal was delivered she handed the napkin to the barkeep. He knew better than to try to talk over the chatter, so he nodded again, taking the napkin back to his seat. She felt very relaxed as she at the succulent fish, washing it down with a beer tonight. None of that sissy cider stuff, she wanted a brew.

Half an hour later the band began warming up and Erika was just getting ready to head back to Anwylyd when the bartender motioned for her to join him at the other end of the bar. She left her coat on her barstool and worked her way down towards him. She could see that he was standing at a table where several men were seated with their glasses of beer. He shouted to her that some of them might be interested and able to help with the work that needed to be done. Two of them handed her business cards and one scribbled his name and talents on a napkin. She tucked them into her purse and thanked them. "I'll be calling you," she said loudly to overcome the cacophony of the room.

Just as she reached for her coat another man tapped her on the shoulder.

"I hear you are looking for some workmen to fix up Anwylyd. So glad someone has taken the old place under their wing. It has a beautiful history."

"Um, yes, my friend inherited it and I am helping her get it out of disrepair."

"Oh, I see. Well, me and my nephew are pretty handy at most anything and I'd love to talk to you about it sometime. But…"

He barely got the words out when the guys in the band began frantically motioning for him to get up on the stage.

"I have to get up there, but my name is Ivan, Ivan Ainsworth. Look me up soon, will ya?" He hopped up the steps to the stage and Erika sat back down. There was something about him that had her mesmerized.

Another hour passed and she tapped her foot along with the music. Ivan was the front man and he sang with a lovely brogue, songs of England and many familiar folk songs. She was thoroughly enjoying herself. By the time she looked at her watch it was nearly ten, so she slid out of her seat and onto the street. She slowly drove back to the manor house where she went straight up to bed and fell asleep with her clothes on. Her mind was mush.

Erika awoke to the vibration of her phone on the night stand. She reached for it and saw that it was Kayla. She fumbled with the stupid touch screen but managed to answer it before it threw the call to voicemail.

"Hello, hello?"

"Where have you been Erika? I've been worried sick. I called your cell about ten times last night and you didn't answer. I texted you and you didn't reply. I was afraid someone had broken into the house and murdered you or something!"

"Calm down there, Kayla. I'm fine. I went into town for some things and had supper at The Red Bull. There was a band there and it was loud. I could barely hear myself think no less hear the phone. I was so tired by the time I drove the cow path back to the house that I fell asleep. No harm, no foul, girl. Everything is under control. And how are you doing?"

"I'm doing fine. We had a fabulous dinner, went dancing and spent the night at another fabulous hotel. Just finished breakfast and going out to see Windsor Castle later today. The sun is shining and it's a beautiful day."

"Hold on a minute. You stayed in a hotel again? Why didn't you go to his place? Doesn't that seem odd to you?"

"His apartment is small and off the beaten path so we got a nice suite on the Thames."

"Have you actually seen his apartment, Kayla? Do you even know where he lives? Or does that not matter to you?"

"No, it really doesn't matter. I'm loving London and enjoying myself. I'll be home sometime tomorrow afternoon. Do you want me to bring you anything since I'm in London? I have access to all the good stuff."

"As a matter of fact, yes. Bring me a few good bottles of wine, some nice chocolates and some potato chips. I need some of the comforts of home. I can't live on fish, fries and wheat stalks for the rest of my vacation! And tea, good English breakfast tea. And Kayla?"

"What Erika?"

"I know you think I'm jealous, nuts, or whatever, but be careful with him. There are just too many red flags coming up. Promise me?"

"Sure, he's an ax murderer. I promise I'll be careful. See you tomorrow."

Erika hung the phone up but not without trepidation. There was just something out of place with all of this. She knew she should be so very happy for Kayla, but she just couldn't. It scared the hell out of her that she would be leaving Kayla here alone in less than three weeks. But life had to go on. We all made our own choices and Kayla was a thirty-two year old woman. She could handle whatever came her way. She would have to.

Erika stretched and sat up on the side of the bed. She could see that the sun was shining and there was a light breeze causing the wind chimes to sing their little tune. She showered, got dressed then headed into the kitchen to fix some breakfast. When the doorbell rang she sat her skillet of bacon to the side and answered it.

She peeked out the window and saw a small white truck, or lorry, sitting in the drive. She grabbed the nearest heavy object and placed it in her left hand as she opened the door with her right. One could never be too careful in a foreign country. It was a pleasant surprise when the open door revealed the smiling face of Ivan, along with a younger version of him.

"Sorry to bother you ma'am, but we didn't get a chance to make acquaintance much last night. I wanted to introduce myself properly and let you know what I can do to help you with the fixing up of the house. Oh, and this is my nephew who works with me on these things."

He handed her a business card and she glanced down at it for a moment. Then she got lost in those damned green eyes of his and stood on the stoop mesmerized. The men lingered on the steps in silence, waiting for her to respond. She suddenly came back to reality, cleared her throat and stepped aside.

"Please, won't you come in, um, Mr. Ainsworth."

"Oh, no. Not Mr. anything, ma'am. I'm Ivan and this is my nephew, Grebe."

"I've just started breakfast, would you like to join me? I'm making eggs, bacon and toast."

"No, ma'am. We've had our breakfast, but I would love a cuppa. One for the boy, too, if that's alright."

She led them into the kitchen and they sat at the massive table, Ivan peering over at the stacks of yellow legal pads. Erika put on the teakettle and turned off the other burners of the stove.

"So what kind of work are you looking to have done, ma'am."

"Honey, there is so much stuff to be done here you could be employed for the next ten years and it will never get done. My friend who owns the place is trying to decide if she wants to just do enough to sell it or to fix it up and make it a bed and breakfast. I think she's nuts wanting to move all the way over here and leave everything she has known her whole life. But it's her choice."

"When is the lady of the house going to be here? Maybe I should talk to her."

"No, no, she will be back from London tomorrow. But she told me to start interviewing people and making lists of who does what kind of work. So I suppose we should start with what type of work you do. What is your specialty?"

"Well, I'm really a farmer, but, by owning a small family farm, I've also learned to do all kinds of work, from laying floor to putting up drywall. My nephew here is good at mechanics and plumbing, plus he knows a lot about plants and such. So we pretty much are jacks of all trades, I suppose."

"Do you have the proper licensing to do that kind of work?"

Ivan smiled and the sparkle in his eyes caught Erika off guard. "Licensing? No. Not too many handymen around here have a license. We just have the ability. But I have lots of jobs that I can show you that we've done. That wouldn't be a problem at all."

"Do you speak, um, what's your name again? Grebe? You haven't said a word since the two of you arrived."

"Um, yes, ma'am. I speak. But only if I have something that needs to be said. Ivan does most of the talking. I'm just his sidekick."

"Please stop calling me ma'am. My name is Erika."

"Miss Erika, there is talk around town that your friend inherited this place from Rebecca MacGowan. She was quite a popular character around here. Everybody loved Miss Becca. She was everything from the crazy dog lady to the riding instructor to the midwife. Shame she never had any children of her own. She really was good with the kids. She gave a lot of her time to the community. My sister, Grebe's mother, spent a lot of time over here when Miss Becca would hold one of her big parties. She really liked the woman a lot. So we are pretty familiar with the property."

"Let me give you a list of the projects in priority order that need done around here. The first list is the 'sell it' list and the second list is the 'B&B' list. Some of the things overlap on the two lists. Take them home and look them over and I'll talk to Kayla. We will probably interview a few more people from the business cards and listings we have been collecting. You should hear something from us by mid-week, then, if we hire you, we'll have you come over and look at the specific items so you can give us some estimates on the work." She turned back towards the stove and turned the burners back on. "As you can see, my breakfast is calling me. I'll see you to the door and then get back to it. Does that sound reasonable?"

"Yes, it sure does. And, um, Miss Erika, will I see you at the pub tonight?"

Erika blushed, something that she hadn't done in years. She felt the curve of a smile creeping up one side of her face. "Maybe you will." She walked the men to the door and stood there a moment as they got into the truck and drove away.

CHAPTER **FIFTEEN**

Kayla didn't immediately realize it, but Erika had said enough to plant the seeds of doubt in her mind. She had always been naïve in some ways, due to her overprotective parents, her low self-esteem and conventional belief that people were good. And right now the attention she was getting from Brent had raised her self-esteem a notch or two. Being with him was good for her. It made her feel like a desirable woman. It was increasing her confidence and making her learn to utilize her assets. She used to always laugh when her grandmother would say "you can't make a silk purse out of a hog's ear." Maybe she thought she was the hog's ear, so why make an effort to improve her appearance. It was good enough for her friends and the dog didn't mind. No men were beating down her door, so why bother? But now she had a sudden interest in makeup application and current fashion trends.

She glanced over at Brent, who was now driving down the M-1 towards Windsor Castle. He was handsome, articulate and, by all accounts, fairly good in bed, although her personal experience was not too varied. He knew what to do to make her feel like a woman. And that was good enough for her. She had missed out on nearly all the sexcapades that should have happened in her twenties, so why not make up for it now? It certainly wasn't unpleasant spending time with Brent and maybe he was 'the one'. She had never been in love before and wasn't really sure about her feelings. She had so many things on her mind and decisions to make. Sometimes she would lay awake for hours thinking, everything was so overwhelming. Her mother had always said 'things take time, girl. Don't always be in such a hurry.' Perhaps it was time to take that advice to heart.

They had a lovely visit at Windsor, taking the guided tour. It was unbelievable to Kayla that people actually lived this way. The grandeur was overwhelming, the decor over the top. Americans barely see the tip of the iceberg when it came to royalty. The White House had nothing on the palaces of Europe.

After a lovely lunch and stroll through St. James Park, Brent suggested that they go to the office so he could show Kayla some of the figures related to Anwylyd. They pulled up in front of the building and hurried inside. The elevator was slow, so they kissed a little while riding up. It was very romantic to her. She had seen movies where people had made love on an elevator. She just couldn't picture it, even now, when Brent had her back up against the wall kissing her, his knee pushing hers apart. Before he could get any further, the bell dinged and door opened, reminding them where they were.

They tumbled out of the car, Kayla's hair scattered and her breaths deep and rapid. Brent's office was down the hall to the left, all glass and metal. A few staff were working diligently at their desks and barely acknowledged them as they passed. He pulled a blue desk chair behind his desk and placed it next to his, motioning for her to sit down. Sliding into his huge leather seat, he pulled out a blue folder packed with papers. Methodically he laid them out in front of them.

"What's all this?"

"Just a few different scenarios you might want to consider before making your final decisions about Anwylyd. I've crunched some numbers and I think you should see what your options are."

"But I want to live there. I'm pretty sure of it."

"Well, now, before you get all sappy about it, let me show you these. Then you might want to reconsider. Just give me ten minutes, will you?"

"Of course, Brent. I am very interested in what you have done here. Please continue."

He patted her hand as if she were a child and then handed her a stack of papers.

"On page 1, as you can see, is the estimated tax liability of the property. Although the taxes have been paid somewhat in advance, you would still be responsible for them in the future. And this spreadsheet shows how they will increase over time. The second page shows you the regular market value of the property as of last year and what it would be worth in five years and then ten years. As you can see, it is actually depreciating due to the age of the house and outbuildings. Unless it is completely torn down and a newer home built, it will continue to decrease. Page three shows the current offers that have been presented to owners of similar properties in Wales, including two in the Cardiff area. You can see that these offers far exceed the current market value. I believe you can really make a huge profit if you choose to sell Anwylyd in the near future to one of these developers. Can you see what I'm saying?"

"Yes, yes, I see what you are saying. But I don't really care about making a huge profit. I feel that this place is part of my heritage and that my Aunt wanted me to have it for some reason. Considering the size of the other components of my inheritance, if managed wisely, I can return Anwylyd to its former greatness and still live comfortably for the rest of my life. Am I not correct?"

"You realize you should probably have three million available if you intend to retire in the near future. Things are not as simple as you think. You could live well into your nineties. By then your 'nest egg' will be gone."

"Not if I live frugally, and I am very good at that. I have always lived that way. And if I can turn Anwylyd into a business, I can easily pay for upkeep by using those profits."

"The tourist business is very seasonal, Kayla. How would you pay the bills in the off season?"

"I'm sure I could find a way. I can work as a radiology tech at the local hospital if I wanted to. Once I get permanently settled, I'm sure I can find something. I can wait tables if I have to. I'm not afraid of working to pay the bills."

"Well, I just want you to take some time to look all this over and seriously consider all your options. You could be laying on the beach in France living the good life if you sell the estate and invest wisely. You would never have to work another day. That is something most people do not have the option of doing. Just think about it, will you? And I am always here to help you with any questions you might have. Enough of this business talk, what would you like to do this evening? Theater, dancing, pubs? You name it, I'll make it happen."

Kayla eyed him warily. That sure sounded like a business pitch to her. He was fondling her in the elevator just minutes before and now giving her financial advice. He was probably just concerned for her welfare, so she shook it off for the moment. She smiled and turned to him.

"I think I'll head back to the hotel and freshen up. How about we go to the theater and then dinner tonight?"

"Sounds fabulous, love. I'll drop you off, then go home and change. Why don't I pick you up at, say, six?"

"Why don't we run by your place, get your things and then go back to the hotel. We can have some quiet time before the theater."

He glared at her. "I have to check all my email, answer client inquiries and shower. That will take a few hours. I don't want to bore you with all that."

"Alright. Then take me back to the hotel and I'll see you at six."

Kayla rode back in silence, her thoughts askew. This weekend had seemed like a business transaction with a little sex thrown in for good measure. Oh well, she wasn't complaining. Being with Brent was still exciting and new, and so much better than sitting at home in her footie pajamas.

She pulled out a sequined dress for the theater and fixed her hair in a wild coif, a bit different than she usually had worn it. Why not have a little fun? Once she was dressed she called Erika but got no answer. She left a short message relaying when she would be back to Anwylyd. Hopefully Erika had gotten somewhere with finding handymen to start on some of the many projects. Hopefully she had not wound up in a ditch somewhere as a result of combining her recklessness, speeding and driving on the wrong side of the road.

The theater was pleasant and Brent stroked her hand through most of the performance. Dinner was in an intimate Asian café and the food was outstanding. Their conversation was very urbane, mostly discussing how the city of London combined the new and the old and how well things blended. Nothing personal came up. When they got into the car, Kayla was feeling tired, worn out from too much overthinking, one of her biggest habits. They returned to the hotel where the valet quickly swooped onto Brent, anxious to drive the shiny black beast. Kayla was already inside the lobby when he pulled away, waiting for Brent to join her.

They stepped into the elevator alone and he pushed the buttons, then switched his attention to pushing her buttons, slowly slipping one hand up the back of her dress. By the time they got to her room Kayla was physically on fire. Their lovemaking was quick and urgent tonight, and when Brent rolled off her, Kayla turned away and fell into a restless sleep. Neither spoke another word.

The clock reflected 4:25 a.m. as Kayla awoke with a sudden jerk. She sat up on the side of the bed, dug into her slippers and wandered over to the stuffed orange chair by the window. Staring out at the lights of London, she pondered over so many questions. Had Erika's opinions jaded her own? Perhaps Brent didn't like to rush into a relationship, but rather let it play out for a while. Had he actually done anything to hurt her in any way? He had been doing his job professionally, trying not to muddy the waters between work and play. He had certainly been a good lover and was always very attentive. She needed to stop worrying and enjoy the ride. She silently slid back into bed and put her arm across his shoulders, deciding to see where this all might lead.

When the alarm sounded at 6:30, Kayla was already showered and dressed, sipping a cup of coffee in the big orange chair. Brent rolled off the bed and stood, completely naked, peering out the huge window.

"You're an early bird today. Did you not sleep well?"

"To be honest with you, I was up and down all night."

"Are you ill? Should I get a doctor for you?"

"No, not ill, just still not adjusted to the time change. And I have a lot on my mind, you know that. Nothing out of the ordinary for me."

"I hate that I can't take you to the station to get the train. I have early meetings today."

"That's fine, really. I think I can find my way back to Anwylyd. I've done it a few times now."

"Maybe I can get a three day holiday soon and go see this wonderland for myself. Would that suit you?"

"Yes, I would love that. Then you can see why I love it so much. It is a beautiful place."

"I'll see what I can do with my schedule. How long are you staying?"

"I know I have to go back home at least one more time to make arrangements for an estate sale, and put the house on the market. I need to pack up my things to have them shipped to Wales and I need to get my dog. So I'm probably here for about a month, then I'll be gone for a month or so. Then I plan to return permanently."

"Just don't forget to look over the papers I gave you before you make your final decisions. You might be packing up to go to the Riviera instead of the harsh Welsh winters."

"I promise to look them over. You'll let me know when you can come to Anwylyd, won't you? I think you'll really like it."

Brent kissed her gently on the cheek, then proceeded to shower and dress. It was 7:30 a.m. when he left the hotel room. Kayla watched him pull away from the window of the suite. Something was tugging at her heart, but it wasn't a man, it was a manor house.

Four hours later the train pulled into the station at Cardiff and Erika was waiting for her. The friends embraced and were quickly chatting away about the things they had done over the past three days. Kayla discussed the theater and Erika discussed the job jar and work sheets she had completed as they sped down the bumpy road to the estate.

"And this man came with his nephew who can do nearly any kind of handy work around here. He is bringing us estimates on some of the jobs. They knew your Aunt Becca and his sister used to help cook here at Anwylyd."

"Hold on, hold on. Just how many workmen did you interview? Surely more than one."

Erika shook her head. "No, just one. But I have a good feeling about him."

"You and your 'feelings'. At least let me check on a few others before we go about making any decisions. Not that I don't trust you, but since it's my money, I want to be sure."

They laughed and went into the kitchen where Erika had been marinating chicken and vegetables to fix for dinner. She put the meal in the stockpot on the stove and brought out a bottle of wine. Pouring two glasses, she handed one to Kayla and placed one on the kitchen island for herself. They continued chatting while the meal was cooking.

"So, how was lover boy this weekend, really?"

"He was just fine. We had a lovely time. And no more of your doom and gloom. Brent has done nothing but be kind to me. I want you to just drop it. What I do with my personal life is my own business."

"Yea, your own disaster waiting to happen! But I will shut up about it. I've said my piece."

They finished their dinner then pulled out the lists that Erika had been working on. Kayla slowly looked over each sheet.

"Very impressive, Erika. You didn't just lay on the couch and eat bonbons all weekend. I'm proud of you."

"I didn't know there were any bonbons or I surely would have eaten them! But yes, I did try to organize things

to simplify getting estimates and prioritize. Go ahead and make any
changes as you see fit. As you can see, I did one list with the heading "SELL" and one list with the heading "B&B". That way if you would decide to sell you can do the minimal list for staging the property."

"I doubt very seriously if I will sell. I have a real feeling of belonging here. Like this is where I'm supposed to be. I honestly have never felt at home in my parents' house. I knew there was something else out there for me. The first time I laid eyes on this place I realized that I was finally home. When I walked through the front door, I knew Anwylyd was my destination. Do you think I'm crazy?"

"You know I believe in fate and all that sort of thing. This place has a certain appeal, that's for sure. At first I thought I would be a little nervous staying here alone, sort of spooked, you know? But I haven't felt so comfortable being alone in a very long time. There is a peacefulness here. Of course, I would probably go nuts being here very long, since it is so isolated, but in small doses it is very therapeutic. So no, I don't think you're crazy."

They had a good laugh and went back to the business of organizing the jobs. Erika had set up a job jar for the two of them, consisting of chores that they could complete themselves with no help from anyone else. She had also made a list of cleaning supplies and equipment they would need that could be picked up at the local shops in the morning. She had found a pile of aprons and dust rags in the pantry and had washed and folded them for use. All in all, she had had a very productive weekend.

After talking to Brent on the phone, Kayla retired to her bedroom. She was exhausted from the travel and lack of sleep. Needing to be fresh for all the work coming up this week, she headed to bed. Erika stayed up a while, listening to the BBC on the radio. That was another thing she wanted to get done this week, television and internet. Those were the priorities!

CHAPTER SIXTEEN

Monday morning came quickly and the ladies were up and at 'em at dawn. They ate a small breakfast of muffins and berries, accompanied as always by some hot tea. They gathered their shopping lists and headed into town so that they could get an early start on their jobs. As they drove by the hardware store Erika noticed the lorry that had been at Anwylyd just the other day and smiled. There was just something about that man, Ivan. She couldn't quite put her finger on it and she surely wasn't going to tell Kayla that she wanted to hire the handyman because she thought he was hot. That wouldn't go over well. So she kept that little item to herself for the time being.

Once all the purchases were made they hurried back to the estate to get started. Each took a slip of paper out of the job jar and gathered their supplies. It was a huge endeavor to clean such a house, so it was time to get cracking!

Erika took the wood soap, a bucket of warm water and a handful of dust rags and headed for the library. It was going to take a long time to methodically remove books from their shelves, clean the shelf, then dust and return the books. She decided to divide the room into fourths and tackle it that way. Then she would have a sense of accomplishment for each section as she completed it.

Kayla grabbed toilet brushes, Clorox bowl cleaner, Windex and paper towels and headed for the upstairs bathrooms. It would probably take her at least an hour and a half to clean each of the nine bathrooms, so it was going to be an all-day affair. Never in her life did she think she would be spending a whole day cleaning bathrooms, but she was looking forward to it. Each one was unique in its way, something she had noticed throughout England, so each room would be a new adventure. As odd as it sounded, she liked that about the house.

By noon each had completed half of their chore for the day, so they were taking time to fix a light lunch and take a brief rest. As they sat at the kitchen island chatting about their tasks, there was a knock on the front door. Kayla's furrowed brow indicated that she was not expecting anyone and didn't recognize the white lorry that was pulled into the drive. Erika, on the other hand was well aware who the truck belonged to.

"Who is it, Erika?" Kayla yelled from the kitchen.

"It's the handyman I spoke to over the weekend. He's probably come to get the list of what we need estimates on. Why don't we invite him in for lunch?"

"Sure, invite the handyman in for lunch. What's next, have the postman over for cocktails? What's wrong with you? We don't even know these people."

"Geesh, Kay, lighten up."

Kayla heard the door open and a mixture of voices. Within minutes Erika was back in the kitchen with two fellows in tow.

"Kayla Battaglia, I'd like you to meet Ivan and Grebe. Ivan and Grebe, this is Kayla."

"Lovely to make your acquaintance, ma'am." Ivan said kindly

Grebe nodded, acknowledging her, his sensuality filling the room. Kayla was captivated by his smile, his eyes and how his crimson locks hung recklessly across his shoulder. She noticed that his eyebrows moved precariously as he smiled. She didn't believe in love at first sight, but lust, yes, that was a definite possibility.

"So that's it, then. You'll take home the lists and get back to us by the end of the week. How does that sound to you, Kayla? Kayla? Hello, earth to Kayla....please return."

"Oh, oh yes, that sounds marvelous. That way we have time to finish all the cleaning and inventory before any work begins. Does that accommodate you, Mr. Ainesworth?"

"Ma'am, my job is to accommodate you and what you need done. If I have the estimates done sooner I'll drop them off. I'll plan on starting next weekend if the estimates are of your liking. It's been nice to make your acquaintance, Miss Kayla. You should come down to the pub for dinner tonight. It's ladies night at the bar."

Kayla giggled and nodded her head. "Maybe we should do that, eh, Erika? And thank you for coming out today." She shook Ivan's hand and reached for Grebe's. He gently stroked her thumb during the handshake. Again he nodded then turned away, following Ivan out the front door.

"What in the hell just happened here Kayla? Have you gone over the edge? I've never seen you like that?"

"I was just taken by surprise, that's all. I've never felt so drawn to a person the first time I met them. There was just something about his, his eyes."

"Who? Ivan? I fancy him myself and you have Brent so back off, girlfriend."

"What? No, not Ivan, His nephew. What was his name? Greed?"

"Nope, Greeb, Greeb. Isn't he a bit young for you? Are you becoming a cougar? And what about Brent?"

"I don't know. There is no harm in looking. Anyway, how old do you think he is?"

"I have no idea. I don't know how old either one is. And we are getting off topic here. Don't you think we need to interview a few more handy men? I know you want to get a variety of estimates."

"Yes, we should talk to a few others as well. There is just something about him. I can't explain it."

"You are going to be the death of me, I swear it."

They went back to the business at hand, Kayla continuing to work upstairs while Erika went to the parlor downstairs. They should have taken out stock in the legal pad company with the number of them they had in use. It was amazing how many items could fit in one house. Kayla wondered how long it had taken her aunt to amass the things that she was now cataloging. It boggled her mind to even think about it. There were items from many countries, probably that she had visited during her time in the military, tons of floral items and a large number of animal related items, especially things canine. At least they shared one thing, their love of dogs.

Several hours had flown by when Erika came bounding up the stairs.

"Time to put away your pen and paper, girl. We need to get ready to go to dinner at The Red Bull."

"Aw, I don't know, Erika. I don't think that's a great idea. We really don't even know those guys and I'm not sure we should be seen out partying with them at this stage in the game. I don't want rumors flying around that the only reason I hired them was because I have a personal interest in it. I'm too new here to be the center of scandal."

"C'mon Kayla! We are two women who need to eat dinner. If we run into people we know what's the harm in it? We have to eat, you know."

"I suppose you are right, but I'm sure there are other eating establishments in the big town of Cowbridge. Let's drive into town and see what else is available. Is that okay?"

"Fine, fine. Whatever you want to do, Kayla. This is your rodeo, not mine."

They quickly changed and headed into town. Of course, as with their previous trips, the whole place was closed up for the night except for the pub. Erika grinned an evil knowing grin as Kayla parked across the street. At least she hadn't whined or forced the issue.

When they walked into the pub Erika looked around for Ivan, but he was nowhere in sight. There was one empty table on the left side so they promptly placed their coats on the chairs and went up to the bar to order. The barkeep was quick to accommodate them.

"Glad to see you back, girls. It's nice to be appreciated." He handed them their glasses of wine and they settled back at their table.

Fifteen minutes later they were being served their roast beef and potatoes, which smelled heavenly to Kayla. Suddenly Erika looked up and saw the dark form of the man she knew to be Ivan standing in the doorway. She waved her arm frantically above her head to get his attention. Little did she know that she was already in his sights. Kayla turned, glancing side to side, trying to see beyond his hefty frame. She felt the disappointment rise up from her deepest recesses. Grebe was not with his uncle tonight. She forced a smile when Ivan joined them.

"I see you've eaten without me, lass," Ivan said directly to Erika.

"When we didn't see you, I assumed you had decided to stay home tonight. And where is Grebe, he isn't joining us?"

"No, he had a meeting and went to the gym this evening. He often works out at night. It is part of his routine. Nothing personal, ladies."

"Oh, that's fine. Just wondering if he would be joining us."

"Lovely to see you as well, Miss Kayla. Miss Erika has been alone the past few evenings which can often get a young woman in trouble around here."

Kayla turned to him. "I've never met a young woman who could handle trouble better than Erika. But I appreciate the warning, Ivan."

They had a good laugh and Ivan sauntered to the bar to place his dinner order. He carried two glasses of wine and two steins of beer when he rejoined them at the table. Making quick work of the first stein, he slowly sipped from the second. The ladies continued eating their dinner while Ivan spun yarns about the area for them. He had lived in the county his entire life except for his time in the military, so he was very familiar about his subject. For the next two hours he kept them entertained with his tales about life, love, and everything in between. When he stopped for a drink and a breather, Kayla glanced intently at him.

"And what do you know of my Great-Aunt Becca? How did she come to be here? Was she ever involved with anyone? Any idea why she never married and raised a family?"

"Now hold on there, young lady. Your aunt was a wonderful person. She gave a lot to the community. She had all kinds of parties for the war orphans and adopted nearly every rangy mutt that wandered onto her property. It is rumored that the property was given to her by a lover, but no one has ever confirmed that to my knowledge. She never spoke of it, at least not to me. She never married and never was involved with anyone after moving to Anwylyd that I know of. She was mysterious about her private life, but she was no hermit. She was always out doing something. She donated a lot of time to the clinics around here. She was practically a saint, I tell you."

"I just wish I knew more about her. What brought her here, what kept her here, and who she really was. My grandmother never spoke of her that I can remember. I think it's odd. I suppose without email and the internet it was difficult to keep in touch across the Atlantic, but still, I should know something about her. Sorry Ivan, it's just frustrating."

"Like I said, my sister knew her a lot better than I did, and you know how women talk. Maybe you ladies should come over to the farm for dinner sometime. We rarely have guests, you know."

Erika chimed in. "That would be great, Ivan! Of course, if your sister doesn't mind. We can bring a covered dish over so she doesn't have to do all the work. What do you like to eat?"

"As you can see, lass, I am not too particular. Just don't care much for brussel sprouts and lima beans. Otherwise, I'd eat almost anything that won't eat me." He chortled, taking another huge chug from his beer mug.

They finished dinner and chatted for another hour, when Kayla began yawning.

"Sorry about that, my brain is shutting down for the night. We have to interview a few more folks, but I'm really looking forward to your estimates, Ivan. I'll be calling your references and going to look at some of your work over the next few days. I am so very anxious to get this work started."

Ivan rose from his seat and accompanied the women to their vehicle. "You can't be too careful at night, fine ladies like you and all." Once they were safely in the car he patted Erika on the arm and winked, then turned back towards the tavern. They returned to Anwylyd and Kayla went straight to bed, not noticing the 'missed messages' alert on her cell phone.

By Thursday afternoon Kayla was feeling a great sense of accomplishment. She and Erika had catalogued all of her aunt's belongings in the house, stable and guest house. She had made arrangements for an appraiser from Cardiff to come the following week to assist with assessing values and selling some of the pieces. They had interviewed many of the local handymen and had narrowed it down to three, based on their abilities, references and actual work that they had done. The pantry in the kitchen was full and she had also located a several farmers, including Ivan, for fresh fruits, vegetables, meat and eggs. She was definitely enjoying the role of mistress of the manor house.

When she had finished all her phone calls, Kayla found Erika sitting in the study with her hands folded in her lap, looking very intense. She sat down next to her friend on the overstuffed leather sofa and took her hand.

"What's wrong, Erika? You seemed to be having such a good time the past few days."

"Yes, they have been some of the happiest days of my life. Everything is so carefree and the people are so nice. No pressure from any angle. But reality is going to set in. I have to go back to Ohio next week. It's not that I want you to come with me. It's that I want to stay here. It is a chance for a new start, leave all the old baggage behind and have a new life. You don't have to worry about paying bills and going to work but, well, I do. I don't have a choice. Sometimes life sucks. And I don't know if I can stand my best friend being three thousand miles away. I guess I'm just sad really."

"So what is the main reason you are going back? Your life? Your job? What?"

"I have to have income, I have bills to pay. I can't just loaf around."

"You rent a crappy apartment for a ridiculous amount of money. You are tired of your job. You have no husband, no children, no nearby family and no serious relationship. So why don't you pack up and move here with me? What is stopping you?"

Erika looked at her in disbelief. "You are kidding me, right? I can't leave America? I can't move to a foreign country just like that."

"You are the one who is usually impulsive, not me. I didn't make this decision lightly, although it probably appears that way. Then I got to thinking. What is holding me back? I have no family left to speak of. I live in an old ranch house by myself with my dog. I have no relationship, there, anyway. I have lived a very boring life. Sure, I made enough money to survive, but now I don't have to worry about money if I am frugal. So I'm taking a huge leap of faith here. I may live to regret it, but I feel in my heart it is the right thing to do. Think about it, will you, Erika? It's not like this place is too little for the both of us, even if we did find husbands and have kids! And besides, if I open this bed and breakfast, I'm going to need a good party planner. And no one can plan a party like you, girl!"

"You are serious, aren't you? You really want me to pack up my bags and move across the pond. Your arguments make sense, but it just feels weird, you know? I never had 'move to Europe' on my 'to do' list. Let me sleep on it for a while. You know I have to weigh the benefits against the consequences. I'm neurotic like that."

"Sure, I understand completely. But I do hope you will consider my offer."

"Can I ask you one pretty personal question, Kayla?"

"You can ask. Don't know if I'll answer."

"Just how much are you worth these days?"

Kayla smirked and stared right at Erika. "Enough, girl, more than enough." She poured two glasses of lemonade and the pair went out on the front porch and sat on the swing, overlooking the vast fields of green that was Anwylyd. She could see the young man she had hired to start mowing the vast sea of grass riding the ancient green John Deere at the far end of the entrance fence. She was delighted that he was able to get it started. This was one of the first, most monstrous of jobs which would take several days to complete, weather permitting. Then she would get the chance to have a glimpse of a more refined estate. A place where she might actually find herself.

CHAPTER **SEVENTEEN**
Ivan

As the ship pulled into port at Belfast, Ireland, young Ivan Ainsworth rocked back and forth with the rhythm of the water pulling the boat into the dock. His knapsack was nearly fifty pounds but he had little trouble hanging it on his powerful shoulder while clutching a fat knotted rope. The one thing he had been able to do a lot of at sea was lift weights on a regular basis. The gym on the ship was well-equipped to keep her sailors in shape.

Being on a merchant marine vessel was not for sissies, and Ivan was worlds away from that moniker, his physique improving with each re-enlistment. Training and conditioning his body made him feel good about himself. His father had not treated his own body well, and he had watched the man succumb to lung cancer after a short and horrifying existence. He vowed not to end that way, but to live a long and healthy life.

Ivan was born into a poor farm family just north of Cardiff, Wales. He was the only son of James and Clara Ainsworth of Cowbridge. His father was a coal miner who owned a large family farm and his mother was a seamstress. He watched his parents work their fingers to the bone to keep a roof over their heads and food on the table for their family. Two sisters, one older and one younger, helped their mother with the household chores and took in sewing to bring in a few coins. Ivan himself spent the majority of his time out of school working the farm, tilling, planting and harvesting the crops. He had a good eye for cattle and sheep, which he took to market every Saturday to sell. There was barely any time for rest or holidays.

    As he neared graduation from high school, Ivan had been feeling the need to get away from the all-female household he had been living in since the death of his father two years before. He felt the need to leave the small village and see the world. He knew the only way out was to enlist in one of the military factions that were heavily recruiting in the area. He joined up just after graduating from high school, much to his mother's chagrin. His younger sister and mother were the only two at the house now, so there wasn't as great a need for maintaining the larger herds and gardens. All he needed to do was hire a gardener to attend to the small vegetable plot and feed the dwindling number of animals that remained. Once that was accomplished, Ivan felt that it was time for him to move on.

    It wasn't that he didn't enjoy the company of his mother and sisters, but he longed for brotherhood and also wanted to serve the country that had provided for his family for centuries. And if he had the opportunity to kick some menacing ass, he was more than happy to do that as well.

    Spending twelve years in the Merchant Navy was very good to him. Alongside the mechanical and leadership skills he had acquired, he also found out who he was. A simple man who longed for the simple things. He merely wanted to be a gentleman farmer with a loving wife and children of his own. He knew he wouldn't have a lot of material things to offer a lady, but he would give her his heart, gentle and true, and give it one hundred percent.

    He wasn't one for a one night stand. As a matter of fact, the two times he had hired a prostitute in one port or

another, he paid the girl without using any of her services. He felt pity that she had to make a living by giving her body to an uncaring savage. The whole thought of it nauseated him. He wanted love to be more than physical, giving oneself completely to another person. He had never married, even though he had courted many fine women. But now, well into
his forties, he had accepted that the hole in his heart was permanent. He was no longer what would be considered a 'good catch'.

Returning to run the family farm and care for his aging mother brought him a great sense of purpose. He again took immense pride in the family farm, raising crops and creatures from
conception to meet their full potential. He understood animals and they understood him. It was a symbiotic relationship that kept him focused. And he somehow managed to squeeze a decent living out of it when other family farms were failing miserably. And he was very thrifty when it came to his military retirement fund. Not that he was miserly, but he was careful with the family budget and rarely indulged in anything excessive for himself.

Four years after his return, his youngest sister, Elizabeth, tragically lost her husband in a motor vehicle accident and was left alone to contend with her difficult teenage son. Ivan moved them into the farmhouse with him and never looked back. If he was never going to be a father, the least he could do was to help care for his troubled nephew, who, at seventeen, had gotten involved with some persons of questionable reputation.

In a small town like Cowbridge, it wasn't difficult to know who the problem folks were. And these were definitely problem folks. Ivan felt that putting the boy to work as a farmhand would keep him busy enough to stay on the straight and narrow. Little did he know that the young man had already been launched into a downward spiral that would impact all of their lives.

    The next three years were worse than he could ever have imagined, but Ivan had to stay strong for his sister, as she would be tested beyond her capabilities and someone had to be the rock. Serving as a role model for his nephew would prove to be one of the most challenging of his entire life. Ivan took this role as seriously as all others, but began to doubt his own sanity at times when the walls of privacy came tumbling down.

    Following the sentencing and imprisonment of his nephew, the family settled back down into some semblance of normalcy, or as normal as one could be after such tragedy. Ivan began working as a handyman to help pay off the legal bills his nephew had acquired. When the opportunity for employment at one of the largest estates in Wales came his way, it was a miracle for Ivan both financially and personally. And who was he to question fate?

CHAPTER **EIGHTEEN**

By the time the weekend rolled around, everything was falling into place. Kayla and Erika had completely cleaned the manor house, started on the outbuildings, finished the interviews, done their hiring and shopped until they dropped. There was a great sense of accomplishment that could be felt when one entered the house.

"It is coming together, isn't it?

"Yes, Kayla, this place is fabulous! You were right. I feel such a sense of belonging here. It is mysterious yet so right."

"So have you come to a decision yet, Erika? I mean, about moving here?"

"No, I really am not sure about that yet. It is a huge step. And I still can't believe you think you will seriously do it. Have you totally dispelled the idea of selling the place? I mean, like Brent said, you could sell it and retire to the coast of France without a care in the world. Keeping Anwylyd would require your time and attention at all times. You can't just go travelling the world whenever you'd want to."

"I have a few more things I want to look into before I make the final decision, like what the true value is, but I just feel that there is something here that I need to do or find. I can't explain it. But I know it's true."

"Maybe there is something that your aunt wanted to tell you or show you and it is here, hidden somewhere in this house."

"I know, right? But we have catalogued everything here. Could I have missed something?"

"That is possible. The whole place is huge. There could be all kinds of hidden cubby holes and hiding places.

We just haven't looked hard enough is all. Now that things are in order and organized, maybe we can poke around a bit deeper. What do you think?"

"I think we need to get back to the matters at hand, taking these estimates and working on the budget, setting things up for the workmen and stocking the kitchen. Why don't we head into town and get this done, then we can go listen to Ivan singing at the pub tonight? I know you want to, Erika!"

"What is that supposed to mean? I mean, he is, like, ten years older than me. I'm a cougar, girl, I go for those young studs. Not an old retired stallion like him. He probably has a woman in every town he works in and a few farm maids as well. No, as handsome as he is, he isn't for me. Not my type at all."

"Ha! I thought if they had a working penis they were your type! But what do I know?"

Erika threw a metal spatula in Kayla's direction, missing her by a mile. The clattering of the metal on the stone floor made the starlings sitting on the back deck fly off in a black scolding cloud. They watched as the birds scattered then regroup before heading off into the woods. Grabbing their purses, they headed out the door into town.

As they were bouncing up the driveway to the main road, Erika began to laugh and turned to Kayla. "Are you going to keep a rental car forever or are you going to buy something? I mean, it's not cheap to use a rental car. And you surely aren't going to keep this puddle jumper! What a piece of junk it is!"

"No, I think I will buy a car when I come back from the next trip home. I have to get all my affairs in order there, put the house on the market, sell my own vehicle and find out the
requirements to bring my dog over here. I do need to do some research on cars here. I have no idea what to buy. I'll drop this one off at the airport and never look back!!"

~ 167 ~

"And when will that be, I mean, when are you going back and how long will you be staying? I have to make plans, you know. Do you and Spinner want to move in with me while the house is being sold? Do you have any idea what it would sell for? I doubt you would have trouble selling it since it is in great shape in a good neighborhood. Are you moving back here before the house is sold?"

"Hold your horses, Erika! Geesh! So many questions! I am playing this by ear right now. I don't know what's happening with Brent, what the total expense is of fixing up Anwylyd, if it can keep its own head above water. There is a lot going on in my head. I know this sounds crazy, but I'm going to let my intuition rule. One thing at a time, one day at a time. I will probably go home a few weeks after you do. I need to find a caretaker for the place while I'm gone, but I don't know who I could trust completely. That is one of the next things on my 'do' list. Is that okay with you?"

Erika nodded and knew it was time to quit talking. One thing Kayla was not good at was handling pressure when making decisions. She decided to let things settle down before pressing Kayla any further. She changed the subject to the shopping list and kept on course through the entire trip to town. That is, until she saw Ivan's lorry parked outside the hardware store.

"I think we need to stop at the hardware store. I've forgotten to pick up hangers for the all of the artwork and photographs. I'm not sure of the weight of some of the pieces."

"All right, but this is the last stop." Kayla pulled into a small spot behind the lorry, realizing exactly what Erika was up to. "Make it snappy, will ya?"

Erika jumped out of the car and rushed to the door of the hardware store where she saw Ivan in the checkout line loaded with bags. She hesitated until he was nearly to the door, then swung it open.

"Fancy seeing you here," she said coyly.

"Aye, fancy that. How are you today, Miss Erika?"

"Fine, fine. Just picking up some hangers for photos and the like."

"Well, don't just go hammering nails into the walls there. You are better off using the newfangled adhesive hangers. They won't damage the place. On second thought, don't go doing it at all. Just show me where you want things and I'll use my laser level and the adhesive hangers. If you are making the house a place of business, you won't want things looking all crooked and such. Make another one of your fancy lists going room to room with how you want it done and we'll take care of it. How does that work for you?"

Erika tried to scowl but it was a half assed attempt to be sure. She nodded and returned to the car empty handed. All she could do was smile and shrug her shoulders when Kayla gave her the evil eye. The car lurched forward headed towards the manor house.

When the car was just past the stone pillars Kayla noticed a dark vehicle sitting in the driveway. She could make out a tall figure seated in the driver's seat but couldn't imagine who would be waiting for them. As they approached she recognized the slick black BMW that she herself had ridden in so many times. Brent! What the hell was he doing way out here? When she climbed out of the car he threw his door open and stepped quickly towards her.

"Where the hell have you been? Who is he? Who are you seeing? Why don't you answer my calls?"

For just a moment Kayla was afraid. She had never seen this side of Brent before. He was always so kind and attentive to her. But feeling Erika's hand against her back gave her a bit more courage to respond to him.

"What are you talking about Brent? I'm not seeing anyone but you. And my phone service out here is 'iffy' at best, so I might not have even gotten your calls. I think I have the right to ask what you are doing here. The last thing I knew we were meeting in London this weekend and that was my plan."

"I do not take well to being blown off for someone else, Kayla." He turned to Erika. "We need to discuss this in private if you don't mind."

Erika turned to Kayla. "I'll be right inside the house with my little friend if you need me."

"I'm sure I'll be fine, Erika, but thank you for giving us some privacy." Kayla took a step towards Brent. "Just what is this all about? You knew I had a mountain of things to do this week and would be crazy busy. I don't have time to be seeing anyone for God's sake! Why would you say such a thing?"

"Because your friend, Erika is, shall we say, fond of the boys and I thought she might have drawn you into her activities. I'm sure she isn't staying celibate."

"That was so rude. She has been as busy as I have, helping me try to get this place in shape."

"In shape to sell, I hope. You can't live here alone. Who would take care of everything? I hope you have taken some of your precious time to look over the paperwork I gave you and some of the brochures showing wonderful town houses in exotic places."

"Yes, I have taken time to look them over. However I have still not made my decision to stay or go. I'll let you know what I decide. Please come in and I'll fix a pot of tea. Then I will show you around."

Brent started to object but relented, following Kayla up on the porch and into the kitchen, where Erika was perched on one of the island chairs. She proceeded to turn on the stove and filled the teapot. Erika eyed Brent warily and he returned her glare.

Kayla served the tea in antique white cups and saucers garnished with red and pink roses surrounded by gold trim. They were part of a complete set that she had found in her aunt's dining room sideboard. They were clearly marked 'Homer Laughlin Company, Newell, West Virginia USA" which thoroughly amused Kayla as she had grown up just across the Ohio River from that company. Either Aunt Becca had taken them with her or she had received them as a gift from home. The set made Kayla smile and feel even more at ease in the manor house.

After some idle chit chat about work and what was being done to the house, Kayla rose to her feet and took Brent's hand. Erika winced at the thought that the scumbag was going to tour Anwylyd, but she sure as hell wasn't going to let him put negative thoughts into her friend's head. She followed along at a polite distance as they went from room to room, Kayla pointing out the improvements that she was having done in each. The atmosphere seemed to lighten a bit during the tour, making everyone feel more at ease. Perhaps Brent was just the jealous type. Nah, Erika thought, he's just a jerk.

Two hours later the tour ended abruptly in the kitchen, just as it had begun. Brent picked up the "Home Improvements" ledger and perused it once again.

"If you plan on selling this place, why would you put this much time and money into it. Surely you could sell it by doing the bare minimum, some paint and flooring. You should easily be able to sell it for a reasonable price. Do you really think you will be able to recoup your investment if you do all of this?"

"Remember that I paid nothing for the estate, Brent, so anything I make less the cost of the improvements is free and clear. There is no outstanding debt, so if, and that's a big if, I would sell, like you said, I could be living the good life in Monaco."

Brent smiled. "Yes, yes, you could. So you will be coming to London on Friday night then?"

"Yes, that has been my plan all along. And Brent, let's do something different this weekend, like a pub crawl or a book reading. Something off the beaten tourist path. I've seen and done most of that." She saw him check his watch. "It's getting late, will you stay tonight?"

"No, that's impossible. I have a trial tomorrow and need to be there bright and early. I have to go home and make sure all my preparations are complete. But I'll see you on Friday evening after work. Just go to the usual hotel, I've already made your reservations." He kissed her gently on the lips and whispered softly, "I do expect you will come alone."

She glared at him as he walked out the door, slid into his Beamer and pulled out of the drive, throwing gravel and mud as he accelerated the engine, mostly for show.

"What a jerk," Erika said under her breath, not knowing that Kayla was starting to agree with her.

They returned to the kitchen and their stack of papers. Kayla went about working on the repair schedule while Erika verified the check list. Yard worker? Check! Painter? Check! Electrician? Check! Woodworker? Check! Plumber? Check! All around handyman? Check! She was amazed at what they had been able to accomplish. Back home it could take weeks to get one of those jobs organized. Of course, several of those jobs belonged to the team of Ivan and Grebe, which made her heart flutter just a little bit. She took her scrub bucket upstairs and started working on the bathtub, where Grebe would be working over the weekend. She wanted to make sure he started with a clean slate.

By mid-afternoon, Ivan had begun bringing supplies to start working on the outside of the house, wood, nails and trim began stacking up at the far corner of the front porch. He had a small spiral notebook and pencil in his pocket and was checking the measurements he had taken prior to starting the jobs. The pounding of the hammer was rhythmic and smooth, just as Erika imagined his lovemaking would be in the bedroom, picturing that in her mind. So what if he had a decade over her, it was a decade of experience, a far cry from the fumbling of younger suitors. She needed to get her mind out of the gutter, or off of sex. It had been a while, that was for sure. Longer than she cared to remember.

Erika went back into the kitchen where Kayla was scrubbing the floor on her hands and knees.

"Kayla, I have to get out of here! Two whole weeks without television, newspapers or internet is driving me mad! And I am sick and tired of cleaning, dusting, scrubbing and cleaning even more! That is not exactly what I consider a good time! You will have to institutionalize me if I can't use my iPad pretty soon!"

"Geesh, calm down a minute, Erika! I need some groceries for dinner, so why don't you take the car into town, pick up some newspapers and find a little café' where you can get WiFi for a bit. I've got things under control here. Just take the car and be careful!"

"Hell, I don't know if I can drive around here! I don't know where any little café is. I might get lost and cause an international incident! Are you crazy?"

Ivan came in the kitchen door, loaded down with wood and nails that he didn't want to leave out in case of rain. He overheard the conversation and glanced at Kayla.

"I have to go into town to get some parts and I was going to grab a late lunch. I would be more than happy to take Miss Erika with me. I can get my things and then take her for errands if that would be alright."

Erika gave Ivan a huge hug.

"Yes, that would be wonderful! You are my hero! Wait here while I get my purse." She certainly knew that she wasn't going to be able to get her mind off sex with Ivan in close proximity. But she readily agreed to join him.

The two of them climbed up into Ivan's lorry and headed into town. He pulled up in front of the local hardware store and told Erika he would only be a few minutes. She leaned her head back against the seat and closed her eyes. This was just crazy. At first when Kayla wanted to stay in this godforsaken country that was decades out of the loop, she knew that she sure as hell couldn't do it. She needed technology! But her attitude was beginning to change. What was really waiting for her back in Ohio? A dead end job? Unemployed men still living with their mothers with no future? Maybe she, too, needed a fresh start.

Her thoughts were interrupted when Ivan opened the door and climbed back into the truck, loaded down with all sorts of handyman items that Erika knew very little about.

"What would you like for lunch, lass? I know a good little place with the some of the best beef sandwiches in the county. Or are you one of those vegans who doesn't eat red meat or something? Seems you Yanks don't like real food as well as we do."

"That sounds fantastic, Ivan. And by café, you mean a little place that has alcoholic beverages?"

"Indeed I do. I fancy a brew myself."

The Hitchcock was a small bistro on the main street in town. Ivan held the door as Erika walked into the darkness. It took a few moments for her eyes to adjust to the poor lighting inside. The place was small but well thought out. There were tables for two along the walls, tables with four chairs towards the center and one larger table that could seat six patrons at the very rear of the room. It was adorned with true Welsh décor, plenty of red dragons to be had and paintings of the area done by local artists on the walls. Quaint was a word that came to mind as she looked around. They took a table for two near the far window.

"It's crowded because it's good, you know. Mostly just the locals are aware of it. Not the damned tourists."

An older waitress was quick to attend to them, smiling sweetly at Ivan.

"A Guinness Stout for you, eh, Ivan? And what for the lady?"

"I'll have the same, thank you. I need it!"

Ivan laughed again and ordered two beef sandwiches with onion while Erika turned her attention to the news on the television. She was dying for any news of home. She pulled out her iPad and sat it on the table.

"They have the WeeFee here, I think." Ivan said.

Erika smiled at him. He probably didn't even know what WiFi was, but she was impressed that they had it in such a small out of the way café. She turned on the iPad and began perusing her email, followed by her social media. She was deeply engrossed in some gossip when their meal came. It smelled so divine she was almost drooling with anticipation. She put her technology away and set about ingesting the delicious meal. She noticed that Ivan had put down his fork and was focused on a news story about some conglomerate buying up property for housing developments in the area. The headline read 'WAFT Offering Huge Stipends'.

"That should be good for the economy, shouldn't it, Ivan."

"Hell no, the bastards are taking advantage!"

"In what way, Ivan?"

"They know that people are in dire straits and have to do whatever they can to survive anymore. These bastards dangle a bag of coin and buy family farms that have been in the same hands for generations and ship the families off to live in some condominium. They sure as hell named it right. Just like a condom, they wrap them up tight and keep them from having a life. The sons of bitches say it's all in the name of progress, that small farms just cannot support a family anymore. They are doing it to 'help out', they say. Building these housing developments on productive land. It's been going on for a while now, but they are getting more aggressive these days. They'd better stay off my farm or I will blow their fecking heads off, I tell you!"

"You think they would try to force you off your farm?"

"Of course they would! Trying to get their almighty dollars! They buy your farm for a pittance, then build some big fancy house on it, landscape it and sell it for quadruple what they pay for it. And they have no concern for you after that, I tell you. I'll not have them doing that to my place, even if I am down to my last cent!"

"Your farm really means the world to you, doesn't it?"

"Other than when I was in the Merchant Navy, I have run the farm my whole life and learned how to be self-sufficient. I have never ask anyone for anything. I have thirty acres and run some sheep and cattle, some of which I sell at market. My sister and Grebe live there as well, and she does the gardening. They have been living there since her husband died a few years ago. You have to take care of family, you know, they are all you really have. We have our own meat, wool and vegetables to keep the house running. And I do the odd job here and there as I need to."

"What about Mrs. Ivan?"

He laughed heartily once again. "There is no Mrs. Ivan, lass. I don't have time for the complications of a woman in my life. Either I wasn't meant to be a married man or I don't want to be one. I'm not sure which. I used to have plenty of women around but now I am too old for that. I do my work, I sleep, I work and I eat. I have what a man needs to survive."

"And just how old are you, Ivan, if I may be so bold?"

"Old enough to know better and young enough to still enjoy it, lass. I'm sure I've got at least a few years on you and Kayla. I'm just a few years past forty, it's the new fifty, you know!" His laugh was rich and hearty and those eyes....

They talked a bit more about their lives as they finished their meal. Erika reached for the bill, but was not fast enough to beat Ivan to it. "Please, let me take care of this, Ivan. As a friendly gesture."

"No ma'am. I don't let ladies pay my way. It is the other way around. I pay their way. It's only right."

"And I thought chivalry was dead, Ivan. You are proving me wrong on so many levels."

"Aye, chivalry is my middle name. We know how to treat a lady around here. You will see if you stay a while."

He rose out of the chair, lifting Erika's hand to plant a soft kiss on the inside of her wrist. Then he turned to the cash register to pay the bill. The heat that rose up out of her core surprised her. That kiss was more sensual than any she had received in her life, and she had been kissed quite a lot. She came back to her senses and grabbed her iPad, meeting him at the front door, which he opened as she stepped through.

The ride back to the house was eerily quiet, both deep in their thoughts, which the other obviously would like the power to read. When they pulled up to the house, Ivan patted Erika on the thigh, smiling from ear to ear.

"I really enjoyed that lunch today. We should do it again sometime soon. When are you leaving to go back to the States?"

"My flight is scheduled for next Friday. I have to get back to work on Saturday. Back to reality which totally sucks."

"Well, we all do what we have to do. I have to go pick up Grebe and take him into Cardiff this evening. We'll see you bright and early in the morning."

"Looking forward to it. See you tomorrow."

Erika floated into the kitchen with a euphoric manner that Kayla had never seen before. Her friend was really getting weird.

"What the hell is wrong with you, Erika? Did you smoke weed or take LSD or something? You look like someone who is trippin'."

"Now you know I don't do drugs. I'm just on a natural high. Must be the country air around here."

"Country air, my ass. You are up to something. Or someone."

CHAPTER **NINETEEN**

Kayla packed her bags to head into London for the weekend with Brent. She made a long list of items she wanted to pick up while in the city, some décor, some clothing and a few foods she wanted to try before considering adding them to the menu that she hoped to someday offer at the bed and breakfast. She heard a commotion downstairs and looked out the window to see Ivan and Grebe unloading more equipment to start working on the house. Grebe glanced up to see her staring at him from her bedroom. He smiled and raised his hand in a wave, then went about his business. Something stirred deep in Kayla's body, something she knew she had to fight. He was just a boy and Brent was a man, the man she had given herself to as of late. A man of means who could prove a worthy husband to the lady of the estate. Steady, girl, steady.

Kayla carried her bags to the bottom of the stairs and joined the coffee klatch in the kitchen. Erika had suddenly turned into an amazing cook and had freshly baked quiche, scones and coffee prepared for everyone.

"Going to London, ma'am?" Ivan asked as she sat at the kitchen island.

"Yes, I have to go pick up some things for the house, look at some samples of wallpaper and carpet and try some foods I'm thinking of adding to the menu here if I stay."

"If you stay? You mean you are thinking of selling off the place?"

"Well, my financial advisor thinks it would be best if I do sell. He says that property around here is selling very well right now and if I wait I won't be able to get what it's worth. But I am becoming pretty attached to the place the longer I stay. I'm going to have to find a job, though, and that might be difficult."

"Your financial advisor is probably up the arse of all these developers that are trying to ruin this country. Don't you want to keep this property in the hands of family? I'm sure that's what your aunt wanted. She had many opportunities to sell it, but she gave it to you. Make sure you think about that when contemplating selling." Ivan grumbled under his breath as he and Grebe headed back outside.

"Your financial advisor? Why didn't you say your lawyer lover? Let's get real here, Kayla."

"My personal life is none of their business. They are working here, that is all, Erika."

"Sure, sure. That's all, my ass!"

"So when did you turn into a domestic goddess, Erika? I didn't think you could boil water or make toast. This is a new side of you."

"I don't really know. Maybe this country living is making me feel more matronly. There definitely is something about being here that makes me want to be a better person. Does that make sense? I can't really describe it."

"Yes, it makes sense. I have such a feeling of belonging here. It's odd."

"Are you serious about trying to find a job? Where would you look?"

"There are two hospitals and several health clinics within 10 miles of this area, a big one in Cardiff. I thought I would make some phone calls and see if they have any openings for CT scan staff. Can't hurt to ask."

"While you're at it, see if they have any openings for phlebotomists, too. That is, if you are serious about staying here and letting me live in Casa Battaglia."

Kayla nodded and the two had a chuckle. "Casa Battaglia, that has a nice ring to it. But I like the sound of Anwylyd much better." She took a deep breath. "Well, I need to head to the train station so I can get to London early. I want to go see Catherine at the law office and surprise Brent for lunch. Are you sure you don't need the car over the weekend? I can have someone drive me into Cardiff."

"No, I don't think so. The groceries and cleaning supplies are stocked. If I need a ride I can ask Ivan or Grebe. And besides, I hate to drive here, it confuses me. I'll be just fine. Now run along and go see your financial advisor."

Kayla threw Erika a glance that only two friends could understand then headed out the door for the short drive to Cardiff.

The train ride was smooth and quick, landing Kayla in London just before noon. She took the tube to her hotel and dropped off her things, then hopped a cab over to Wickett and Wickett. She had grabbed a small bouquet of flowers from a street vendor to give Catherine and was feeling very good as she stepped off the elevator. A young blonde was seated at Catherine's desk and she was perplexed as she approached.

"Ring Mr. Dankworth and tell him I'm here, please."

"He asked to have all his calls held this morning, miss."

"Just tell him it's Kayla. He'll take the call."

The woman eyed her and chewed her gum like a cow chewing cud. "I'll try, but I'm not making any promises." She turned her back to Kayla and began punching numbers on her phone. Moments later she wheeled back around. "Have a seat. He'll be with you in a few minutes."

Kayla shook her head and plopped down in one of the uncomfortable leather chairs in the lobby. She wondered where they get these young temps today. This one surely had poor communication skills. She was checking her email when Brent came through the big oak doors. She rushed to him, throwing her arms around him and tiptoeing to kiss him. But he turned his face away, placing his hands on her waist to lower her down.

"Not here, Kayla. I'm at work."

"Oh, oh, sorry. I wasn't thinking. I've missed you."

"And I missed you. But you weren't supposed to be here until this afternoon."

"I wanted to surprise you."

"I don't like surprises. I am a busy man."

"I know that, but maybe you should ease up a bit. You are always working so hard. I was thinking we could have lunch, then I could finish all my errands before this evening so we have the whole weekend to ourselves. And, by the way, where is Catherine?"

"I already have plans for lunch. You should have let me know you were coming in early. And I have a meeting tomorrow that I can't miss. So you will have plenty of time to do your errands."

Kayla was disappointed, but was trying to understand. She knew his job came first above all else. "Well, I'm sorry I didn't notify you. I thought you would be happy to see me. But I understand that your job is very busy. Maybe Catherine would like to do something tomorrow. Is she at lunch? And who is the bimbo?"

"Um, that bimbo is the new executive secretary, Rachel Maddrow. We felt that Catherine was no longer fitting our forward moving image. She has cut down to part-time as a fill in whenever Rachel is not available. I can give you her number if you'd like."

"That won't be necessary, I have her number. I can't believe the firm would give up such a great asset. She impressed me from the beginning as woman who was in control of her life and put the firm ahead of anything else."

"She was getting close to retirement age, Kayla. I assure you that she was well rewarded for her time here. Now is there anything else? I have to get back to work. I will see you at the hotel around five."

"I suppose there isn't. I'll go on my merry little way and see you there for dinner."

He leaned forward and kissed her on the forehead, making her feel small and inconsequential. She was being dismissed like a child. As she walked through the doors she heard him say to Rachel Maddrow. "Hold ALL my calls as I had requested earlier."

Well, that certainly took the wind out of Kayla's sails. She had been treated like a pest, an insect that had landed on his expensive wool suit that needed to be flicked off quickly. Tears were forming at the inner corners of her eyes. She had been treated this way before by a man years ago. He was only with her when it was convenient. She had not been the center of his world, although he had been the center of hers. Was she so gullible to believe everything a man said to her, or was she just so desperate for attention she would take it however it came? Thoughts were whirling through her head as she tried to reconstruct her relationship with Brent, especially what had just happened. She had a lot of thinking to do and a lot of time to do it. That was a very dangerous thing.

She handed the bouquet of flowers to an elderly lady who was seated at a table outside the café she had chosen for lunch. The woman smiled and thanked her profusely, immediately sniffing the flowers one by one. Kayla went inside and picked up a newspaper along with her lunch and sat at one of the tables near a window. One of the minor headlines on the front page caught her attention – WAFT Continues Buying Land In Wales As Property Owners Protest. As she perused the article she learned that a large conglomerate was buying large pieces of farm land for development in the area outside of Cardiff, very close to Anwylyd. Local farmers were being offered large sums of money for their properties, often more than the property value and it was affecting the local communities in the areas of food and employment. Local governments were being promised that the properties would be developed into high income housing which would provide construction jobs and income to the communities. She saw no mention of concerns for impact on environment of the area, which she found disturbing. She went on the read up on the London scene, entertainment and shopping. When she finished her lunch, she pulled out her 'to do' list and city map, making the plan for the afternoon and tomorrow. Maybe she would call Catherine and see about doing lunch.

Time passed quickly as Kayla set on the task of deleting items on her list. She perused home interior shops, choosing paint colors and wall paper designs. She explored small groceries in search of items she wished to sample and picked up several of them to take back to the estate to try out on friends. She took hundreds of photos of designs and colors that she felt would fit well into a country estate. And when she came upon an item she wanted to use in one of the rooms at the house, she had it shipped to Anwylyd rather than burden herself to carry it back on the train. All this helped keep her mind off the earlier confrontation with Brent. But she couldn't avoid it for much longer. It was already four in the afternoon and she would be seeing him in an hour. She headed back to the hotel to prepare her strategy.

Kayla took a long, hot shower to clear her mind. She had to be completely sharp and aware to deal with Brent this evening. She had been so enamored by him that she hadn't noticed all the little nuances surrounding their relationship. Just recently he had begun showing his true self, and she didn't like what she saw. She had used every excuse in the book to try to ignore all the red flags that were waving above her head, but this afternoon's behavior really cranked it up a notch. He was an ass, a self-serving pompous ass. Perhaps Erika had been right all along. Brent was a scumbag. She couldn't exactly put her finger on it, but there was something rotten going on and she was in the middle of it. She needed to find out what his angle was and not just go flying off the handle. After all, they had an intimate relationship which obviously meant nothing to him, but had meant everything to her. She couldn't just let that go. Not yet, anyway.

She slipped into her little black dress that he was so fond of and accessorized with new jewelry she had picked up that afternoon. She spritzed her perfume on her neck and wrists and let it waft into the bedroom. Stepping into her black heels she knew she was ready for battle. When he rang from downstairs, she grabbed her purse and gently closed the door, her mind cleared of the fog that usually formed when Brent was around.

"You look fabulous, darling!" Brent said as he leaned forward to kiss her. But Kayla turned her face, allowing him to barely peck her on the cheek. She wondered how he felt being blown off for once. She doubted that happened to him very often.

"I'm famished, Brent. Tell me you are taking me someplace marvelous for dinner." She brushed past him and slid into the black Beamer without his assistance. She could tell that he was perturbed at her behavior.

He climbed into the car and closed the door, hesitating before starting the engine. She could see the wheels turning in his head as he pulled out of the drive. "We're going to St. George's Tavern for dinner if that suits her highness." The sarcasm was dripping from his tongue.

"Yes, I think that will be just delightful. Tavern food is really the best, isn't it?"

Brent didn't say another word until they pulled into the parking lot of the tavern.

"Just what were you trying to pull showing up at my office today? Do you not understand that I am a very busy person and don't have time for personal calls? You might as well have sent a clown with balloons if you wanted to cause a distraction. Showing up unannounced is not acceptable."

"I was trying to be spontaneous and fun, Brent. You know, fun? Something people do with the ones they care about? I had no idea it would be such a burden for you. Next time I will send that clown with balloons. Then at least you can't just send me away like a naughty child."

"You can't be serious! I have my 'fun' after work hours. My job is very high profile and professional. I don't suppose you would be able to understand that since you only have an associate's degree. My education cost a fortune because I want to make a fortune. Can't you understand that? I am a lawyer, not just some tech with a learned skill set."

"Ouch. Excuse me, Mr. Lawyer man. I am just a little old tech with a learned skill set…and two million dollars. Don't forget that, sir. I already have a fortune. So you might want to rethink your attitude." She paused. "Now let's go get that nice tavern dinner, shall we?"

They sat through dinner in silence, Brent with his nose in a newspaper while Kayla was pecking away at her iPad. She barely touched her meal, her mind too busy to focus on food. She snatched the bill immediately when it hit the table, reminding Brent again that she already had her fortune and that he should keep saving for his. He scoffed and went back to his paper while she paid the waiter.

There was no sign of chivalry when she climbed into the car. He made no effort to assist her. She was clicking away at the iPad once again when they pulled into the hotel driveway.

"What? You're not coming up for a night cap?"

"I really don't think you want me to, Kayla."

"Oh, don't be silly! Of course I do! I'll go freshen up while you park the Beamer." She leaned into him and planted a kiss on his cheek before heading inside. He watched as she cleared the revolving door, then pulled out his cell phone as he handed the keys to the valet.

When Brent arrived at the room the door was slightly ajar. He slowly opened it, the scent of flowers and perfume enveloping his senses. Kayla was sitting sideways in the big orange chair by the window dressed in skimpy black and red lingerie.

"That's a different look for you," he said as she approached him. Before he could say another word she was on him, her tongue probing deep in his mouth while her hands slid inside his neatly pressed beige JCrew slacks. Passion overcame him as he succumbed to her touch, her hands controlling him, her mouth overpowering him.

The sex was rough, quick and impersonal, just the way he liked it. No complications or emotional involvement, just raw, physical pleasure. Kayla rolled off him and went into the bathroom while he lay in bed listening to her shower, imagining how she was rubbing her body, touching herself to remove his scent and sperm. He felt the need rising again in his loins but quieted them, knowing Ms. Maddrow would satisfy those desires later tonight. He needed to get back to the business at hand.

When Kayla came out of the bathroom in her robe, strands of her wet hair encircling her face, Brent was completely dressed less his tie, staring out the window as a heavy fog began descending on London. Without turning to face her, he asked, "What was that all about?"

"I don't know what you mean, Brent."

"That sexual aggression, you taking over. Not that I'm complaining."

"Oh, I was just using one of my learned skill sets. You know, things you taught me and some things I've leaned on my own over the years."

"Cut the crap, Kayla. What in bloody hell is going on?"

"I need to ask you a question, Brent."

"And what would that be?"

"Who, or what, is WALF?"

Brent swung around to face her, moving dangerously close. He glared at her for a moment, then composed himself.

"I believe it is a conglomerate that is doing new construction all over England."

"At what cost?"

"What do you mean at what cost? They are providing housing and jobs where they are desperately needed."

"And do you know what kind of environmental impact this will have? Have any studies been done as to what will be destroyed?"

"How the hell would I know that? I read it in the papers just like everybody else. And you know the press exaggerates everything!"

"I read that it is going to impact family farms, forestry and water supplies in Wales, particularly around Cardiff and other major southern cities."

"Those damned tree huggers are all doom and gloom. And what does it matter to you, Kayla? You are going to sell Anwylyd and move out of England permanently, jet setting around the globe with your, um, fortune! I don't even know why we are having this conversation."

"We are having this conversation because I think you know more than you are indicating, and, of course, because I want your professional insight as my financial advisor."

"Why would you think I have more information than you do? You obviously have done your homework. I told you I read about it in the same newspapers you have."

"Perhaps I got that impression because the "W" in WALF stands for the lead firm in the group, Wickett and Wickett."

He opened his mouth to speak but she placed her finger over his lips and continued. "One of the four major law firms with plans to develop lowlands in southern Wales into luxury homes for the privileged of London and Edinburgh to get away from the cities on holiday. Does any of this sound familiar to you?"

"I have nothing to do with corporate decision making."

"But you have everything to do with real estate law for Wickett and Wickett. And I have a feeling you plan to make your little fortune off this venture, correct?"

"And what if I do? How does that affect you? Or have you started getting cozy with the locals? You sell the estate and walk away with an even grander fortune! No harm to you at all! I can't see why this is so bothersome to you!"

"Really? You used sex to get to me so that I would sell my property to your firm. I think the little Law Society of England and Wales might be interested in hearing that. Hmmm….no job for you after that, is there? I guarantee you that I have no intention of selling Anwylyd! Not to you or anyone else! It has grown on me and I plan to make it my home. It is part of my heritage and the one thing that ties me to family."

"For god's sake, Kayla! You didn't even know the woman!"

"I am getting to know her and I like her! I want to be like her, supportive and generous, part of the community."

"You will always be an outsider, don't you see that? Everyone is suspicious of Americans. Soon you will come crawling back to me begging to sell the place and you will never get a better offer than this one." He slid a sealed envelope bearing the Wickett and Wickett logo into her hand, running his other hand between her thighs. He leaned in close enough that she could feel his warm breath on her neck and whispered, "I planned to fuck you and make you an offer you couldn't refuse tonight."

She tore his hand away, leaned forward and whispered, "I guess I fucked you first!" She tore the envelope to shreds, letting the pieces drop to the floor in front of his feet. "Now take your garbage and get out of here! If I ever see you again it will be at your disbarment hearing! Get out!"

Brent kicked the slivers of paper off his shoes and grabbed his jacket. "You will see me again, that is a promise. I'm quite sure we can find something illegal going on in Cowbridge that will require my legal prowess. And, by the way, I'm off to make love to a real woman, not some lonely desperate Yankee!"

Kayla threw the remaining shreds of paper at the slamming door before sliding down the wall into a shivering mass.

CHAPTER **TWENTY**

Kayla was awakened by the sound of her phone vibrating against the surface of the bedside stand. She was slightly disoriented due to the amount of wine she had consumed last evening along with her sleeping pill. Snatching up the phone, she saw it was Erika calling, so she decided to answer.

"What is it, Erika?"

"Oh, rough night, hmmmmm? I hope I didn't interrupt anything."

"No, definitely not. What do you need?"

"I wanted to find out when you are coming back because Ivan has some questions about a paint color or something for the front porch. I told him I thought he had the right one but the minute I say it is you will say it isn't. So I had them start on some inside work until you get here to clarify. Is that okay?"

"Yes, sure. No problem. Have them work on the bathroom off the kitchen and the few little things in the kitchen itself. I'm coming home tomorrow. I would have come back today but the soonest I could change my ticket was from 4pm to 10am in the morning. So I'll be back around noon. Ok?"

"Um, sure, okay. I'll see you then. Don't do anything I wouldn't do."

Kayla laughed and hung up the phone knowing she probably already had.

After showering Kayla picked up the phone and called Catherine Adamson, who seemed both surprised and delighted that she called. They made arrangements to meet for lunch and spend some time visiting shops and designer houses. Kayla was really looking forward to seeing her friend.

They met for lunch at a small bistro and talked about Kayla's plans for Anwylyd. Catherine listened attentively to every detail, delighted that Kayla had decided to stay in Wales. Kayla sat silently for a moment, then turned to face Catherine.

"So how much did you know about the development project, Catherine?"

"I'll be perfectly honest with you, Kayla, I knew very little about it until after you and I made the trip to Wales. Then I kept having to type letters to the other firms and witnessed quite a few documents with regards to the conglomerate. I was very upset at what they were doing, but what could I do? I had to keep my job and I had signed various forms ensuring my confidentiality. After you became involved with Brent more seriously than most of the women in the past, I worried about what would become of you and Anwylyd. But I had to honor my employer and those documents. So I kept silent."

"Why did they cut your hours and get that nasty Ms. Maddrow in there? Surely she doesn't know a whit about anything!"

"I think they were worried that I would break under the pressure of all the dirty deals that were going on. Or, they seriously thought I was too old to front a law office. I'm not really sure. They are paying my full salary for one year while I work a few days per week then I am being let go. Retired, they said. But I'm too young really to be retired. I don't know what I'll do. But I wasn't given much choice in the matter."

"Well, if you ever need something to do, just come to Cowbridge and you can work at Anwylyd. There's plenty of room there for you and I'm sure you can handle the phones and visitors just fine."

"That's so very kind of you, Kayla. I really appreciate that. Enough of this small talk, let's eat and shop!"

The two women spent all afternoon enjoying each other's company. Kayla checked her phone frequently, thinking she would hear from Brent somehow, but that was not to be. She was a dangerous depression shopper, and purchased many new items for the estate, especially for her personal bathroom. The thought of Grebe working in her private space made her smile. She knew she couldn't get back to Wales too soon. When the women parted both vowed to keep in touch. Kayla returned to her hotel room with a new attitude.

She did not hear her alarm go off, but luckily awoke with just a few hours to spare before her train was departing from the station. She crammed her clothing into her suitcase and left most of her toiletries on the sink in the bathroom of the hotel. Raking a brush through her hair, she grabbed her purse and bag and fled to the lobby, grasping a smashed muffin in one hand while she dragged her totes with the other. She managed to flag a taxi and hopped into it on the move. Within minutes she was rushing into Victoria Station, through the turnstile and onto the train car.

She barely had the strength to drag her heavy bag onto the dais, no less lift it into the luggage rack. As she struggled with the weight of it, a massive, rough hand slid into the handle, easily lifting the fifty pound load onto the top tier. She turned to thank the person for their assistance and found herself face to face with the largest man she had ever seen. He was well over six feet tall wrapped in solid muscle. His long, dark hair framed his face as she stared into his dark brown glimmering eyes. She had never seen such a mountain of a man.

"Toby Markham, ma'am," he said as he shook her tiny hand. "Glad to be of service."

Kayla introduced herself and he was very excited that she was an American. It seemed that Toby was the top amateur boxer in Ireland and had won Olympic medals in the sport. He was headed for Wales for his last amateur bout and would be leaving for Canada to train for his first professional fight which would take place three months from now in New York City.

Toby was surrounded by his entourage, including his wife, Sandra, his brother Thomas, and their trainer. Rather than spend time drowning in her own sorrows as planned, Kayla spent the entire train ride conversing with Team Toby, who were very interested in sightseeing in America. They were amazed at the size of the United States, thinking they could easily visit multiple sites such as Washington, D.C. and Philadelphia in one day. She gently explained that they might want to plan a few days to accomplish that.

Their company served as the diversion she sorely needed. By the time they pulled into the station at Cardiff, she and Sandra had exchanged numbers and emails, promising to keep in touch. She wished Toby luck in his final amateur bout and promised to try to make it to cheer him on, knowing she never would as she abhorred sporting events.

Getting into the rental car to head back to the estate, Kayla again promised herself that she would buy a new vehicle as soon as she returned from that trip home that she needed to make, feeling the aches and pains that came with driving the 'puddle jumper' down the road to Anwylyd. But the driveway was welcoming to her and she knew she was home. This was where she wanted to make her bed every night, come what may.

Grebe met her at the front door and took her suitcase out of her hand, their fingers touching ever so slightly as she passed the handle to him. He lowered his head and turned as if he didn't want to meet her gaze. Kayla shrugged and headed into the kitchen where Erika had made
vegetable soup and biscuits, along with both hot and iced tea, something the English were not accustomed to.

The two friends greeted each other warmly and Erika grabbed Kayla's hand, leading her to the bathroom off the kitchen.

"Close your eyes. I want you to be surprised."

Kayla obliged and let herself be lead inside. Upon Erika's prompting she opened her eyes and was delighted at what she saw. All the bronze fixtures were shining like a new penny, the new baseboards were in place and the mosaic tiles that had fallen out of place were all cleaned and in place. It looked amazing! She just had to grab the chain that hung down from the tank on the wall and pull, listening to the sounds of a properly functioning loo. Who knew that a working loo could put such a smile on her face? And, of course, she knew that the plumbing was done by none other than Grebe. He was certainly a genius! Kayla turned to see him standing in the doorway.

"Does it suit you, ma'am?" He asked quietly.

"Oh yes, yes, it suits me just fine. Thank you!"

The trio returned to the kitchen just as Ivan came through the back door. The girls set up a lunch buffet and everyone helped themselves. It was a very pleasant afternoon at Anwylyd and Kayla was looking forward to many, many more.

That evening the ladies retired to the library and were having a glass of wine. Erika was pacing anxiously behind the huge desk as if she were unsure of where to sit.

"What's wrong with you Erika? You are acting really weird."

"Well, I want to ask you what happened in London, but not sure if you want to tell me."

"Sure, I'll tell you what happened in London. You were right about Brent, he is a scumbag and we broke up, as if there was anything really to break up. It's over."

"Really? I was right? I knew I was right! So what will you do now? Will you leave Wales altogether?"

"No, definitely not. I am here and here to stay. No scumbag is going to run me off. Is that what is making you crazy?"

"Well, there's something else. I want to tell you something but I don't want you to be mad at me."

"You have decided not to come back after you go home. Hey, I can understand that. There is no reason to think I'll be mad at you."

"No, no, that's not it at all. I slept with Ivan."

"What? You did not!"

"Yes, yes, I did. And I'm going to do it again, too. I think I'm falling in love with him."

"What? How? Not you! You don't fall in love! You love 'em and leave 'em, remember?"

"I know. This is so unlike me. But I do think I'm falling in love with the man. It's crazy, right?"

"It's only crazy if you don't hang around to see what happens next."

The following week flew by as the estate was beginning to take shape. It was just as Kayla had imagined it had been under the tutelage of her Great Aunt Rebecca. The color and design choices that she and Erika had made maintained the historical look of the place giving it just a pop of color where it was needed. She had her bedroom painted in pale poppy with light
green trim, accentuating the flowers that her aunt had held so dear. The linens matched perfectly and she was thrilled

with her private space. Grebe had even found a bronze floral faucet set for
the master bath that finished it off beyond chic. There was only one thing she could think of to make this place home.

Friday morning Kayla accompanied Ivan when he took Erika to the train station. She would be making the trip into London then boarding her plane at Heathrow to head back to the States. Ivan took Erika into his arms and kissed her ever so gently, then released her to board the train. From the look in his eyes, she could see that he was falling for her best friend, hook, line and sinker. If only a man looked at her that way, her world would be complete.

CHAPTER **TWENTY-ONE**
Grebe

It had been four years, three months, sixteen days and ten hours since he had walked through the stone gate through which he was now exiting. He had been just over eighteen years of age when his sentence was passed down, five years in prison for vehicular homicide and possession of cocaine with intent to deliver.

Grebe Hascall had been born the youngest child of happily married parents who nurtured and supported their children. His two older sisters were married with families of their own. Their father had worked hard as a gardener while their mother worked as a part-time cook at the local hospital. He'd had a fortunate childhood, being surrounded by supportive family and mates. They weren't wealthy but they had what they needed. He would learn during his incarceration how lucky he had been after hearing stories of abuse and abandonment from his cellmates.

Grebe had been a high school athlete, rugby being his sport of choice. He was popular with the ladies and his lads, and brought home good marks in academics. He earned a pittance or two working with his uncle doing odd jobs around people's houses and became particularly good at plumbing. He liked the feel of cool water and cold metal on his hands and wasn't afraid to get dirty to make a few pence. He saved and scrimped his money to buy his own car and, when he finally did, his family was proud of his efforts.

The year before he was to graduate he lost his father as the result of an automobile accident on a foggy night. His mother was inconsolable and no longer as involved in his life, trying to deal with her own grief. His sisters were both living quite a distance away from them, only visiting occasionally to the chagrin of his mother. After a few months, his uncle took both he and his mother in to live at the family farm, selling off their home to provide needed income to keep him in school.

As his mother drifted away from him, Grebe, himself, drifted into a different crowd at school. His academics suffered and he quit playing sports, trying to find alternative ways of making money to help his mother out. He knew most of his new companions were peddling drugs, but he avoided that part of it. He never asked questions and that was the way they liked it.

That spring, he met a girl at a party, Marlene Siegel, who he became quite fond of. They were soon a couple and rarely spent time apart. Although she was the sister of one of the known players in the drug ring, that didn't bother Grebe. She herself was an innocent, not involved in the process, and she always treated him as if he were the only boy in the world. Three months later she told him that she was pregnant with his child. Although he initially was shocked, he found it soothing somehow, that a baby would keep Marlene close to him forever.

On one fateful Saturday, Marlene's brother, Milo, asked Grebe to take a package over to Swansea for him. Although he was suspicious, he reluctantly agreed to do it, hoping that Milo would approve of his relationship with Marlene. Marlene insisted that she ride along with him to help keep him awake during the drive. He told his mother they were going to the beach for the weekend and then headed down the M4 towards Swansea.

An hour later as they were nearing their destination, Marlene was asleep, leaning against the headrest and Grebe was barely able to keep his eyes open. He heard the sirens before seeing them and slowed his vehicle to let them pass. But they didn't pass, rather they stayed just behind him and he realized that they were signaling for him to pull over. Panic overtook him as he remembered that he had an unknown package in his vehicle, one which he suspected contained an illegal substance. It took only a few moments to make the fatal decision to run rather than be caught, so he lowered his foot on the gas pedal and took off.

The high speed chase lasted only twenty minutes although it seemed like a lifetime. When the car hydroplaned and slid into oncoming traffic, the chase ended in a heap of gnarled metal, squealing tires and black skid marks. As Grebe became more alert, he saw Marlene's limp body covered with glass and blood.

Against his lawyer's advice, he pled guilty to the charges and was given a reduced sentence of five, rather than ten years for his cooperation in apprehending the dealer, Milo Siegel. He knew that he was making himself a target, but he also knew it was better than putting his mother through any more drawn out financial and emotional beatings. He did the crime and would do the time.

The first few months of his incarceration had been difficult, but he eventually learned to store his grief in an impenetrable corner of his mind. He kept to himself and didn't trust anyone, speaking only when it was necessary. He was a model prisoner and obeyed all the rules, never even smoking a cigarette or looking at the porn magazines that made the rounds. After the second year, he was offered a spot in the work program, taking the position of gardener's assistant.

In the garden he could get away from the heavy concrete walls and spend his time in the serenity and solitude of nature. After finishing whatever chores he was assigned, he would lay on his back in the freshly cut grass staring up at the sky and imagining what life would have been like if he had only said 'no' to Milo. He knew that what was done could not be undone and that he would carry his guilt to his grave. And when his demons rose up from that dark place inside his head, he turned to the gym to work against them. It was there that he found boxing and was able to learn at the feet of some of the greats whose alcoholism or intense rage had landed them behind those gray walls.

Grebe was an excellent student, learning by observation and asking questions. As his body built up and his mind sharpened he became very good at the sport. Within a few months he was representing his facility in matches across Wales, and earning respect from the warden. He always fought a clean fight and never lowered himself to some of the dirty tricks others used against him. It wasn't necessary, not for Grebe. His talent exceeded any ruse they could imagine. Over the next few years he had gained the respect of the other inmates and the admiration of the guards, whose pockets he had lined with many pounds from their unsanctioned bets.

At a little over four years into his sentence, he was given a parole hearing at which time he was offered an early release with three years of probation for his good behavior. He was quite surprised, really, knowing that the warden had taken great pride in having him as 'his' pugilist. But he nodded his head and accepted it, finding his way back to the gates and reality.

CHAPTER **TWENTY-TWO**

The ride back to Anwylyd was lovely, the sun shining brightly over the emerald fields and the smile on Ivan's face making it even more brilliant. They discussed how the renovations were going and Kayla complimented him on the detail that he had accomplished in each and every job.

"You have a great friend there, you know. Ms. Erika is truly devoted to you."

"And I to her. We have been friends for many years, through each other's ups and downs. I can't imagine living away from her."

"Oh, has she decided not to come back to Wales? I understand it is very intimidating to move to a foreign country."

"No, not that. She hasn't decided yet. I keep trying to convince her to stay here and live at Anwylyd. She would be the perfect activity planner for the B&B. She is so enthusiastic and upbeat about life in general. I think she is going home to try to make some decisions. I, myself, need to go home in a few weeks to get my affairs in order, sell my parents' house and get my dog."

"You have a dog, Ms. Kayla? I really love animals. Of course, that's probably because I've been on a farm my whole life. All of us fancy our creatures, really. Grebe has always had a dog since he was a small boy. And his mother is smitten with kittens!" He let out a deep laugh at this own rhyme. "I'm not too fond of cats, but at least they keep the barns free from mice and other vermin."

They pulled down the driveway of the house and Kayla noticed that the lights were on at the barn and a tall ladder was leaned against one side. Ivan didn't turn the car off, telling her that he had forgotten to stop in town to pick up the rest of the baseboard he was going to put down in all the upstairs bedrooms. She thanked him for the ride, jumped out of the car and went into the kitchen.

Seeing that it was almost noon, she decided to fix a small lunch and some tea for Grebe. She packed two chicken sandwiches, some scones and vegetable sticks in a brown bag and filled a thermos with steaming tea then set off down to the barn.

When she walked into the aisle way it took a few moments for her eyes to adjust from the bright sunlight to the artificial light. The faint smell of manure and fertilizer was somehow earthy and appealing. She closed her eyes remembering her youth which was spent mostly on horseback and in a barn. It relaxed her.

She heard the sound of footsteps approaching and she opened her eyes only to see his silhouette against the background of the huge open door. His muscular frame stirred something in her as no man had ever done. What was it about this boy that attracted her? He certainly had nothing to offer her but himself, and she was content with that. How silly all this was! She was nearly seven years older than him, what could he see in her?

"I've brought you down some lunch in case you get so involved in your work that you don't stop to eat. I certainly don't want to find you passed out from starvation."

"I thank you, ma'am. I was just starting to get hungry and thinking about taking a break. But I didn't want to leave without finishing up the water closet here. Whoever is going to be managing the barn will surely appreciate the nice office and facilities. Have you considered hiring a stable manager?"

"Well, I really hadn't thought about it because initially I was going to fix the estate up and sell it."

"Oh, you're not staying?"

"Yes, yes, I'm staying. At first I didn't think I would. Now I can't imagine not living here. I love it."

"You've not seen nearly anything that Wales has to offer, what with you running off to London every weekend. You need to take some time to familiarize yourself with the area."

Kayla blushed. "I don't think I'll be running off to London any time soon. That is for sure. I would love to see the area and get to know the people better. Are you offering to be a tour guide?"

"I think I could do a bit of it. I know my way around since I have spent most of my life here. What is it you like, I mean, hobbies and such?"

"Oh, many things. I like animals and music and, oh, can you possibly take me to some local hospitals?"

"Are you not well?"

"No, not that. I am very well. But I want to look for a job as a Cat Scan technician and try to find a job for Erika. If she decides to come back, she'll need a job."

"So your friend plans to come back here to live as well? There are several good hospitals around here and they are always looking for help. Why don't we go around on Monday, if Ivan will give me a day off?" His smile lit up the hallway, a mischievous twinkle running across one eye.

"That sounds wonderful. Oh, here's your lunch, I packed two sandwiches, some scones and brought down a thermos of tea with lemon and honey. I think that's how you like it, right?"

"On the money ma'am. Sounds delicious! Thank you again."

He reached for the bag and slowly drew his finger over the back of her hand. Sparks flew up her arm and into her core. There was something happening here that could easily spin out of control if she let it. She slowly pulled her hand away.

"I'll be up at the house if you need anything. And Grebe, don't be afraid to ask."

He watched as she strode through the sea of emerald and cinnamon grasses and ascended the front porch. She turned to look towards the barn before closing the front door. Maybe she was the angel he had been waiting for.

The rest of the afternoon proved futile for Kayla as her mind kept wandering back down to the musty smell and sights of the barn. She wondered just how it would feel to have a roll in the hay with the Grebe, feeling his powerful arms around her, stroking her hair and whispering sweet nothings in her ear. Silly, silly thoughts be gone! She had much planning and work to do without having these afternoon daydreams! But oh, how she wished they would come true.

Her thoughts were dispersed by the sound of Ivan's truck pulling up out front and the clamoring that occurred as he unloaded it. Funny, she thought, that Erika has already staked her claim on the man with no guilt. And here she was, fantasizing about his nephew. Life surely was as crazy and unpredictable as they claim it to be. It had been fate and fate alone that had brought her here, she was sure of it. So why not go with it? If Grebe was unattached and interested, why shouldn't she be with him? Only time would tell.

A few hours later Ivan and Grebe came into the kitchen to let her know that they were done for the day. They would be working half days over the weekend since there was a big farmer's market in the square and they would be helping Grebe's mother with the crops there. They invited her to come and join them at the market so she could get to know some more of the local people and businesses. Kayla vowed to make every effort to attend and she watched them drive away.

She was alone in the house for the first time and, initially, it was a bit unsettling to be in such a huge place where no one could hear her scream. She decided to start on the upper floor and walk through each and every room, checking on their progress and making sure there was no boogie man waiting to jump out after dark. How she missed her dog and knew she would have several once she returned from the trip back to Ohio. It was a lonely place for one person. This was a house that was meant for parties and dances and company all the time. It wasn't meant for solitude. She strode down the halls as if she owned the place, and, as a matter of fact, she did. It was finally sinking in.

After walking through the downstairs and checking every lock and window, Kayla felt safe enough. She went into the kitchen and poured her tea, then pulled out the phone book. She would have the internet service put in next week so she could keep in touch with Erika and make her plane reservations. She knew she needed to get back to Ohio so that she could tie up her loose ends, find a realtor, get the house on the market and pay off all her outstanding debt. She could easily sell her car as it was in excellent condition with low miles. A month seemed like the amount of time she would need so she penciled the trip into her calendar and texted Erika to let her know what she was thinking. Then she leaned back in the desk chair and smiled. No running to London to be manipulated by Brent. Sure, the sex was good and she needed that to boost her self-esteem. But she would no longer be used, not by him or anyone. She didn't need that anymore. She needed to be herself.

Kayla was awakened to the sound of thunder while the lightning touched the sky somewhere very close. There was a ferocious storm blowing about and it caused goose bumps to raise up on her arms. As the storm escalated she could hear the shutters banging against the stone. Rushing outside to secure them, she was blinded by the torrential downpour. It was only when she was under the stoop near the windows that she saw him. Grebe was on the ladder tightly gripping the last shutter, latching it to its tether against the house. When he spotted her he stepped off the ladder and removed his jacket. He reached for her and wrapped it around her shoulders to protect her from the cold drops that were pelting them. As he escorted her back up onto the porch, she heard him whisper, "I'll not let anything harm you, lass. Let's get you inside."

She headed into the kitchen and put the teapot on to brew while she went upstairs, dried off and donned her robe and slippers. She grabbed an extra robe and some socks to give Grebe when he came in. The teapot was just starting to rumble when she heard the front door close. He was standing on the stoop, water running down his body, making his clothes cling as if they were a second skin. His fiery red hair was hanging down, glued to his forehead and cheeks, raindrops dripping off the ends. He looked up and smiled at her with a boyishness that had never left him, but she could see an intense sadness as well. She watched him move with catlike precision as he removed his boots and socks, leaving them on the mat.

"How did you get here so fast? The storm came up very quickly."

"I have to admit that I set myself up in the guest house. I was worried about you here alone."

Kayla blushed. "I can't thank you enough! I've brought you down some dry things to put on while I dry your clothes. And there is tea boiling to warm you. Don't be afraid of dripping on the floors, I have a mop. Now come on in here and change. You'll catch your death of cold in those wet jeans. Please."

As he moved slowly towards her, his clothing revealed what lay beneath. She could see every ripple of his muscles beneath the cotton shirt as he moved. She handed him a robe as he passed her heading into the nearby bath. She heard him turn on the faucet and tried to imagine what he looked like standing naked in front of the mirror, the hot water steaming up his reflection. She turned her attention back to the pressed copper teakettle that was demanding her attention and poured two cups of the steaming brew. As she sat the kettle on the back of the stove she felt his arms envelope her from behind. She could feel his body pressing up against her robe and was certain that he was naked. His hot breath on her neck began to melt her into his arms.

"I can think of other ways we can warm up on such a night."

She could barely remember being carried up to her room, but was conscious that she was now laying on her bed with Grebe, who was completely naked next to her.

"If you want me to go, just tell me. But I don't think that's what you want, and I know it's not what I want."

He reached across her and pulled her on top of him, bringing her face to meet his. She pushed his wet locks back and stared into his eyes, losing herself in those deep green pools. Their lips met and he probed deeply into her mouth, drawing her into him. His hands explored her body in ways she had never imagined. She impaled herself as their bodies became one, rocking as a boat does on an angry sea, crashing as the storm raged all around them. He buried his head in her breasts as they reached a crescendo, his breath ragged against her smooth ivory skin. Her hands were entwined in his crimson hair, then fell, raking his shoulders as she reached the highest of heights. She felt him empty himself within her and she shuddered against him again and again. Making love to Grebe had exceeded her every expectation, making her daydreams seem nothing but whimsy.

    They rolled to one side, still conjoined. He stroked her hair with one of his powerful hands, using the other to keep her close against him. He continued planting tiny kisses on her shoulders, a contented growl rising up from his throat. Kayla closed her eyes, taking in the scent of him, the feel of his body against hers. It felt so right. No other lover had made her feel so alive, so safe. She knew this was where she belonged. This house was not her fortress against the world, it was her redemption.

    They laid in silence, listening to the thunder as it faded into the distance. There was nothing but peace in the house, its sounds changing with the intensity of the storm. The lights flickered for a moment, then settled back to their normalcy. But the old normal would no longer be part of Kayla's life. The new normal was taking over. All doubt and self-loathing was gone. Her world had changed in an instant and she was never looking back again.

    Kayla slid out of bed and into her gorgeous master bath, turning the brass knob to initiate the flow of warm water in the shower. Grebe joined her and they gently stroked each other's bodies with sweet smelling herbal soap. They shared gentle kisses as the lather fell from their bodies, leaving the faint hint of jasmine on smooth skin. They dried each other with soft fluffy towels and slipped into robes and slippers, then headed back down to the kitchen where their tea patiently awaited.

    "Why did you come here tonight, Grebe?"

"I told you I was worried about you. The storm was approaching and the word is out in town that you are here alone, and some people might find it an opportune time to um, bother you."

"I have to admit that I was a little bit nervous being here alone for the first time. I walked from room to room checking all the windows and locks. I wasn't really scared, but I was cautious, wishing I had my dog here with me."

"Aye, you need a few dogs to keep an eye on the place. It isn't safe for a young woman to be alone anywhere anymore. I should see to getting you some canine companionship."

"I'll be bringing my own dog back with me when I go home in a few weeks."

"And what of the place while you are gone? It would be a shame to have done all this work only to have it ravaged by some hooligans."

"I had thought of hiring someone to stay here while I'm gone. Would you be interested in the job?"

"Aye, that I would. I could be working all hours and resting when I pleased while keeping the place safe. Are you asking me to take on that job?"

"Yes, yes I am. And wondering if you'd like to stay on afterward."

"It's something I would certainly consider. I'd like to stay on, stay here with you."

"And which bedroom would you like?"

"Yours, of course. It's the only one that suits me."

Kayla blushed and nodded. Yes, it was the only one that suited him. And that suited her just fine. They finished their tea and went back to bed, spooning with a vengeance.

CHAPTER **TWENTY-THREE**

Kayla reached for Grebe but the other side of her bed was empty. Had it only been a dream? If so, it was the most realistic dream she had ever had! Or had he loved her and left her like all the rest? She should be used to that by now. She wasn't long-term relationship material. An old boyfriend had told her that long ago. She was too trusting, too easily roped in by any story, too desperate to make things work.

She slid on her slippers and started down to the kitchen when she smelled the most delightful cinnamon aroma wafting up the stairs. Her smile was hard to hide when she entered the kitchen to see Grebe in her aunt's rose emblazoned apron over her pink fuzzy robe taking a pan of biscuits out of the oven. The kitchen island held large plates of eggs, bacon and toast, and now the biscuits were added as well.

"Isn't this a big surprise? Where did you learn to cook like this?"

"I grew up in a household of women, two sisters and my mother. If I wanted something to eat that they weren't ready to fix, I had to learn to fix it myself."

Kayla grabbed a plate and began filling it with all the wonderful food that he had prepared. She couldn't believe that he was still there and was fixing breakfast. It was like a fairy tale. She kissed him on the cheek and whispered 'thank you' as she sat down at the table to enjoy the fare. Within moments Grebe had joined her sitting just across so that they were facing each other.

"I hope it's edible, ma'am. I did my best."

"That you did, sir. And it all looks delicious. And I think you can stop calling me ma'am, now. We are a little better acquainted than that."

He grinned at her and tapped his fork on the side of his plate. "I do think I need to tell you a few things before this goes any further. I don't want you to be blindsided by anything people might tell you."

Kayla could hear the seriousness of his voice, although it never waivered. "What is it, Grebe? Please tell me."

After taking a few bites of his breakfast, he put his fork down, took her by the hand and told her all about his young life, from the drugs to the death of Marlene to his incarceration. Kayla listened intently, knowing what it had taken for him to open up to her about these things. She acknowledged him as needed, never saying a word. He knew from her eyes that she was not judging him, but trying to understand how he could cope with the burden that he would carry for the rest of his life.

"I would give anything to not have let her come with me that day. My only regret is that her family has to suffer for my poor decision. It will haunt me to the end of my days. But I don't want you to get involved with me if you have any concerns about all this. You are the first woman I have wanted to share it with."

"Oh Grebe, my heart aches for you after all you have been through. But you did your time and paid for what you did. The incarceration was nothing compared to the pain you have to live with. Did you love her, Grebe?"

"I don't think at seventeen we have a true concept of what love is. Was I attracted to her? Yes. Did I want to spend time with her? Yes. Did I love her? I don't really think so. It wasn't something deep and intense. It was superficial at best. All boys want to drive a hot car with a nice looking girl on their arm. And that's what I did. After I lost my father I didn't care much about anything else except fitting in."

"I understand. I never was one to fit in. I wasn't in the right cliques, the right clubs and I was not very attractive. I protected myself by living in my own little world with my horse and my dogs. I related much better to animals than to people. I think I still do."

"So, do you think you can relate to me? Are you bothered by what I did? Are you afraid of me?"

"Afraid of you? No. I just gave myself to you without any remorse. I'm definitely not afraid of you. I'm afraid of what I am feeling for you, though."

"And what is that?"

"I, I think I'm in love with you, Grebe. Even though I know that's impossible. We barely know each other."

"I knew it the first time I saw you. And tonight confirmed it. You are the woman I have been waiting for. Tell me you knew it too."

"I, I was involved with someone when I met you. I couldn't think of you in that way. But yes, I was attracted to you the first time we met. I am so much older than you, though. How can it ever work?"

"Age has nothing to do with it. I am a man and you are a woman. We are attracted to each other and want to be together. What could be wrong with that? Why must you question your feelings?"

"If you hadn't noticed, I'm not exactly a swimsuit model. Look in the mirror, Grebe, you are beautiful. You could probably have any woman you wanted."

"Don't be so hard on yourself. I'm no fancy lawyer in a silk suit, but does that matter to you? It is what's inside that matters. You are beautiful inside and out. Most of all, you are beautiful to me. Anyone else's opinion does not make any difference. If you can accept me with my flaws, then why wouldn't you expect me to do the same? Give us a chance Kayla, you won't regret it. I promise you."

She loved the way her name rolled off his tongue, a touch of brogue laced through it. She loved the way his hand felt on hers, the roughness of his skin, the strength of his grip. With him she did feel safe, safer than she had felt since the death of her parents. Someone wanted to be with her. She had forgotten what that felt like and it felt good.

"I must get home and help Ivan and ma get the things to market. You will be joining us won't you, Kayla?"

"Yes, definitely. Should I bring anything along with me?"

"No, love. Just your gorgeous self. And a chair, bring a chair unless you want to wind up sitting in my lap the entire day. Not that I would mind."

Kayla pulled his clothes out of the dryer so he could get dressed to head home. He kissed her passionately on the lips before leaving. She watched him until he was out of sight, feeling a tingling all over her body. She could barely wait until she saw him again and again and again. It was six in the morning. Only three hours until then.

She sat down at the table and again worked on her lists, but they could barely hold her attention. One minute she was writing down airlines to call and the next she was in bed with Grebe, reliving last night over and over in her mind. For the first time she felt truly loved by a man. Was this how it really could be? Or was she setting herself up again for a heartache? All Kayla knew was that she had never been loved so well. She had to believe that Grebe was the one she had waited for all along.

When she was finally able to focus on her travel plans she knew one thing, she couldn't get home and back fast enough. If there was any way to get the business done by anyone else, she would do it, but, alas, she alone had to sign all the paperwork involved with selling the house and car, as well as make arrangements to move. She also wanted to personally go through all her parents' things, in hopes that she could find more information about Aunt Rebecca and the life she'd had here at Anwylyd. There was one thing of which she was certain - if Erika was as anxious to get back to Ivan as she was to get back to Grebe, all that business would be taken care of record time!

CHAPTER **TWENTY-FOUR**

The day at the farmer's market went well. Kayla was a bit nervous about meeting Grebe's mother, but Elizabeth Hascall was a charming woman, albeit a bit mousy. Elizabeth discussed all the produce with Kayla, from the first planting of seeds to harvesting. The woman actually seemed to be happy to have another female with her in the sea of farmers and their sons. Kayla could see how proud she was of her own son and how he had overcome his demons as well as the fact that he never backed down from his responsibility for the accident. All in all in was a pleasant distraction from her deep desire for him.

Elizabeth invited Kayla out to the farm for dinner and she obliged, anxious to see what Grebe's life was like. Of course, Ivan was very happy that she accepted, most likely so he could get any news of Erika. How funny that everything had happened the way it did. Her grandmother had always told her that the world worked in mysterious ways. Now Kayla was becoming a believer.

Dinner was simple yet delicious, a fresh salad from the garden, homemade chicken soup and biscuits. Kayla could see where Grebe's wonderful recipe came from. Elizabeth was a superb cook and baker, a talent she might want to use when the bed and breakfast came to fruition. Ivan poured the local wines and described each of the vineyards' specialties. There was a real feeling of family here, in the old farmhouse. It was a feeling Kayla desperately yearned for.

After dinner they moved to the living room where she found herself surrounded by family photos, including Grebe's deceased father and his sisters. They looked like a very happy group of people and there was no denying they were all related. There were many stories of young Grebe's escapades and athletic prowess, as well as Ivan's stories of the Merchant Navy.

"If I may ask, how did Grebe get that name? It is so unusual."

Ivan chimed in. "My lovely sister here loves birds and she decided to name her children after birds. His sisters are Robin and Wren, don't you know."

Elizabeth blushed when Grebe added, "I'm surprised she didn't name me Cardinal, hoping I'd become the next fucking pope!"

The room was filled with joy and laughter, something which soothed Kayla. With all the trials and tragedy that had befallen this family, she never imagined they would be so resilient. It touched something deep within her soul.

Grebe looked at his watch and went somewhere back in the house, returning with what looked like a duffle bag. Ivan grabbed their coats and turned to the women.

"I've got to get the boy into Cardiff so we need to be leaving soon. Shall I walk you to your car, Ms. Kayla?"

"No, I'll be fine." She looked at Grebe and hesitated.

"I'll be staying at the guest house again tonight. Not to worry, ma'am. It might be around ten when I get there so don't be alarmed when you see the lights on over there."

"Should I turn the porch light on at the guest house for you since it will be quite dark when you arrive?"

"That would be appreciated. I don't need to be falling down now, do I?"

Elizabeth nodded her approval as the trio went to the door. Kayla turned to the older woman. "Thank you so much for your hospitality. I learned so much about plants today. I have a black thumb, I even killed a cactus once."

"That's one way you don't take after your great aunt. She was a master gardener who did all the original landscaping at Anwylyd herself. It was one of the most celebrated gardens in Wales at one time. Perhaps we can find some photos of her in her glory. Would you like to see them?"

Kayla smiled and nodded, thankful that Elizabeth had been so welcoming to her. As she drove the short trip back to Anwylyd, she decided to try to get to know this woman better along with Becca.

After getting settled into the manor house, Kayla took a long shower and put on her pajamas. She pulled her robe up to her face and took in the scent of him, anticipating his arrival later tonight. Did Elizabeth or Ivan suspect that they were getting involved? If they did, they made no reference to it today. And what would they think about the older woman going after the young man? With Grebe there was a craving deep inside that she had never felt before. Sex with Brent had been raw animalistic desire, lust, if you will. But this was something much deeper, not as readily out of control. It was something that would last for the long run, she was sure of it.

She was sitting at the desk in the library reading *Pride and Prejudice* when she saw the headlights coming down the drive. She leapt out of the oversized leather chair and went into the bathroom, primping her hair and straightening her nightshirt. Her hand was on the doorknob when he stepped up on the porch. She swung it open and pulled him inside, pressing herself against his powerful chest.

She felt his strong arms envelope her as she leaned forward to kiss him.

"Ow," he whimpered.

Kayla stepped back and saw that his lip was swollen and that he had a small cut over his right eyebrow.

"What on earth happened to you? Are you okay?"

"I haven't had a chance to tell you what I do for a hobby, love. Don't you wonder why I'm going off to Cardiff nearly every night of the week?"

"I have been curious, yes, but didn't think it was any of my business, really."

"I think it's your business now, girl. Remember when I told you I boxed in prison? I still box. I am the Welsh middleweight amateur boxing champion. When I go into Cardiff it is to go to the gym where I train. Tonight my mind was on other things." He cleared his throat. "I think you could be very dangerous for me. But I like it."

Kayla was stunned by this announcement and his appearance. She remembered the meeting with Toby on the train and his upcoming final amateur bout.

"You don't have a big fight coming up do you? With a Toby somebody from Ireland?"

"Hmmm, I didn't think you followed sports, love. Toby Markham is a heavyweight and I'm a middleweight, so I won't be fighting him, no. I'm fighting his brother, Thomas. We are the opening fight of the big night."

"Oh no! You can't! If his brother is anything like he is, he is huge!"

"Thomas and I are in the same weight class. What I lack in size I make up for in speed. I promise you I can handle it."

Kayla stepped back for a moment, looking into the eyes of her lover. "I'm sure you can. I just don't want to see you get hurt." She thought better of continuing that line of discussion. "You are so good at so many things, repairs, gardening, cooking, and now boxing. Is there anything you aren't good at?"

"Aye, lass. I can't sing, I can't dance and I'm no artist. I'm not of that type of mind, I suppose. But I am good at strategizing and designing, and boxing is mostly strategy, how you move, how you respond to the other man's movements. I had a lot of time to watch people when I was in prison. I can read their eyes."

"Can you read mine now?"

"Yes, and you are having naughty thoughts about me, aren't you?" He lifted her into his arms and proceeded up the stairs for another night of simple pleasures.

The following week was one of the most remarkable of Kayla's life. She felt a new sense of urgency to finalize her plans to go back to the States so she could quickly return to Grebe's arms. She sent emails to her realtor, insurance companies and banks to make arrangements for sales and transfers of her assets. She was finally able to secure her flight but left the return date open. She didn't want to commit to being in Ohio any longer than was absolutely necessary. And she also wanted to be able to book Erika on the same return flight if she chose to return to Wales with her.

After several conversations and texts with Erika, she convinced her to put in her 30 day notice at work and with her landlord so that she could be ready to move as fast as possible. So what if she didn't work out her 30 days? What would it matter? Within a few months she would be working for Kayla, and it wasn't like they weren't financially stable. But Erika did have a few concerns still eating at her.

"Are we going to be considered communists if we leave the U.S.?"

"Of course not, silly. We are going to apply for dual citizenship. That way we are still Americans living in Wales. We have to live here for at least two years before we can even apply for citizenship. And we also have to have proof of employment. It will take at least that long to get the B&B on its feet. So just try to keep calm. It will all work out fine."

"Whew! I was worried about that. And, your friend, Ron Marshall, keeps asking about you. He wants to see you when you come home next week."

"You can tell Ron Marshall that I will be very busy while I am home. I'm not sure if I'll have time to visit. That man is exasperating!"

"So you will be home next Monday morning, right? Am I supposed to pick you up at the airport?"

"No, I'm going to rent a van so that I can fit in boxes for storage and donation and shipment. You need to start going through your things so we can figure out what is staying, what is going and what is being donated. I don't plan to stay in Ohio more than two weeks to get all this done. I need to get back to Anwylyd as fast as I can. It is the only place where I feel sane."

"Are you leaving the house empty while you are gone?"

"No, Grebe has agreed to stay there and keep an eye on things. I feel better having him there."

"Grebe, eh? Anything you want to tell me?"

"I don't have that many minutes left on my phone. I'll tell you everything when I get there. I promise."

"Pinky swear?"

"Yes, yes, pinky swear! See you in a few days."

Kayla started packing her smaller suitcase for the trip. She had all the toiletries and clothes she would need back at her house in Ohio. It would be a monumental task to get things in order in just two weeks, but she knew they could do it. She worried about the fact that Spinner would have to be in quarantine for several months when they came back, but she knew he could handle it. He would be very close by in Cardiff and she could see him every day until his release. Grebe had been a great help in educating her on the importation of dogs. She was grateful for all his insight on the move.

Kayla spent Sunday morning at the farm with Grebe, Elizabeth and Ivan. They had a wonderful full English breakfast outside on the patio. She was delighted when Elizabeth brought out a photo album filled with pictures of Anwylyd at various times of the year. The gardens were everything she had been told and the landscaping was magnificent. Although most of it had grown over in the past few years, the layout remained and Grebe offered to help her return it to its previous majesty.

As she was glancing through the album her heart skipped a beat. There was a photo of her aunt standing with another woman and a young man. The man looked so very familiar to her but she couldn't exactly place him. Was it the same man in the gilded frame in her bedroom? She asked if she could take the photo with her and bring it back when she returned from her trip. Of course Elizabeth obliged, saying that the photos actually should belong to Kayla, since they were of her family. Kayla thanked her profusely and slipped the photo into her purse.

Just before noon she and Grebe climbed into her rental car which she would return at the train station. Grebe would then walk over to the gym where Ivan would pick him up later that evening. The ride to Cardiff was quiet, but the silence was sweet. They were both at a place they hadn't been in a very long time. The contentment of feeling secure overwhelmed Kayla. She knew she was where she was meant to be.

Grebe carried her bag to the train and kissed her gently before releasing her through the turnstile. He watched until the train pulled out of the station and then stood on the platform a few minutes more. She would not be back in his arms soon enough. But he had to shake it off so he could be completely focused at the gym. No more sucker punches when he was daydreaming!

CHAPTER **TWENTY-FIVE**

Erika was standing in her driveway when Kayla arrived, waiting with open arms for her best friend and hopefully, lots of juicy gossip from Wales. The two friends embraced, laughing and crying at the same time, full of fear, joy and anticipation resulting from the choices that they had made. There was so much to ask and so much to tell.

"I can't believe you only brought that one small bag with you, Kay!"

"I don't plan on being here long. I have everything I need at the house which I will dispose of before getting back on a plane. I'm sure I'll have bags to check for the trip back. But we will probably go ahead and ship most of it so we don't have so much to carry."

"It's really hard trying to put thirty years of your life in boxes to ship across the ocean. I never realized how many clothes I have of the before and after dieting sizes. I guess it's time for a major purge."

"Let's go and get some brunch first, I'm starving. Then I'll tell you everything that is happening."

"It's a deal!"

They stopped at the local Denny's restaurant to get a bite to eat. When they were nearly finished, Kayla pulled the photograph out of her purse that she had borrowed from Elizabeth.

"Does this man look familiar, Erika? I mean, from some of the old photographs we looked at when we were going through mom's things."

Erika shook her head. "Where did you get that? I can't be sure, but I do think so. His facial features are very familiar, I think. We'll have to pull out your mom's boxes to check, of course."

"I just can't shake the feeling that I know him. It's weird, isn't it?"

"Yes, very weird. Now let's get to my place and pick up your crazy dog who is dying to see you and then I expect you to spill, girl. I want to know everything!"

They stopped at Erika's apartment, where Kayla noticed her friend had been hard at work packing and cleaning up the place. Spinner was so delighted to see his mistress that he didn't stop wagging all the way back to Kayla's place. When they went into the house Kayla realized that this wasn't her house at all. It was her parents', particularly reminiscent of her mother. Nothing here showed who she was or who she wanted to be. Although it had always been her house, it had never really been her home. Her anticipation that she would feel sad to leave was gone. She knew where she belonged. She belonged at Anwylyd.

The first day went quickly as they began to sort through everything in the house. They ordered a pizza for dinner and rented a movie on Pay Per View. Kayla told Erika everything about what had happened between herself and Grebe, meeting Elizabeth and going to the house several times. Erika listened intently and finally asked how Ivan was doing. It seemed funny how they had both met lovely men who they felt belonged in their lives. Neither had any regrets about their decision to move to Europe.

    The girls spent the next week and a half working with three mind sets, things to donate, things to sell and things to ship. Kayla had never imagined how much a person could accumulate when living in the same house for over thirty years. The things that she had amassed were mindboggling. Erika hadn't had the same stability and therefore didn't have nearly the amount of items to deal with.

    With the help of Grebe, Ivan learned to use Skype to talk to Erika on the computer. He was a quick study and it made the separation a little bit easier. But seeing him made her want to get to Wales even faster. Kayla promised Grebe that she would be back in time for the fight, even though she doubted she could attend. She just didn't have it in her to watch the man she loved being pummeled by someone who couldn't care less about him. He told her he understood but did want her to come home to when the fight was over.

    By the following Thursday all the packing was completed, most of the boxes were being shipped to Wales, she had a buyer for the car, and the contract for the house was signed so that the realtor could take over. Kayla took Spinner to the veterinarian to have his travel papers completed and a pet passport established. Everything was falling into place. They would spend the evening making their travel arrangements and booking their flight so that on Monday they could return to Wales forever.

Erika emerged from the master bedroom with four boxes balanced precariously on her forearms. Kayla cleared a spot on the dining room table for them and Erika slid them down onto the flat surface.

    "I think these are the boxes that had most of the photos and things from Aunt Rebecca."

"Yes, now let's see if we can find this fellow," Kayla said, placing the photo she had brought from Elizabeth's house in the middle of the pile.

They each took two of the boxes and started sorting photographs, making separate piles for each family member, and placing any cards or letters in a pile by themselves. Just as Kayla was opening the second box in her care, Erika jumped up out of her chair.

"Holy crap, Kayla! You are not going to believe this!"

"What? What is it?"

"The man in the picture with Aunt Rebecca is your grandfather, Ian! Look, here is a picture of your grandparents at a family party. Now look at the man in the photo with Rebecca. It's the same man! You can't mistake the scars on the side of his neck."

"Now wait a minute! That's not possible! My grandmother met her husband when she was working in Cleveland. I'm sure the photo of Aunt Rebecca was taken at Anwylyd. How could that be?"

"Read the back of the photo, Kayla. It says "Rebecca MacGowan and Ian Williams on holiday at Anwylyd, Summer 1940. It is him, I swear it! When did your grandparents get married?"

"1942, I think. Dig some more in the boxes and see what else we can find! This is so weird! How can they be connected?"

They spend the next three hours looking at photos, reading letters and verifying postmarks. They found Marguerite and Ian Williams' wedding photos but Aunt Becca was nowhere to be found. Why wouldn't she be at her own sister's wedding? And it was strange to see that the number of letters from Aunt Becca dwindled in the years following her grandparents' wedding. Yet there was a large number of letters from a woman named Thelma Williams, who was evidently Ian's mother and Kayla's great-grandmother, in which she often mentioned Becca and the work she was doing in London. Just how did all this happen? And how did Kayla figure into the picture? It was something that was going to require a lot of research when she returned to Wales. She carefully packed those boxes and placed them in one of her carry-on bags so that they would be easily accessible.

Kayla wanted to have a farewell party for herself and Erika so she set about calling all their mutual friends to come over to the house on Saturday night. They spent the day preparing tons of food and drink. It would be an intimate get together of approximately ten friends and co-workers. It seemed strange that she would never see most of them again. It made her realize that she really didn't know a lot of people all that well nor did she care to. Her heart was across the big pond and that was where it would stay.

The guests streamed in starting at seven, some bearing small going away gifts for each of the girls. Several thought they had gone insane thinking about leaving the US for Wales and tiptoed around them at times. But Kayla and Erika were full of life, and so very happy about the decision they had made. They actually felt sorry for those who would never get out of the godforsaken valley that was heading for a complete depression.

Kayla was relieved that Ron Marshall had not crashed the party, especially since one of the neighbors had told her that every few days while she was gone, a man in a red Chevette had stopped at her house, knocked on the door, then walked around it. The neighbor told her it was a good idea to have someone keep an eye on her property. She didn't dare tell them that she had not done that. Was Ron stalking her? It was a scary feeling that sent chills down her spine. The sooner she could get out of Ohio the better. And she was sure that someone from work had spilled the beans about the party. She pushed that to the back of her mind so that she could enjoy the comradarie with her co-workers. All in all in was a pleasant evening with a lot of reminiscing and storytelling going on. By eleven o'clock the last straggler had left and she could turn their attention to cleaning up and getting some rest.

Both she and Erika headed to bed around midnight and Kayla drifted off into a deep sleep with Spinner at her side. Her dreams were filled with Grebe and everything that had happened between them. Suddenly, Spinner leapt out of bed and began growling with a vengeance. He was jumping up at one of Kayla's bedroom windows, deep guttural noises emitting from his throat. His hackles were standing on end as Kayla pulled back the covers and touched the lamp on her bedside stand. The hullaboo stopped as quickly as it started, with Kayla sitting up on the side of the bed. It was three a.m. 'Stupid deer', she thought as she crawled back into bed. 'Now where was I in my dream?'

Sleeping in was not usually on Kayla's agenda, but Spinner's wakeup call in the middle of the night had worked on her. When she opened her eyes and checked the clock it was nearly nine in the morning! That might be Erika's normal, but it was way past her normal. She climbed out of bed, grabbed her robe and went out to the kitchen. Much to her surprise the coffee was made and Erika was seated at the table with the laptop in front of her. It took Kayla a minute to realize that Erika was on Skype with Ivan. Thank goodness she hadn't stepped in front of the computer! She looked like the wrath of the Hespers! But she did shout a good morning to her friend's lover and he responded in kind.

Kayla then went to the back door and let Spinner out in the yard. He immediately went around the corner and was sniffing at the outside of the fence. Kayla walked over to see if there was some type of dead vermin waiting for Spinner to roll in and bring the fragrance indoors to prep the house for viewing. She surely didn't want that to happen! But she stopped in her tracks when she saw what he was really after. There was a bouquet of red roses laying on the ground below her bedroom window surrounded by large boot prints in the mud. She decided not to tell Erika about this. There was no reason to upset her. They were flying to Wales in the morning, leaving all this behind them.

Brunch at their favorite mom and pop restaurant sounded good, as it would probably be the last time they enjoyed the place, so the girls got dressed and headed into town. They found their favorite booth and ordered their usual breakfast special; two eggs over easy, hash browns with cheese, bacon and wheat toast. They both knew that if they wanted a breakfast without baked beans after the move to Wales, they would have to make it themselves!

The conversation was filled with excitement when they realized that tomorrow they were going to change their lives forever. The dismal valley would be behind them and they were in control of what lay ahead. Erika excused herself to go to the rest room as Kayla pondered the rest of the day. The hairs stood up on the back of her neck seconds before she felt his hand on her shoulder.

"Good morning, Kayla. How are you doing?"

"I'm doing fine, Ron, fine. And how are you?"

He slid into the booth across from her and cleared his throat. "I was hoping to see you last night."

"Oh, why is that?"

"You had a party with your friends and I thought I was one of your friends. But evidently I'm not. And you haven't been at work for almost a month. I've been keeping an eye on your house. I thought maybe something had happened to you."

"You knew that I was going to Europe, Ron. Don't be coy about that. I didn't think you would be that interested in my comings and goings."

"Oh, I'm very interested in your comings and goings. I like to know that my friends are doing okay."

"We aren't exactly good friends, Ron. We are co-workers, that's all. And now I no longer work at the hospital so we aren't really that either. I'm not sure where you are going with this."

"I've just been worried about you. That's all. Running off to a foreign country isn't really like you. You are always dependable and steady, not doing crazy things."

"I had to go settle a family matter, it wasn't a 'crazy thing'. It actually is none of your business. It's a private matter."

"Maybe I want to make it my business."

"Oh no you don't, Ronald Marshall," Erika's voice boomed from a few booths away. "This is a private breakfast and you weren't invited. So be off with yourself, now, or I'll have to call the local constabulary."

"C'mon Erika. Give me a break. I'm just having a conversation with my friend, Kayla, here. I was just about to ask her where you are moving to. I saw you packing off a lot of boxes the past few days."

Kayla was shocked to think he had been watching Erika. It was just too creepy to even consider. But Erika handled it in her tough bitch style.

"Oh, are you looking for an apartment? Mine's available. I'm not living in that shit box any longer. I'm moving up in the world."

"Finally found a man who can put up with you more than one night, huh? That's a surprise. Or maybe it's a woman!"

"You'll never know. Now why don't you just go feed the chipmunks under the hood of your little red Chevette and head on home?"

"I know when I'm not wanted so I won't prolong the torture. See you soon, Kayla, and I hope you liked the flowers." With that he turned and strode out the door.

Erika threw Kayla a grimacing look. "What the hell is he talking about, flowers?"

Kayla took a deep breath and explained to Erika about the noise last night, Spinner growling and what she found under her bedroom window. "I'm sure he's perfectly harmless, Erika. A peeping Tom maybe, but perfectly harmless."

"Jesus, Kayla, why didn't you wake me up? Why didn't you call the cops? We are not staying there tonight. It's a good thing he doesn't know we are leaving tomorrow. He might do something desperate like kidnap you or something. I'm calling my friend, Jim, who is a deputy sheriff and have him keep an eye on your place. And we are packing up, taking the limo to the airport and spending the night in Pittsburgh. And I won't take no for an answer. OK?"

"Okay, okay, Erika. I agree with you. It's not worth taking any chances when we are so close to getting out of here."

Erika was on the phone to her friend Jim immediately and brought him up to speed on the day's events. "Thanks, thanks so much, Jim. Just text me if anything happens. You're the best."

Kayla gave a huge tip to the waitress and hugged the owners, promising to come back as soon as she could, knowing that she never would. A tear formed in the corner of her eye but she repressed it, well aware that she would never regret leaving.

They hurried home to get their belongings in order. Erika called and made a hotel reservation near the airport at a pet-friendly hotel while Kayla made the arrangements with the airport limousine service. They would be picked up at six o'clock to be whisked away to Pittsburgh. Kayla made a list of people to call in the morning before take-off and then when she arrived in Wales. The whole thing was so surreal, but it was so exciting. Soon they would be back in the arms of the men they loved.

All afternoon Kayla noticed that a patrol car came past the house about every hour or so which gave her a feeling of security. Although she truly felt that Ron was harmless, she still liked the idea of someone keeping an eye on the place. You never knew what the combination of crazy and creepy might do. Her mind was taken off that eerie subject when the computer began beeping indicating that a call was coming in. Erika raced to the machine but was sorely disappointed when the face she saw on Skype was that of Grebe, not Ivan. "It's for you, Kayla, dammit."

Kayla was thrilled to see Grebe and was also touched that he had taken the time to make the call. Of course, he was at Ivan's house since there was still no internet access at Anwylyd. They spoke for a while, never indicating just what the nature of their relationship was, perhaps because Elizabeth and Ivan were in hearing distance. Fifteen minutes later Ivan appeared on the screen asking for Erika. Kayla smiled at him with a Cheshire Cat grin and moved away so that Erika could be center stage. She went on about the business of making sure everything was ready to go, including Spinner's crate and travel documents. She taped his papers to the top of his crate, attached the food and water dishes, and then slipped her passport into her purse. By the time she had accomplished all of that, Erika was turning off the computer and putting it into her briefcase.

"We can't get back to Wales too soon, Kayla. I think I'm in love."

The limousine pulled up outside of the house as Kayla was checking her watch. Exactly six o'clock, right on time. The driver came up to the door and assisted them with their baggage, putting the large pieces in the trunk while they held onto the crate and their carry-ons. Spinner was happily bouncing about until Kayla put his leash on, ushered him into the back seat and then joined him. Erika climbed in and closed the door, just as the realtor finished pounding the 'For Sale' sign into the front lawn.

The night went quickly and they hurried to go through security and down to their gate. Spinner had been dropped off at the cargo desk but he was so happy-go-lucky that Kayla didn't have much to worry about. He had befriended all the airline staff and she was sure that they would make him comfortable. They grabbed a latte' and salad to eat at the gate while waiting for boarding. Who knew what time they would get their meal on their overnight flight to London? And what it might be. Airline food was pretty lousy unless you are in first class, they supposed.

CHAPTER **TWENTY-SIX**

Both Kayla and Erika slept most of the flight, visions of their new lives dancing in their heads. Although there was some trepidation, neither was afraid of what was to be, but excited to be moving forward. By the time the pilot announced that they would be landing within thirty minutes, the girls were wide awake and ready to go.

Kayla rushed to the baggage claim area to check on Spinner leaving Erika to collect their things. She heard him barking before she could get to the desk which made her feel good. He had made the flight with no problems. The clerk allowed her to take him out for a walk to relieve himself before she had to put him back into the crate. He would be shipped on the train to Cardiff where he would be put in kennel for the duration of his quarantine. Thank goodness he was such a happy fellow. This quarantine would be tougher on Kayla than it would on him.

Kayla rejoined Erika at the baggage claim and helped her get everything loaded up on the cart. There was no line at the taxi stand so they were quickly on their way to Victoria Station. Normally they would have taken the tube, but with all the luggage they had with them, it would have been nearly impossible. Springing for the taxi was the only way to do it.

As they stepped up onto the train Kayla again heard the familiar bark of Spinner somewhere towards the rear of the baggage car. She smiled, knowing her friend had made it to the train on time.

Ivan and Grebe were waiting at the platform when the London train rolled into Cardiff. They stood back to let the passengers off and waited until Erika appeared in the doorway. After giving her a huge bear hug, Ivan boarded the train to help with their bags.

"Good lord, lass, what do you have in here? Everything but the kitchen sink? And how many bags do the two of you have? You'd think you were moving here or something! Oh, you are moving here!" His deep laughter was soothing to Erika's ears.

Grebe had stood back while his uncle made over Erika, knowing it was really now or never when it came to his relationship with Kayla. He lifted her off the step with ease and kissed her longingly for what seemed an eternity.

"Here now, boy, what are you doing there? You don't kiss your employer as if she were your lover, you know."

Grebe smiled at his uncle as he hopped up onto the train. "I know," he answered, shooting an intimate glance at Kayla. Ivan looked at her quizzically, but she just shrugged her shoulders. She didn't want to reveal too much about their relationship until he was ready. Although with the kiss he just gave her, she thought he might just be ready. They rushed through the pouring rain to the warmth and security of Ivan's truck, which was just yards away from the station entrance. The men secured the luggage while Kayla and Erika climbed in. It was going to be a tight fit so Kayla waited for Grebe and slid up on his lap, much to Ivan's chagrin.

"Hold on tight, lasses, it's going to be a rough ride!"

They were are Anwylyd within an hour and the rain had begun to subside. The girls grabbed a few of the smaller pieces of luggage while the men carted the big bags. When Kayla stepped into the entryway of the manor house, she let out a huge sigh of relief. She was home. Even though the entire hallway was full of boxes that they had shipped, it still looked like heaven to her. Erika shook off her cloak, hanging it on the coat rack by the door. She motioned for Kayla to join her in the kitchen and Kayla complied. They put the tea pot on and settled down at the kitchen island.

"Holy crap, Kayla! Didn't Grebe tell Ivan about the two of you?"

"No, I don't think he did, Erika. I don't think he was ready. But obviously he is ready now, don't you think?"

"Um, yea. The way he nearly sucked your lungs out of your throat when you got off the train made it pretty clear."

"I just hope it doesn't cause him any issues with family. It just, happened, and I don't regret it."

"Doesn't look like he has any regrets, either!"

Ivan came into the kitchen first with an odd look on his face. He sidled up to Erika and put his arm around her waist, then turned his attention to Kayla. Suddenly a huge grin began forming in the corners of his mouth.

"So you and my nephew have grown a bit fond of each other have you, Miss Kayla?"

"As a matter of fact we have, yes, Ivan. Grebe and I have a lot in common and we are both adults who have chosen to explore our relationship a bit more. And what about you and Erika there? It certainly appears that you two have grown very fond of each other."

"Aye, 'tis true. I haven't had an interest in a woman for many years, but Erika is very special. We are, like you said, exploring our relationship. I like that way of putting it."

Grebe joined them in the kitchen and immediately went to Kayla's side.

"So the cat's out of the bag, so to speak. It certainly wasn't my intention to get involved with your employer, Ivan, but it couldn't be helped. She had me the first time she said the smell of the barn was soothing to her. Although I later found out that she has a penchant for killing plants. I'll have to give her some lessons in that department."

"Your mother is expecting us all for dinner so we need to get a move on. She's anxious to talk to Miss Kayla a bit more about the history of Anwylyd. It's odd. Although our father worked here, I had no idea she had such an interest in the place."

Ivan grabbed Erika's coat off its post and helped her slip it on. Kayla and Grebe were close behind as they dodged raindrops en route to the truck. Once inside, Ivan fired up the engine
and turned toward the farm. They arrived shortly and tumbled out of the vehicle and into the house.

Elizabeth met them at the door, taking Kayla by the hand and dragging her into the kitchen, which smelled of beef roast, gravy and biscuits.

"I found so many old pictures of Anwylyd while you were gone. I can't wait to show them to you! And several of Rebecca and her friends as well. I even have one color photo from sometime in the late 60's of the gardens.

My father tended them, you know. So we as a family are quite proud of them. I'll show you after dinner!"

Kayla smiled, happy that Elizabeth was cherishing time with her. But would she feel the same way when she discovered Kayla's relationship with Grebe? It might not be as civil once the truth were told. She asked Elizabeth if she could help out and was put to the task of setting the table. Once the place settings were finished, Kayla went to the living room to join Erika and the men.

"She's put you to work already, hasn't she Miss Kayla? She's not used to having any females around since her daughters married and moved away."

"It's nothing Ivan, and I don't mind. I genuinely like Elizabeth and want her to at least like me a little bit. But I am trying to figure out how to introduce Erika to her. She is fluttering around in that kitchen like a mad butterfly."

"Not to worry. I'll introduce Miss Erika to her since she is essentially my guest. My sister likes to cook for the masses so one more is no bother."

"She told me she's found more photos of Anwylyd and Aunt Becca. I'll be very anxious to see them. I have been doing some research myself and there is some connection between Aunt Becca and my grandfather, Ian Williams. I found several photos of him which convinced me that he is the man in the photo Elizabeth gave me."

"Of that I am sure. There is a connection of some sort."

Before Ivan could say anything else Elizabeth came into the room to summon them to dinner. She stopped for a moment, looking at Erika and then back to Kayla. Ivan put his arm around his baby sister.

"Elizabeth Hascall, this is Erika Livingston, and she will be my guest for dinner this evening."

Elizabeth turned to Erika. "So very nice to finally meet you."

"And it is nice to finally meet you as well. Kayla has high praises for your cooking and gardening skills."

"Really? That's lovely! Come now, don't want the food getting cold!"

Dinner conversation was light and the food was delicious. Of course, Kayla expected nothing else as Elizabeth was a wonderful hostess.

"You'll have to teach me how to cook like this, Elizabeth, or else become the head of dining at Anwylyd when I finish converting it to a B&B! We would have the best food in all of Wales under your supervision!"

"You flatter me too much, Kayla, dear. But I do enjoy cooking and the pleasure it brings to people. My mum was so very good at it and I'm glad I paid attention to her in the kitchen anyway."

"Here, let me help you clean up," Erika said, rising from her chair. It struck her that she and Elizabeth were not that far apart in age. It was a very strange feeling, but she knew it would not prevent her from becoming more involved with Ivan. "It's the least I can do being an unexpected guest."

Elizabeth smiled and nodded while Kayla and Erika began clearing the table. The dishes were done and the kitchen cleaned up in record time. They soon joined the gentleman on the front porch, Kayla trying to not get too close to Grebe, at least not yet.

Ivan went into the house, quickly returning with a bottle of wine and five glasses. "I think it's time for a toast. It has been too long since we have had one at this house." He popped the cork and poured the honey colored liquid into the glasses.

"So what are we celebrating my dear brother, may I ask?"

Ivan moved very close to Erika, handing her a glass then placing his arm around her waist, which caught her by surprise.

"First we have to raise our glass to Miss Kayla, who has taken on the monumental task of restoring her Aunt's manor to its previous grandeur and keeping those money-grubbing bastards

from London out of our back yard." He took a long sip of the wine, encouraging the others to join him.

"And secondly?" Elizabeth asked.

Ivan turned towards Erika and went down on one knee. The terror in her face was unmistakable as he reached into his breast pocket.

"I'm a simple man of simple means, but I have met the woman of my dreams and I am asking her in front of all of you if she will be my wife." He took a ring out of the box and slipped it onto Erika's finger. "Erika, you make me want to be a better man. You give me a reason to wake up smiling every morning. And I want to wake up next to you for the rest of my life if you'll have me. Will you marry me, Erika Livingston?"

Kayla was surprised that there was no hesitation from her friend. She had never seen Erika like this.

"Yes, yes, I will marry you, Ivan! A thousand times yes!!"

The only silent shock in the room was from Elizabeth, who looked at her brother in total surprise. But she managed to find her voice.

"Isn't this a bit rushed, brother? You have known the woman how long? Two months?"

"Aye, who cares about time, Elizabeth? I'm not getting any younger, you know. There are some things that you know are right and this is one of those things. From the moment I laid eyes on her, I knew she was the one for me. Although I wasn't sure she would want such an old bull."

His eyes were shimmering in a way that Kayla could only describe as sheer delight. She knew deep in her heart that Ivan would treat Erika like a queen, and she even had a brief twinge of jealousy that her friend had found her true love.

Grebe raised his glass. "A toast to the happy couple! Now drink up everyone, drink!"

Everyone joined in the toast and Grebe refilled their glasses. The room filled with sheer joy and laughter as the reality of what had happened began to set in. Even Elizabeth found herself hugging Erika warmly and welcoming her into the family.

"Now you girls have a lot of planning to do because I want Erika to have the wedding she has always dreamed of. Spare no expense, well, maybe some expenses, but still, I want to make it a day we will remember for the rest of our lives!" Ivan patted Erika playfully on the rump. "I do love you, lass. You make me feel like a young man again."

Erika kissed him ever so gently on the lips. "And you make me feel loved in a way I never imagined, Ivan. Although even I think it's a little bit crazy, it just seems right. And Kayla, I want to be married at Anwylyd, your first formal affair. Holy cow, we have a lot of planning to do!"

"Of course you will be married at Anwylyd! There is nowhere else! And you know I love weddings, Erika!"

After a few more minutes of chatting Kayla stated that she needed to go down to Cardiff to see Spinner.

"I need to go down to the gym to pick up some things, Kayla, so why don't we go together. Then I can help you get some of your things unpacked at the manor house."

Kayla looked at Erika and then to Ivan. "Now you two don't get too crazy tonight, will you? Should I wait up for you, Erika?"

"I don't think that will be necessary Kayla. I have a key, so don't worry about me."

"I think for the first time in our friendship I finally don't have to worry about you. I think you will be in good hands from now on!"

She thanked Elizabeth for the lovely dinner before joining Grebe outside in the car. She slid in close to him and let out a deep sigh. The separation had been just the thing she needed to appreciate him. She promised herself she would never leave him again.

The conversation was, of course, about Ivan's marriage proposal and the upcoming nuptials. The ride went quickly because of it. They soon pulled into the parking lot of the Welsh Boxing Association and went inside. Kayla had never been inside a boxing gym in her life and was surprised by the neatness of it all. Although the room smelled of sweat, it was not an unpleasant smell, but a powerful aphrodisiac. She felt a sudden urge to pull Grebe into her arms, but thought better of it. This wasn't the place or time. She stood with her hands clasped in front of her as he went about gathering his things, stopping frequently to chat with one man or another. Kayla took the time to check out the decorated walls of the facility. She couldn't help but smile when she saw Grebe in his boxing attire, silky shorts and large brown gloves. She rubbed her hand across the plaque at the bottom of the photo, 'WABA Champion 2011-2012'.

Kayla glanced around and saw the mountainous figure of Toby in one of the rings across the gym. She walked over to see if his wife was with him. When she saw Sandra they hugged like old friends. They chatted away and the next thing Kayla knew she had invited them to dinner at Anwylyd the following weekend. What was she thinking? Would Thomas come along as well? Would Grebe be upset by her being in the 'enemy camp'? He always said the only time it was 'on' was in the ring. She kissed Toby on the cheek and strode back over to Grebe, who was involved in another discussion at the moment. He turned and introduced Kayla to Jarod, his trainer, which flattered her. She had no idea that he was ready to actually confirm that he was in a relationship, especially with the bout looming.

But he made no mistake that she was with him, as he placed his hand around her waist and pulled her close to him.

When Jarod left, Grebe picked up his things and directed her towards the door. They climbed into the car and pulled out of the parking lot.

"So where were you off to, love? I missed you."

"Oh, remember when I told you I had met Toby Markham and his wife on the train? I saw them at one of the rings and went over to say hello. I hope that's alright."

"Of course it's alright. I certainly cannot tell you who you can be friends with. Besides, they are a pretty decent lot, nice folks and all."

"Um, I invited them to dinner."

"Dinner? Tonight? We just had dinner!"

"No, next weekend at Anwylyd. They are out of their comfort zone, staying in hotels and eating in restaurants. I wanted them to be able to relax and have a good home cooked meal."

"Is Thomas coming?"

"I, I don't know. It wasn't mentioned. I just told them to bring their group over. I didn't think. I'm sorry."

"Don't apologize Kayla. I know where your loyalties lie. Besides, the boxing circle is a big family. The only time we get into it is during the bout. If he comes along so be it. You are okay with me being there, aren't you?"

"What? Of course. You are my, my, what exactly are you, Grebe? I don't like the word boyfriend, because we are adults. I don't want to say lover because it is too intimate. Just what should I say?"

"Say I'm the man of your dreams and I'll do anything you want me to do. But for the sake of this dinner, let's just say I'm a dear friend. Does that work for you?"

"Yes, I suppose it does. I wouldn't be having my plumber for dinner, would I?"

"Oh god, I certainly hope so."

Kayla gave him a playful shove on the arm, the thought of it causing a pale red blush to creep up her neck. The intimacy between them was so easy, nothing strained. There were no awkward expectations. They just knew how to satisfy each other's needs. It was unlike anything she had ever known.

The visit with Spinner went well and Kayla could see that he was being well tended to by the staff. He was bouncing and playing with everyone. When they started to leave, she turned to watch him walk back to the kennel. He glanced back at her with an 'it's okay, mom, see you tomorrow' look, which made her feel more at ease leaving him there. She knew he would love the estate once he was able to get out of there.

As they were driving back to Cowbridge, Grebe's phone began to ring. He glanced at it for a moment, then picked up. The conversation was definitely one way, with Grebe only replying with short yes and no answers. At the end he said "I love you too. We'll talk about it when I get there," and hung up.

"It was my mom, Kayla. She is not sure what to do about this 'awkward', her words, situation with Uncle Ivan and Erika. She doesn't know if she should stay at the farm or get a room at a hotel or what. What do you think about it?"

"In all honesty, Grebe, I don't see why she can't come over to Anwylyd. There is plenty of room there and I am thinking that once Ivan and Erika marry, she will want to move away from the farm. The only catch is us. I don't know what you are thinking about that situation. Do you want her to know we are together? Are you worried about how it will affect her? I mean, the guest house is perfect for her, don't you think? But then she would know that you are staying in the manor house with me. What are your thoughts?"

"I can tell you that both Ivan and I would not ever see my mother left alone. There have been several attempts at matchmaking by her friends and all were dismal failures primarily because mum already found the love of her life, my father, and I don't think that she could ever love another man. She has engrossed herself in many other interests and seems quite content with those. I do think she would be thrilled to help out at Anwylyd where she spent a great deal of childhood. She has many great memories of the place since her father was the grounds steward for your Aunt Becca, Ian Williams, and his father before him, Gerard MacCarthy."

Kayla was stunned. "What? Ian Williams? That's it! That's the connection! Well, part of it anyway. Somehow my Aunt Becca met Ian Williams but when he moved to the U.S. he gave her Anwylyd for some unknown reason. It's a mystery really, that I am trying to unravel. Oh how I wish I had asked my mother and grandmother more about family. I was too busy trying to find myself and fit in with everyone else that I didn't spend enough time with them learning about who I really was. I wish I could get some of that time back so I could find out! This is going to drive me nuts!"

"I'm sure you will be able to put more pieces of the puzzle together as time goes on. Don't be too hard on yourself. When we are kids we only think of ourselves and our place in the crowd. It's not until either a tragedy occurs or we just get older that we consider what family really means. I know I was the same way. It's just that now family is much more important."

"Are you saying you want a family, Grebe? All I ever wanted was a loving husband, two children and a little house with a white picket fence. But I think I'm getting too old for those kinds of illusions."

"You are not too old at all, Kayla. But I don't think you'll have a little house with a white picket fence. I think you will have to settle for a huge house with a massive stone fence!"

"So are you saying that you want children? I know this is a weird conversation and I don't want you to feel pressured. But you brought it up."

"Aye, I want children. I want to be a good father and supportive husband. I want to prove to society that someone who has been incarcerated can be a good person. But most of all, I want to love someone unconditionally and get the same in return. Is that too much to ask?"

"No, no it isn't. Perhaps one day we will both find what we are looking for."

He reached over and took her hand, squeezing it gently. It wasn't until he turned into the driveway at Anwylyd that he released his grip. There was a chill in the air as they went inside, but it was one that wouldn't last for long.

As soon as they were inside the door Grebe pulled Kayla against him and began planting passionate kisses on her neck, the heat of his mouth dragging her into him. He backed her against the cool oak wall, his hands working their way up under her shirt to release her bra. He slid one arm down low on the small of her back as the other cupped her breast, rubbing it gently with his thumb.

Kayla found her voice and whispered 'upstairs', running her own hands down his back, letting her thumbs rub circles just below his belt loops. Grebe picked her up into his arms so easily, as if she were a feather and carried her to her bedroom, their bedroom, where the passion was so intense that Kayla felt she could be enveloped by his fire and never return. The power of his lean body was incredible against her soft skin. She could feel his muscles tense and release with each stroke, causing her to arch up to meet him. He knew how far he could go before bringing her to her peak, his rhythm increasing until they both could take no more. They fell into a heap and held each other tight. There was no one else in their private world.

After showering and getting dressed, Kayla headed into the kitchen while Grebe began opening boxes in the hallway. She put on the tea kettle then assisted him with sorting items into piles according to their location. She was amazed at all the things she had packed and sent to the house, it seemed so long ago. Many things she had even forgotten that she wished to keep. It was fortunate that nothing was broken, considering the fragility of many items, her mother's china and crystal, for one thing. It amazed her that she finally had somewhere to display all the things that her family had considered precious.

After unpacking two boxes they took a break during which Grebe called Elizabeth to see how things were going at the farm. She told them she hadn't seen Ivan and Erika and was unsure what she should do about locking up for the night. He told her he would call her back shortly and asked Kayla to text Erika to find out what her plans were.

Kayla readily obliged and shot off a text to Erika which was answered very quickly, much to her surprise. 'We're at the damned guest house, Kayla, right under your nose. Do not disturb, if you know what I mean!'

Kayla laughed out loud as did Grebe when she told him how Erika responded. He immediately called Elizabeth back and told her not to worry about Ivan. She could lock up the house for the night, his uncle surely had keys. He assured her that everything would be worked out over the next few days and if she needed anything to give him a call. He wished her good night and rejoined Kayla on the couch.

CHAPTER **TWENTY-SEVEN**

    Kayla was awakened from a beautiful dream by the sound of someone knocking on the big front door. She looked over top of Grebe's shoulder and saw that the clock was reading seven. Who the hell would be knocking at that hour? The shift of her body leaving the bed brought Grebe to his feet as well, pulling on his jeans and boots to beat her down the stairs. Kayla was hot on his heels, sliding the sleeves of her robe over her arms.
    They looked out the side window to see Erika and Ivan standing on the porch, holding tight to one another.
    Kayla swung the big door open. "Oh, it's you two!"
    "If you had your cell phone turned on you would have known that I actually forgot my key, missy. We hear you have an excellent breakfast cook on the premises and wish to be served a huge English breakfast."
    Erika turned to Grebe. "So get at it, sir. My stomach thinks my throat is cut." She plowed past him towards the kitchen with Ivan right behind her.
    By the time Kayla and Gaebe got to the kitchen the pair was seated at the kitchen island. Kayla continued to give Erika the stink eye. "Why are you up so damned early?"
    "We're farmers. We have to be up early. We've already been to the farm, slopped the hogs, fed the chickens and threw hay out to the cows!" Erika offered.
    Kayla rolled her eyes. "I don't know if I can stand happy Erika or not! Miserable Erika never rolled out of bed until noon if she didn't have to!"
    "I never had anything to roll out of bed for, Kayla. Now I do. Can you believe it?" Erika asked, staring at the

ring on her left hand. "I'm engaged to marry a farmer so I had better adapt to the lifestyle!"

"I never would have believed it if I didn't see it with my own eyes. But I have to say it looks good on you." Kayla turned to help Grebe who already had the teakettle on, bacon in the skillet and eggs beaten. She got the dishes out of the cupboard and sat them on the island buffet style. "It's every man for him or herself this morning!"

Ivan looked like the cat that ate the mouse, he was grinning so much. Kayla couldn't remember ever seeing a man look so happy. It warmed her heart to think that this man was so in love with her friend that he could see nothing or no one else. And Erika's face reflected his, a couple so in love. She hoped that others could see the same happiness when they saw her with Grebe.

"I think you ladies need to start planning a wedding, don't you? I don't want to have to wait too long to make Erika an honest woman. I'd go to the constable to marry us if she would agree, but she is having none of that. She says that she only plans on having one wedding and she wants a good one. So I'll leave it up to the two of you to make that happen."

While the ladies became engrossed in wedding chatter, Grebe finished making breakfast and brought it over to the table. He and Ivan filled their plates with little encouragement, although the girls barely came up for air to get some food.

"So that's settled then. You will get married on the side lawn, weather permitting. We'll put up a huge tents all around, then have the reception here in the house. Have you any idea how many guests we are talking? I'm hoping we can fill the B&B as well for its first weekend of business. That way we all win!"

Ivan tilted his head towards Erika. "And when are we thinking this might occur m'lady?"

"In about two months, Ivan. Probably around November 2nd."

"Two months?!?! I don't know if I can wait that long! I want to shout it from the highest heavens right now, lass!"

"Well, you can go about shouting all you want. There is no reason to keep it a secret that we are engaged. I just want to make sure Anwylyd is ready. And there is still so much to do. So you had better get your fine handy ass in gear to get things done. The sooner the projected finish of the house, the sooner the wedding will be."

"I'll get right on that, dear. And Grebe, you will have to work faster, too…after the fight that is. But your priority is making sure you are good and ready for that. Just defend your title this one last time, my boy."

"Oh, forgot to tell you Uncle that we are having the Markhams over for dinner next weekend. Do you wish to join us?"

"What? What the hell are you doing that for? Just a few days from the fight?"

"Because Kayla is friendly with Toby's wife and they were having a nice chat and she invited them to dinner, being they are out of town and all. So what could I say?"

"Do they know that she is your girlfriend, Grebe? Maybe they will suspect a bit of potion, if you know what I mean."

"No, she forgot to mention that. And she is my dear friend, not my girlfriend. We are too old for that, so she says. So they will be in for a little surprise dinner guest. Will you and Erika be joining us?"

"Hell yes, we'll be joining you. I'm not missing out on that tomfoolery!"

Erika and Kayla cleared the table and started on the dishes while the men turned their attention to unloading more of the boxes in the hallway. Grebe instructed Ivan to pile things according to their probable room and/or purpose and let Kayla mark their ultimate destination. Very soon there was a viable assembly line moving things into their places. Within a few hours all the contents of the boxes had been dealt with and the manor house was starting to look like home.

"I hate to leave such good feminine company, but Grebe and I need to get over to the farm to tend to a few things. I want you two working on the wedding plans and trying to get that date moved up a bit. I'll talk to Elizabeth about doing some of the cooking and we will choose some hearty plants to landscape the front of the house with." Ivan took Erika into his arms. "Don't fret, my love. I'll be back for you soon."

Erika giggled when he let loose of her waist. "I would expect nothing less."

When they were alone, Erika brought up several of the items she had on her mind for the wedding. They made their usual lists to cover any and all scenarios. From the food to the seating to the music, notes were being jotted down. But Kayla noticed that something important was missing.

"What about the dress, Erika? What will you wear?"

"Oh, I really have no idea, Kayla. Ivan said he didn't care if I wore a gunny sack as long as I showed up and said 'I do'. And I'm not exactly a size 2. I don't have any idea what I want to wear."

Kayla pulled out the computer and, much to Erika's delight, signed onto the internet. "Grebe hooked it up for me last week. Isn't it wonderful?"

They pulled up every wedding shop in Wales and started looking at dresses. But nothing was catching Erika's eye. "I might have to go naked."

"I don't think Ivan would mind," Kayla said with more sarcasm than was necessary. "So are you going to go ahead and shack up with him now or stay here with me?"

"Um, I haven't thought that far ahead, I guess. I mean, I think I should stay here with you so we can get everything done to get the business open. I still have a job here, don't I? Ivan says I don't have to work but I want to. I would go nuts if I didn't have some kind of gainful employment. And I'll need to get off the farm once in a while to keep my sanity."

By the time the gents had returned to the house there were lists for everything related to weddings and everything that still needed to be finished. They sat at the formal dining room table for the first time, spreading out all their sheets of paper. Ivan set about making his own priority list and had Grebe do the same. The house repairs came first, then everything else. Kayla wanted to make the weekend of the wedding the first weekend of business for the manor, so everything had to be in order. And, as a team, they vowed to see it done.

"And what about the big dinner party next weekend? Do you have some lists for that? Who is cooking? Who is sitting where? How many guests will there be? You aren't as organized as you'd like to think, Kayla. Now that we have dispersed the long term chores, we need to get down to the short-term. We want things looking fabulous now, don't we, for the fancy Irish Markhams."

"Yes, you are right, Erika. We need to get things in order for next weekend. Grebe, do you think Elizabeth would be interested in taking a job cooking for the dinner? Her food is to die for!"

"I think mum would enjoy that very much. Why don't you ask her?" He shoved his phone at Kayla after dialing the number. She peered at him over her glasses, rolling her eyes as she punched in the numbers.

Kayla took the phone into the library to speak to Elizabeth while the cacophony continued in the kitchen. When she returned she was nodding her head in approval.

"Elizabeth is delighted that I asked her to take care of the dinner. You were right, Grebe. I offered her decent pay for a day's work and she said she would be glad to have some of her own money. I told her if it worked out well I would hire her for the B&B. She immediately accepted the challenge. So, now I have work for you, sir. You have the green thumb and great ideas, so we need some landscaping done before next weekend. Are you up to the challenge?"

Grebe stood and saluted her, that oh-so-appealing grin on his face. "Yes, ma'am. Let me take a gander out front and get some ideas. And we'll want something really nice at the entrance to the property. You put together the budget and I'll put together the 'wow' factor."

"Erika, you and I will go through Aunt Becca's linens and find a proper tablecloth, placemats and napkins. We'll need to wash and iron those and polish the silverware. Not to mention making sure the china is rinsed and the glassware is spotless. Get ready everyone. We are having our trial run for accepting guests. Oh, and should I invite them to spend the night? We'll have to figure out who would be staying in a room with whom and how many. I'll get with Sandra later today to get a list. And do all of you wish to attend? The formal dining room seats twelve."

Ivan raised his hand in the air. "Now hold on, girl. You need to back up a bit. I won't give my opinion of you having the enemy in here for dinner. But, on second thought, I really am not interested in attending that bash. I can't even believe that you, Grebe, are a willing participant."

"I hold no ill against my challenger, Ivan. I think it is a good thing to extend our hand to them before I flail him into submission. And besides, it wasn't my idea, it was Kayla's, and I will stand by her. I hope you understand."

Erika put her hand around Ivan's waist. "I will stand by my man, as well. I won't be attending the dinner, Kayla, but I will help you with all the preparations. I hope you don't mind."

"Not at all Erika, as long as you can help me get this shindig ready. Then you two lovebirds can have the evening to yourselves."

"That's settled then. Enough of this chit chat, I have work to do. Grebe, when you're done working on the landscaping ideas, I'll expect you back outside with a hammer and wrench."

The week flew by quickly. By Thursday afternoon the transformation was becoming evident. The Anwylyd signs on the stone pillars at the entrance had been removed, cleaned and replaced, shining like a new copper penny. In huge stone planters at their bases were a combination of Welsh poppies, Snowdon Lilies and Spotted Rock Roses with wild leek mixed in. New perennial ryegrasses lined the driveway and the front of the house sprouted fresh plantings of butterwort, lilies and poppies. The colors brought out the stone of the house and the new paint on the porch. Two rocking chairs and a swing, also painted poppy, were very inviting with their floral patterned cushions. From the outside, things were looking very good.

Inside another mass cleaning with Murphy's Oil Soap had the woodwork shining and smelling incredible. All the glass had been cleaned in each of the china cabinets so that the contents was easily visible. The table was set with lace linens and Aunt Becca's poppy china. Red crystal glasses complimented the settings. Gold tone tableware set off the 24K rimming of the plates themselves with gold chargers underneath. All in all, it looked like the cover of "House Beautiful" magazine.

Kayla could not have been prouder of the work they had done and Grebe's amazing landscaping abilities. He had an eye for natural beauty. She watched him in the gardens, gently caressing each flower as if it would crumble should he apply too much pressure to them. He softly stepped between each row so not to disturb a single leaf. She found herself staring at his jeans, the way they clung to him as he moved, the drying mud rippling across the creases. He was as distant from Brent as a man could be, causing a ripple of her own to radiate across her body.

The next two days they would prepare four of the guest bedrooms with en suite baths, two in masculine tones and two in feminine tones. Although she had not noticed it initially, each room had a large steamer trunk at the foot of the bed that was filled with matching towels and linens. She grinned thinking of how organized Aunt Becca had been. And it really was a good exercise to prepare for opening a B&B.

On Friday the two friends drove over to the farm to discuss the menu with Elizabeth and make a shopping list. Incredibly, the older woman had already prepared some of the foods and had her own large list going. The three went into town for a 'working lunch' and to finish the shopping. Kayla offered Elizabeth a room for the night at the manor house so she wouldn't have
to travel in the morning, but she declined, stating that she still hadn't decided on her attire and would probably make that decision when she got up in the morning. The threesome had a good laugh, knowing that was often a woman's dilemma.

Saturday morning started out overcast and damp, which delighted Grebe as his plants needed a good watering before noon. He joined Kayla and Erika downstairs, watching them skittering about like ants at a picnic. He sipped his cuppa and walked through the house, admiring all the work that the women had done, as well as the craftsmanship of his uncle. This house could be the heaven he had been waiting for. And sharing it with the woman he loved only made it even more desirable. As far as he could see, the manor was perfection and sharing it with the world was a gift.

When Kayla finally sat down for a breather, he joined her on the big leather sofa, putting his arm around her shoulders. She lay her head across his chest and began giggling softly.

"What is it, Kayla?"

"I think we bit off more than we could chew."

"What are you talking about? The place looks fantastic. And besides, Toby is dull as dishwater. We won't be so bored if we are taking them on a tour of the manor."

"Do you really think they'll like it? I mean, Erika and I have broken our backs just getting it ready for a dinner party. Do you think we can handle having a multitude of guests?"

Just then the doorbell chimed and they heard Erika call out "I've got it."

They heard Erika and Elizabeth's footsteps approaching the library. Kayla sat up and tried to lift Grebe's hand from her shoulder.

"It's time she knew, Kayla. I don't think my mother is stupid and I have nothing to hide. She suspects it to be true, so now she will confirm it."

The ladies entered the library and Elizabeth hesitated a moment, then seated herself in one of the large leather chairs. She looked directly at Grebe.

"I have a lot of things that need brought in from the car, my son. Would you mind getting them and taking them into the kitchen for me, please?"

"Of course, mum. It's not from the takeaway is it?" He laughed, his eyes shining in the morning sunlight.

Grebe excused himself and headed out the door, quickly followed by Erika, leaving the two most important women in Grebe's life alone together. Elizabeth turned to Kayla.

"And what are your intentions for my son, Kayla? He has been through a lot in his life and doesn't need any failures or disappointments."

"I'm in love with him, Elizabeth. I want to spend the rest of my life making him happy."

"There is quite an age gap between you. What if he wants marriage and children?"

"That age gap is barely six years, Elizabeth. If marriage and children are what he wants, I certainly would try to oblige. All I ever wanted was to be loved by a good man, live in a little house in the country and raise a family. There was a point in my life when I thought that would never be possible. When I came to London I was overwhelmed. I have never been what you would call wealthy nor romantically involved, actually I have been ignored, especially by men. I was taken in by someone who was a bit of a charlatan, only out for his own benefit. Erika saw it and tried to warn me, but I was so enthralled by his attention, I ignored her warnings. Then I came here, to Anwylyd, and I felt something so incredible. I felt like I belonged. By some twist of fate I met Ivan and Grebe. I knew from the moment our eyes met that he was my destiny. There is no other way to describe it. I hope you can understand."

"I have been in love, Kayla, so I do understand. I physically lost my love but he is still with me in so many ways. All I ask is that you don't hurt my son. He has been through enough. He is a simple man of simple means. He doesn't know how to be rich. But I know he loves you. I see the way he looks at you, you are part of him."

"I promise you that I will never hurt him, Elizabeth. I know those are big words, but I mean them. And I thank you for all your hospitality towards myself and Erika. She and Ivan…"

"Ivan is a man who can take care of himself. It is not my place to discuss him. My only concern is for Grebe."

"I understand. I don't know what it feels like to be a mother, but my own parents were very protective of me. I respect your concern for him. And I really appreciate your expertise in the kitchen. My main menu consisted of microwavable meals. Your prowess is spectacular. I would love to discuss future employment with you in the next few weeks."

"I am delighted that you asked, Kayla. Cooking is my passion. But let's see how this evening's dinner goes before we make any kind of commitments. Come, let's see what those two are up to in the kitchen, shall we?"

The women made their way to the kitchen where Erika and Grebe were seated at the island, sipping on a cup of tea.

"No time for relaxing, my dears. We have a large dinner party tonight and I need to get control of my kitchen. So out of here unless you are helping." They all laughed and left Elizabeth to her own devices.

Kayla grabbed the camera and began snapping photos of the various rooms of the house. She was planning a brochure and webpage for Anwylyd as it got closer to the opening. She shooed Erika and Grebe out onto the front porch then started snapping photos of them in the rockers and porch swing. She took several shots of the flowers and then had Grebe drive her to the entrance so she could photograph the pillars and planters. Just as they were getting into the car Ivan's truck pulled in beside them. He stopped the engine and rolled down the window.

"And where is my love? Cooking with Elizabeth? From what she tells me she could stand a lesson or two."

"No, she is sitting on the porch swing waiting for Prince Charming to take her away."

"Then I'd better get there before he does, shouldn't I?" With that he pulled on down the driveway.

Only seven hours and counting before dinner. Kayla's anxiety was on the rise while Grebe had other things in mind. He took her by the hand and they walked across the sea of swaying grasses. They made slow, uninhibited love in the guest house, the sounds of nature swirling around them as a steady breeze prompted the wind chimes to break into song. It was just what Kayla needed, soothing her whole being into a calm, steady state. Definitely just what the doctor ordered.

After showering they joined Elizabeth at the manor house to complete the finishing touches. Kayla was overwhelmed by how delicious the house smelled. Her stomach was growling for attention. They reviewed the menu and courses as well as how a proper English dinner was served. Kayla felt a twinge of regret at asking Elizabeth to also help serve. She didn't want Elizabeth to feel that she was beneath her. But Grebe's mother was used to working in this capacity and she was not offended at all. As a matter of fact she was happy to do it.

An hour before the guests' planned arrival Kayla felt that everything was in place and they were ready to receive them. She dressed in a simple black number with black pumps. Grebe dressed in a black polo shirt and grey slacks with grey tennis shoes. Some things were not worth arguing about, Kayla thought. She finished her hair and makeup then joined him downstairs.

They were expecting five guests plus the two of them at this point, so dinner for ten had been reduced to seven. That was a nice number for socializing and showing off the house. The only thing she was unsure of was her guests' reaction to Grebe's presence. But she wasn't about to shoo him away. She wanted and needed him by her side and that was where he was going to be. Grebe put on some music and they sat in the library discussing the upcoming nuptials.

Grebe saw the SUV coming down the driveway before Kayla did and sprang to his feet. He put his hand on the door knob despite the quizzical look she gave him. When they rang the bell he slowly pulled the huge oak barrier open.

Toby, his wife, and his trainer were the only ones on the stoop. Toby arched a brow causing the worry lines in his forehead to ripple.

"You? What are you doing here, Hascall?"

"My dear friend Kayla forgot to mention that I was invited. She wandered away from me at the boxing club and the next thing I knew we were having Team Toby for dinner. I'm sure she wasn't aware that I was fighting your brother, Thomas, who, by the way, doesn't appear to be with you."

"Aye, he said he didn't want to get too fond of the Welsh before he had to smash one of their heads in. Nor did he want to eat some delicious cooking and put on ten stone before the match. Had he known it was you, he might have wanted to come just out of curiosity."

Kayla stepped in between them. "Welcome, welcome to Anwylyd! I'm so delighted that you could join us for dinner. And I have to tell you that what Grebe said is true. I had no idea it was your brother, Thomas, he is fighting. I don't really follow boxing. I just wanted to invite some friends over for dinner. I do hope you will stay."

"Of course he'll stay," Sandra chimed in. "We are thrilled to get out of the hotel and have a great home cooked meal. And your home is gorgeous, Kayla, dear! I remember you telling us on the train all the work that needed to be done. It looks like you've gotten to it and everything looks fabulous!"

"Oh, so rude of me. No need to stand in the doorway! Come in, come in! May I take your jackets? Grebe will show you to the French room for a drink. I'll be right with you."

She quickly joined them just as Grebe was pouring scotch for the gentleman. Kayla poured herself a glass of Riesling and offered one to Sandra who declined. She whispered to
Kayla "We're trying to get pregnant", then winked. Kayla nodded to let her know the secret was safe with her.

Toby and Thomas' trainer, Henrique Kochalka, was from Mexico where he had been the national champion at one time. He had trained at all the famous gyms in North America, moving to Ireland eight years ago to open his own gym. There he had met the young Markham brothers and taken them under his wing, aiding Toby in his rise to fame and eventually to his national title. It was obvious that Toby liked and respected the man by his tone when addressing him.

As was to be expected, the conversation surrounded the upcoming bouts, but mostly it involved Toby's competitor. Kayla excused herself to check on dinner and Sandra asked if she could tag along. The two women left the cacophony and went to the kitchen. Elizabeth was welcoming and gave them a sneak peak. As soon as the Yorkshire puddings were done dinner would be served. That would be approximately fifteen minutes. Kayla took her friend by the hand and began a mini-tour of the downstairs.

Elizabeth used the bell in the kitchen to summon the diners to the meal. They converged on the dining room and found their place settings. The two open chairs stood at the end of the table and Kayla asked her to join them once the food was on the table. Elizabeth declined, however, preferring to stay in her private space at the kitchen island.

The first course consisted of artisan salad and several types of bread. Elizabeth had outdone herself in the baking department. Everyone savored the delicious wheat, rye and barley selection. Dinner itself consisted of pot roast with vegetables and gravy accompanied by Yorkshire puddings. Nary a word was spoken as everyone was busy enjoying the stupendous fare.

Kayla went to the kitchen to help serve tea and bring out the selection of desserts, which included a strawberry tart, chocolate layer cake and blackberry cake with caramel icing. It was difficult to decide which she wanted, so she decided on a small sliver of each.

After dinner was over, the ladies went into the kitchen to aid with the clean-up while the men retired to the library for a brandy. Grebe offered the gentlemen cigars, knowing both he and Toby were not smokers, but Henrique gladly obliged and took a spare for later. They sipped their brandy and continued talking about boxing for a short time. Toby asked Grebe to take him to the kitchen so that he could compliment the cook.

Both Kayla and Sandra were working on the dishes while Elizabeth was wiping off counters. The huge man took Elizabeth's hand and brought it ever so gently to his lips.
"It has been my pleasure to partake of your culinary masterpieces this night. I hope to hire you away from all this to work for me. You could travel the world with us and I would make your life an adventure."

Elizabeth blushed and turned her head away from his glance.

"Thank you, kind sir, but I don't think that would be possible."

"And why not? Surely Hascall here is a slave driver and not nearly as good looking as I."

"Aye sir, that he is. But the problem is that he is my son."

Toby let out a huge roar and his laughter filled the room. "I suppose you have beaten me this time, then, Hascall. But should your mum ever grow tired of you, I will be happy to whisk her away."

Elizabeth looked at her watch and suddenly began hurrying through the rest of the clean-up.

"What is it, mum? Do you need to get home?"

"No, I want to get to the pub because Ivan is singing there tonight and I think he is going to announce his engagement. I want to be there for it."

"Old Ivan is engaged? And a singer, to boot? Who is the poor girl he has fooled into thinking he is a gentleman?"

"Kayla's friend, Erika. He is head over heels for that girl, I swear it!"

"That does it, then. Let's all go down to the pub. Sounds like a good time. Is that okay, darling Sandra?"

"Yes, yes, it does sound like a lovely time. I'm sure Ivan would love to see you, too, Henrique!"

Kayla retrieved their jackets as they headed for the door. They all piled into the SUV and pointed it toward The Red Bull.

CHAPTER **TWENTY-EIGHT**

Parking was very scarce on the street outside the pub. Henrique let everyone out in front of the door while he went searching for a spot. There was a banner outside showing Ivan's band as the evening's entertainment along with the dinner specials. The doorway was small and crowded, but with a man the size of Toby Markham it wasn't difficult to get through. The masses parted ways for the Irish national boxing champion.

Once their eyes had adjusted to the dark inside, Kayla quickly found Erika seated at a table near the front of the bar. She had texted her to save some seats and she had been able to commandeer half a dozen of them at her table. Introductions were made and the friends were all seated while Grebe took their drink orders. When Ivan returned from his trip to the loo he was shocked to see both Toby and Henrique at the table.

"Why you old war horse, Henrique! I didn't think I'd be seeing you here! And you, Toby, isn't it past your bedtime? You're in training, you know."

Henrique rose to his feet and hugged Ivan tightly. "I had to see for myself that a woman would have you, Ivan. I just can't believe it!"

Ivan moved around the table to Erika and kissed her on the cheek. "Aye, I never thought it in a million years. But she is making an honest man out of me."

He pulled up a chair and joined the group as Grebe served the drinks. When the band came back out on the stage, he rose to join them.

"Betcha never thought I could sing, either."

The band performed a fifteen minute set of a mixture of old songs and regional favorites. As the other members wandered off to find their beers, Ivan stepped up to the mike and carried it down to the table where he stood next to Erika.

"I have an announcement to make to all my friends, fans and whoever else might give a damn. I have met the woman of my dreams and, believe it or not, she said yes! So we are going to be married soon and we'd love to have you all join us. I'll leave the details to my bride. So raise your glass to my betrothed, the beautiful Erika Livingston! Slainte!"

Erika stood beside him as everyone toasted them. Ivan walked back up to the stage and joined the band for a rousing rendition of "Do You Think I'm Sexy?" Everyone was laughing hysterically, especially Erika.

Suddenly Kayla had an odd feeling come over her and the hair stood up on the back of her neck. No one else seemed to notice as she looked up towards the bar entrance. There, in the doorway she saw him. She recognized the silhouette immediately. It was Brent. He pushed past the revelers, getting dangerously close to her group of friends. It was funny how the intimacy she had once felt had now turned into loathing. As he drew closer to their table, he reached for her arm but hesitated, choosing rather to get as uncomfortably close to her as he could.

"So this is the vermin you have chosen to fraternize with? A jailbird with no possible future?"

"I shall fraternize with whomever I choose, Mr. Dankworth. It is none of your affair."

"Do you know anything about your stray dog, Kayla? Or didn't he tell you he is a murderer?"

Grebe sprang to his feet, standing just behind Kayla. She could feel the tension in his body and turned toward him. His hands were rolled into loose fists and his facial muscles were twitching as he tightened and released his jaw. She spun back around to face Brent.

"What he has told me is between the two of us. He has paid his dues and makes an honest living, which is more than I can say for you!"

"An honest living? Doing what? Placing illegal bets on boxing matches and taking falls for money? At least that's what I've been told."

Now Ivan joined them. "Then you've been told wrong, barrister, and I suggest you take your leave of this place."

Kayla felt a sharp pain shoot up her arm as Brent tightly gripped her wrist. Grebe stepped forward but Brent just stared him down.

"What are you going to do? Punch me? If you did, that would be violating your parole and I don't think you want to do that. I just have some business to discuss outside with Ms. Battaglia. We won't be a moment."

Ivan shook his head. "You'll not be taking the lady outside alone. And be assured, the boy can't hit you but I sure as hell can."

"As can I," Toby said as he towered over the entire congregation. "Let go of the lady, please. Now."

Brent lifted his gaze to meet Toby's, then released his grip, shoving Kayla aside. "You don't scare me, you big ogre. If you throw a punch it is assault with a deadly weapon. I know your fists are registered as such, Mr. Markham. I should have assumed that you boxers would stick together." He turned to Kayla. "I am warning you, Kayla, we want that property and we will find a legal way to get it. I'm sure there is some kind of illegal activity going on out there, what with your lover's drug running history."

"Give it your best shot, Brent. I have already contacted both the Solicitors Regulation Authority and the Law Society of England and Wales about your indiscretions. I believe it is a major violation of ethics to physically abuse or have sexual contact with a client in order to obtain either information or property. I suggest you leave now or I will add assault and battery to the charges. I'll make damned sure that you never practice law in England again. By the time I'm done with you I will be surprised if you can get a license to sell peanuts on the street at Piccadilly. I'll see you in court, sir."

"I'm looking forward to it, you bitch." With that, he stormed out of the bar.

It took Kayla a moment to catch her breath. She took Grebe's hand and squeezed it ever so gently.

"I'm so sorry I couldn't defend you, Kayla, but he is right. I would surely go back to prison if I struck a lawyer. He will always be able to control me."

"Oh no, he won't. He won't be a lawyer for long. When I get done with him he will be crawling at the court's feet begging for mercy, lucky to get a job selling popcorn at a tennis match! And, thank you Ivan and Toby for stepping up. I really appreciate it."

"Twas nothing, lass. I could see that he was just trying to bait Grebe into doing something stupid."

Toby shook his head. "Who the hell was that?"

Ivan glanced at the door then back at Toby. "Just some uptight arse from London. Now let's get back to the good partying, mates!'

They partied well into the night and the Markhams were glad they didn't have to go back to Cardiff to sleep. Everyone piled into the SUV and back to Anwylyd, where warm, cozy beds were awaiting them. Once her guests had settled into their rooms, Kayla laid down next to Grebe, the rhythm of his breathing lulling her to sleep.

"Bore da, good people!" Ivan's voice boomed through the house as he returned from the farm. Kayla glanced over Grebe's sleeping form to see that it was eight o'clock. The smell of bacon and toast got her attention quickly. She was starving, suddenly realizing that while she had spent the evening being the hostess with the mostess, she hadn't eaten much of Elizabeth's fabulous meal. She slid out of bed and jumped in the shower, trying not to awaken Grebe from his slumber. When she came out of the bath he was seated on the side of the bed, watching her move toward him. He pulled her close and kissed her neck, a low guttural sound coming from his throat.

"Not now, darling, we have guests. Why not get yourself ready and join us for breakfast? There will be plenty of time for your carnal desires later on today. I promise."

She pulled away from him and dressed, then ventured down the hall to the stairs. It occurred to her to try to slide down the bannister, but she thought better of it. If she was going to injure herself, better to do it when there were no visitors in the house. She bounded down the steps to find Erika, Ivan and Elizabeth in the kitchen with stacks of pancakes and bacon ready to be devoured.

Within minutes Toby, Sandra and Henrique joined them. "This looks and smells delicious! Are you sure you won't reconsider, Elizabeth? Other than my beautiful wife, no woman has been so tempting in the kitchen!"

"No, no. I appreciate the offer, sir, but I will stay with my family. They are everything to me as I'm sure yours is to you. But I am happy that you are enjoying my simple fare."

"Don't mind him, Elizabeth," Sandra said. "He would weigh four hundred pounds if you cooked for him. He loves a home cooked meal. If I don't watch him, he would sneak four or five scones before his protein shakes in the morning. This weekend is a big treat for him."

Everyone served themselves buffet style and met in the dining room for their meal. By now Grebe was up and moving around upstairs and Kayla expected to see him any minute. She sat down at the table with her guests to consume the scrumptious food. Soon they were joined by both Grebe and Elizabeth. Grebe had a few slices of bacon, some fruit and tea.

"I don't know how you can just eat that Hascall when the rest of it is so good."

"Number one, I'm in training, and number two, I can eat her cooking any time I want. She's my mother. And I guarantee you, after this Thursday, I plan to indulge in several of my favorite foods."

"I have to say that this whole thing went much smoother than I had anticipated. I know Thomas is your foe this week, but we are really just people. He respects you a lot, Hascall, and was pumped when the card added the two of you as the opening fight. Just fight clean and treat each other with respect, that's all we can ask."

"I ask only the same, Toby. But I have to tell you something. You should have seen Kayla's face when she thought I was going to be fighting you instead of Thomas. It was priceless!"

The big man roared with laughter. "You? Fighting me? You are nothing but a gnat, an insect to be squished. HAHA! That would be a sight wouldn't it?"

Henrique and Ivan were bidding one another good bye as everyone else gathered their things for the trip back to Cardiff. "Jarod Marsh is still Grebe's trainer, isn't he? I'm sure I'll see you on Thursday evening, Ivan."

"Aye, Jarod and I will be in his corner."

"Thank you all for your fine hospitality. It has been so delightful to visit. We will surely come back and stay once the B&B is up and running any time we are in this area. Why stay at a bloody hotel when we can stay in style? And Elizabeth, I do hope you will be staying on in the kitchen. I am looking forward to more of your delights!"

The friends bid each other farewell as the Markham entourage climbed into their SUV. Grebe watched as they pulled out of the driveway, joining the others in the kitchen after the car had pulled out of sight. He moved in next to Kayla and started drying the dishes as she washed them. Ivan and Erika helped put things away and the team made quick work of the mess. Elizabeth sat at the kitchen island watching them all, the men she loved and the women who loved them.

"So have you thought any more about the wedding, Erika? When is it going to be? Who will officiate? What is on the menu?"

Erika turned around and looked at Elizabeth thoughtfully. "Well, with everything else going on we haven't gotten into too many details. I'd love to have your input on things. As soon as we get done here why don't we have a real girls' sit down and make some decisions?"

"Sounds wonderful! I never get to do any 'girlie' things with these hulking men lurking about. I have a great friend who does cakes and one who makes dresses. Perhaps one of them or both could be of service to you."

"That sounds great, Elizabeth. I have been having a really difficult time finding a dress. If you can get a few of those yellow legal pads out of the drawer there, we can get started in a few minutes." She turned to Ivan. "And what are you up to today, my darling?"

"The boy and I are going to go to the gym for a few hours to make sure he is ready for this bout. I hope you ladies don't mind, but the fight takes priority right now."

"Of course we understand. We'll have a fun day working on wedding plans and a quiet evening once you get home. I love you Ivan, with all my heart."

"And I love you, lass, more than anything in this world. I will see you this evening then."

Grebe closed the cupboard and turned to Kayla, leaning in very close to her ear. "Once I get through this week, I am forever yours. I promise you that." He kissed her and joined Ivan as he headed out the door.

Kayla, Elizabeth and Erika gathered around the kitchen island with the legal pads, several well-worn copies of BRIDE magazine, swatches of material and two large recipe books. They would spend the next three hours making up and then changing Erika's mind. It was the perfect day to make plans for the future.

CHAPTER **TWENTY-NINE**

On Monday morning Kayla awoke to the sounds of men at work. The tractor was running, hammers were pounding and a table saw was singing. She had felt Grebe get out of bed earlier, but easily fell back into a quiet slumber. Being with him was all she ever wanted. The feeling of contentment that washed over her was so complete, so comforting. It was hard for her to imagine life before Grebe.

She noticed that her phone was vibrating and she grabbed it, sliding it to the 'on' position. "Hello?"

"Hey Kayla, this is Erika. You need to get yourself down here to Cowbridge Outpatient Clinic right now. They called me for an interview and are asking me about you. I told them I would have you come down. They want some instructors for in-services and they think we might have a lot of in-depth knowledge due to our experience."

"Hell, we aren't qualified to teach!"

"Not in the States, but here we can be. Come down and at least talk to them."

"Stall them for an hour, Erika. I know you can. I'll jump in the shower and be right there."

She hung up the phone and took a quick shower, then slid into her black business suit. She practically tumbled down the stairs in her haste, but managed to right herself about midway down. Grabbing her purse, she ran out onto the porch, realizing that if Erika had Ivan's vehicle, she didn't have one. How the hell was she supposed to get to the clinic? She vowed to buy a car as soon as this fight was over.

Glancing around, she noticed that the lawn man's truck was sitting off to one side of the driveway. She trotted down the driveway to where he was working and flagged him down. Grebe saw him handing her something as she ran back down the driveway. He met her at the truck door.

"What the hell are you doing, girl? Running off with the lawn man's truck?"

She explained the situation to him and he opened the door for her. "Good luck, my sweet. I'll see you when you get back." He gave her a kiss for luck and she drove off.

Kayla and Erika spent several hours in the application process, but, in the end, they both had an offer in front of them, working two to three days a week training staff. Orientation would be on Wednesday at this site and Thursday they would be filling out all their paperwork at the main branch of the hospital in Cardiff. Both were part-time jobs that covered two different shifts, and that suited them fine. They decided to stop for lunch and a glass of wine to celebrate on their way back to Adwylyd.

They stopped at what had become one of their favorite little bistros for lunch. A poster on the wall at the entrance stopped Kayla dead in her tracks. It was a picture of Grebe in his trunks along with the Welsh fighter who would be taking on Toby, hawking the fight. 'The Pride Of Wales', it said, with all the ticket information below it. She felt a lump form in her throat as the realization of it all became clear. The fight was this week. Erika grabbed her by the arm and led her away from the picture.

"Now don't go getting any ideas, girl. You knew he was a boxer before he met you. He still is a boxer. The man takes a lot of pride in his pugilistic abilities. He has been honest with you. You cannot mess this up for him. You know that, don't you?"

Kayla nodded slowly. "But what if he gets hurt? What if, if, something terrible happens?"

"Life is full of risks, Kayla. We work in a profession where we see it every day. You have to let this go. Trust him. He has been boxing for eight years now, he knows what he is doing. He loves you and wants to spend the rest of his life with you. He won't do anything stupid or make mistakes. He is focused. But one word from you and, well, you know he would do anything you asked of him. Don't be selfish."

"I know you are right Erika. He would cancel the fight if I asked him to. But I won't. You know I can't go, though. I can't do it."

"You can't go anyway because we work three to seven on Thursday. And that's perfectly fine. You told him that from the beginning that you couldn't be there and he is okay with it. I'll stay with you. Ivan will be with Grebe. It will be fine, I just know it."

Kayla took a deep breath. "Okay, I'm holding you to that. It had better be fine." She took a sip of wine and stared out the window, trying to pull herself together.

Dinner was pleasant and simple, Grilled cheese sandwiches with soup accompanied by a fine wine and beer. Elizabeth had gone back to the farm that morning after the busy weekend at Anwylyd. The discussion focused mainly on new jobs and wedding plans.

Erika sent Ivan on his way back to the farm alone, telling Kayla that they were not going to live together before the wedding. They didn't want to make Elizabeth feel uncomfortable as she was a devout Christian. Expecting them to be celibate was ridiculous, but they didn't want to be right under her nose with their passion. They agreed to be extremely discreet.

Kayla set Erika to doing the dishes while she took Grebe down to the barn to show him where she wanted to set up a chicken coop so they could have their own eggs. She also had decided that a few horses would be nice, not only for herself, but also for any guests that might want to take a ride around the estate. Erika agreed that it was a very good idea to offer horseback riding to the clients on some sound, sane animals. She would love to help pick them out when Kayla started looking.

Kayla and Grebe walked hand in hand down the path that parted the sea of ryegrass. The scent of the recently planted flowers mixed with fresh soil filled their nostrils. They returned to the house, grabbing a cool beverage before sitting together on the swing. Grebe had told Kayla that he didn't think he should participate in anything that could be physically exerting for a few days before the fight. So tonight they would just hold each other and focus on the future. Soon they would be together forever.

They could hear the blare of Erika's television from the second floor while they were sitting on the porch. Evidently she was going to make an early night of it. They chose to remain on the porch swing holding hands and making plans for the future. Grebe seemed a bit out of sorts, though, not really making eye contact with Kayla.

"So that's it, then. You are sure you no longer have any feelings towards Brent Dankworth. He is in a much better position financially than I am. He is much better educated than I am. He could give you so much more, Kayla."

"Do you hear yourself, Grebe? Were you not there at the pub? Yes, of course, I am done with Brent! He is a self-serving pompous, um, what's the word? Scumbag! Am I not here, now, with you? Did I not just promise to love you forever? What brought that on?"

"I just want to make sure that you have your eyes wide open. I want to make sure that you see the situation as it is. I love you so much, Kayla, but I don't want you to have any regrets down the road."

"I have a lot of regrets, Grebe, but loving you isn't one of them. Now I won't hear another word about this from you. Do you understand? I am yours and you are mine."

He kissed her gently on the lips and drew her closer just as the wind whipped up around them. The motion of the swing rocked Kayla into a deeply relaxing state. They sat together for nearly an hour before they headed upstairs to bed. It was going to be a busy week.

When Kayla finally stopped to catch her breath it was Tuesday evening. She needed to get a good night's sleep so she could be coherent for orientation on Wednesday morning. She had very little appetite for the shepherd's pie that was being served for dinner. Instead she went into the library and got online to read some up-to-date information on new types of CT scan equipment that was in use. She knew Erika would be doing the same sometime before tomorrow morning. When Grebe came in from helping Ivan move a load of stone, they went up to bed and held each other, making small talk to prevent their physicality from overwhelming them.

Kayla was up before sunrise, sitting on the front porch swing sipping her cup of tea. She heard the creak of the front door as Erika came out to join her, drinking coffee, of course, one of the very American habits that she, herself, had never become controlled by.

"So, are you ready for this? Do you think we'll be able to understand everything? I mean, sometimes the accent is hard to follow."

"I'm not too worried about that Erika. I think we've been here long enough to have a pretty good ear for it. And it's not like we aren't familiar with the subjects. It has been a very long time since I've had an orientation, though. We both worked in the same hospital since we graduated from high school. New things are always scary. But we are in this together, which helps. If you hadn't come over here with me I don't know what I would have done. I would be all alone."

"I have to tell you, Kayla, you have really surprised me. I never knew you had it in you to make such a huge move. I was wrong about you, my friend, and I have to admit it. You have bigger balls than those bulls we saw out in the country. My hat's off to you!"

"No one has bigger balls than you, Erika. Coming over here, marrying the first man that asks you. Aren't you even a little bit nervous about it?"

"Nervous? No, not in the least. Meeting Ivan has been the most calming thing in my life. I am no virgin, Kayla, I've had many men in my life, but I have never wanted to stay with any of them until I met him. I truly believe it was fate that brought me here, that brought us here. I can't explain it and neither can you, but your grandfather and Aunt Becca wanted you, maybe us, to be here. All the stars aligned and every other cliché you know of. But it's true. So let's get dressed and head out to work. And don't let that damned Welshman drag you back into bed!!"

Their four hours at the hospital consisted mostly of touring the facility, meeting staff and having a snack at the food court. The conglomerate consisted of five hospitals throughout Wales, serving twenty-three different clinics. They would be rotating their in-services between the twelve facilities in the southern counties as each held new staff orientations and updates. They would be based in Cardiff, keeping the staff education curriculum current, utilizing videos and hands-on techniques. It was a very good situation for all involved.

By the time they got back to the house it was just after two in the afternoon. Kayla knew that she had just missed Grebe as he was going in to the gym for a training session at three o'clock. She went into the house and changed into her casual clothes, joining Erika in the dining room.

"So, when is the wedding going to be, Erika? We need to get a timeline going."

"I'm looking at October 18th, which is the middle of the month. It should still be warm enough to be outside, but not interfere with anyone's holiday plans. What do you think of that date?"

"Well, what I think doesn't really matter much. But I think that is good reasoning. Most of the work is done here, so I'm sure that everything will be in place by then. It gives me time to start working on an ad campaign for Anwylyd and get my business licenses in order. I'll have Grebe determine what to plant so that things are looking beautiful for you."

"I'm sure everything will be stunning. I called Elizabeth's friend who makes dresses and we are meeting this coming Friday afternoon to discuss my gown. Oh, and Kayla, I do hope you will be my maid of honor. I couldn't do any of this without you. My only other option would be to elope."

"No eloping for you, girl. I'd be in your suitcase if that were the case! We will pull this off as the wedding of the century! I swear it! Okay, maybe not the wedding of the century, but the biggest wedding ever held in Cowbridge! Remember that your beloved Ivan invited everyone in the pub!!"

They shared a few laughs and memories of their days B.W. (before Wales), still grateful that things had fallen into place. Kayla made a pot of chili and cornbread for dinner and the two women spent the rest of the evening working on wedding plans.

It was after ten when Kayla heard the lorry pull into the driveway. She heard Grebe come into the house and up the steps, but he didn't appear at her door. She waited a few minutes, then heard water running in one of the other bathrooms. Stepping into the hall, she could see the light on in one of the suites down the hall. She started towards it, but thought better of it. Maybe he needed his space tonight with the fight looming tomorrow. Or maybe, just maybe, he didn't think he could stop himself from loving her tonight, which would jinx his routine. She crawled back into bed, accepting the man she loved and what he needed to do. Her faith in him was strong and she knew he would be back in her bed tomorrow night.

The sound of pots and pans banging in the kitchen shook Kayla from a recurring nightmare. It had been a very rough night without Grebe by her side. She had no recollection of the dream, only that it had occurred several times during the night. It took a moment for her to realize where she was. She surely wasn't in Kansas anymore, or Ohio, she wasn't in Ohio anymore! She slid out of bed and jumped into the shower, quickly dressing and heading downstairs.

Grebe was at the stove cooking eggs, bacon and gravy, with the smell of baking biscuits wafted across the room Ivan was at the kitchen island reading the morning paper. Kayla couldn't help but notice one of the lesser headlines "The Pugilistic Princes of Wales take on Ireland Tonight", with photos of both Grebe and Randall MacFarland, the Welsh heavyweight champion just below it. As if she needed a reminder of the fight.

She stepped up behind Grebe and put her arms around his powerful chest, kissing him lightly on the neck.

"Now, now, Miss Kayla, there will be none of that," Ivan stated, lowering the newspaper just below his nose. "The boy has to focus on the fight, not making love to some gorgeous American woman. I hope you understand."

Kayla backed away from Grebe and poured herself a cup of tea, joining Ivan at the table. "Yes, I know you are right, Ivan. I just needed to hold him for a moment."

Grebe turned with the skillet full of eggs and dumped them onto a plate, then did the same with the bacon. He pulled the pan of biscuits out of the oven and set them on the table as well.

"You don't hear me complaining about being loved, Kayla. But Ivan is right, I have to put all my energy into disliking someone enough to punch them in the face today.

I know you don't like boxing nor do you understand it, but when you have so much anger pent up inside yourself, it is one of the best ways to channel it, and it's legal. I swear to you on my father's grave that this is my last fight. I hope to become a trainer at the gym and a gentleman here at home."

"I believe you, darling. I know you have to do this. It is a commitment you made and you have proven to me time and again that you take your commitments very seriously. I will not bother you today. Besides, Erika and I are doing our orientations at Cardiff General this afternoon so we won't even have time to think about it. I'm going to see Spinner before we go to work, so I'm leaving here around one. Your bout is at six or seven? I can't remember."

"It's at seven, Kayla." Ivan said. "And we will call you as soon as it is over. If he wins we will have to deal with the press and all that goes along with it. But we will meet you ladies for dinner sometime afterward. If he loses, well, we'll have dinner sooner. I promise to look after him."

"I know you will, Ivan. I know you will."

Very shortly Erika came bounding down the steps and threw herself into Ivan's arms, planting sweet kisses on his face and neck.

"So what are my favorite men up to this morning?"

"The boy here is powering up with a high protein breakfast, then he is going to walk five miles, take a short nap and then head into Cardiff. I'll be joining him, of course, except for the five mile walk."

Erika patted Ivan's belly. "I think maybe you could use that walk, darling."

"Only if you want me to drop dead before the wedding! I promise to try to get in better shape for the nuptials, my dear. But I can think of some better ways of exercising and burning calories if you know what I mean."

Erika blushed and kissed him again. "Oh, you are quite the Casanova, aren't you?"

She grabbed a plate and fixed herself some breakfast, joining the others at the table. They spoke very little about the fight itself, just the preparation. Kayla turned the conversation to their training the day before and what was coming up today. She talked about Spinner, counting down the days until he could join them at Anwylyd.

Just as they were finishing up, Grebe took her by the hand and led her outside. They sat on the porch swing in silence for a few moments, then he stood in front of her. Lowering himself to one knee, he kissed her hand and slipped a narrow gold band with emerald stones onto her finger.

"I'm not a wealthy man, Kayla Battaglia. I don't have anything to offer you but myself. But I want you to know that I love you with all my heart and I want to spend the rest of my life proving that to you. So if you will have me, I'd like you to be my wife. I don't want to stir up everyone else right now nor take away the importance of Erika and Ivan's wedding, so I am hoping we can have a simple civil ceremony and then join in the party at their wedding. I can't wait for months to marry you, I want to do it right away after the fight. I know this may seem sudden to you, but I have thought about it for quite a while. I want to go into this fight and my retirement from boxing knowing I have something immense to look forward to. Kayla Battaglia, will you marry me?"

Kayla was overwhelmed by a rush of emotions. This wasn't exactly what she was expecting this morning. But there was no hesitation in his eyes. She knew he was speaking from the heart. And she knew that this was what she wanted more than anything in this world.

As Grebe stood up she leapt into his arms. He lifted her off the ground and spun her around as she whispered, 'yes, oh yes' into his ear. They kissed gently, softly, holding it for what seemed an eternity. He slowly lowered her to her feet and their eyes met, both knowing that this was their destiny, to be together forever.

"I know it will be difficult, but I'd rather we didn't say anything until after the big wedding. We can get married this weekend if you'd like. There is a place up north, Gretna Green where couples marry all the time. I'll get the paperwork done in Cardiff today before the fight. That is, if you are okay with it."

"I'm fine with it, Grebe. All I want is to be your wife. I don't need any pomp and circumstance. It will be hard keeping it from Erika, but I promise I will try. Like you said, I don't want to take anything from her big day and I think she would be upset if we married first in a big ceremony."

Erika opened the front door and peered out. "Is everything okay out here? I was getting worried about you."

Kayla turned towards her friend, tears of joy staining her face. "Yes, yes, everything is okay. Just saying our goodbyes for the day. You know I'm worried about the fight and all."

"I know that Kayla. Grebe, Ivan said to get ready to go, you have a big day ahead of you."

Kayla slid the ring off her finger and placed it on the gold chain around her neck before following Erika back into the kitchen. She started on the dishes as Erika cleared the table. The men grabbed their duffle bags and headed out the door for the drive to Cardiff. It was all Kayla could do to keep her secret from her best friend. She hoped that her emotions would not betray her. She set about doing busy work, dusting and rearranging furniture to keep her mind of both the fight and betrothal

After lunch the girls put on their scrubs and headed into Cardiff themselves. A short stop to visit with Spinner, then off to the hospital. They were joined by eight other new employees in the huge conference room. A parade of hospital officials and personnel officials passed through, each giving them a new form to fill out. Of course, they all hawked the facility, making sure they knew they were working for the most compassionate, most equipped and most reputable facility in all of Wales.

"Some things are no different wherever you go," quipped Erika.

At the first break, kitchen staff brought in trays of finger sandwiches, cookies and beverages for everyone to enjoy. Most of the people stepped outside for a cigarette, while others took a water closet break. Kayla turned on her phone to check for messages, but there were none. She was tempted to send Grebe a short text but thought better of it, remembering that Ivan had said any disruption to his routine could be upsetting. After fifteen minutes they returned to their seats for more drivel.

There was another hour of boring rhetoric, then they were divided into groups to visit their departments. Erika and Kayla parted ways, following their appropriate team. Everyone seemed fascinated that they were American and were asking why they would leave the land of opportunity to come to a small country like Wales. The girls tried to answer their questions but no one really seemed to understand that the grass isn't always greener in the U.S.A.

Kayla was surprised and happy to see that the CAT Scan machine was the same one she had been working with for the past four years. The hospital had just gotten it so there was a lot of staff training to be done. The group leader introduced Kayla as the new CT trainer so all of the new staff would be under her tutelage. Then they did a complete orientation and walk through of the entire hospital and met back in the original conference room, Erika's group not far behind.

Another short break and then they returned to the conference room to watch the usual videos on Universal Precautions and Safety. All in all, it had been a busy afternoon and Erika was glad to see it nearly done. They went to the staff locker room to retrieve their coats and purses before heading out to dinner.

The oncoming staff had arrived and were putting their things in lockers as Erika went outside to start the car. Kayla was stopped by her new boss to be introduced to some of the long time staff that she would be working with. Report was being given in an alcove off the locker room where Kayla was standing. She was nearly out the door when she overheard it.

"We have one coming in from the boxing match with a closed head injury. We need to get the CT scan ready as well as IV's for possible dye injection."

She stood in the doorway stunned. She could not breathe for a moment and was having difficult moving her feet. Boxing match? It was awfully early for that. Or was it? The match was to start at seven and it was just now seven twenty. Could it be over that quickly? Could it, could it be Grebe? She saw that her hands were shaking so she tried to take a few deep breaths to settle herself down. Standing back, she waited until the staff shuffled out of the alcove and followed them, desperate to get to the ER.

Erika was sitting in the car waiting when the ambulance pulled in. She kept glancing at her watch wondering what was keeping her friend. She turned the car off and ambled back towards the hospital to find out. From the corner of her eye she saw it coming, a large white truck moving much too quickly for a parking lot. She was about to give them the one finger salute when she noticed that it was Ivan's truck. She chased it down as it pulled into a slot. Before the men could exit the vehicle she was at the driver's door, winded from her run.

"What is going on, Ivan?"

"Good lord, lass, I could ask you the same thing."

"Seriously, why are you here?"

"Damned Thomas was such a plodder that he couldn't keep up with Grebe's speed. The boy hit him with a cross that buckled him to his knees on the mat. Thomas fell back and hit his bloody skull on the bottom of a ring post that wasn't covered with padding. He was out dead cold, I tell you. So they brought him in to emergency."

"Jesus, Ivan! She thinks it's Grebe! We need to get in there!"

"What are you talking about, girl? Who thinks it's Grebe?"

"We got off work and I left the report room with Kayla right behind me. I waited fifteen minutes but she never came out. She must have heard something about the injured boxer and thought it was him!"

They jumped out of the truck, hot on Erika's heels. She went to the ER desk to see which room Thomas was in. She saw Kayla standing at the end of the hall, hands to her face, a look of terror in her eyes. Erika grabbed Grebe by the hand and dragged him towards Kayla, who had turned her back for the entrance just at that moment.

"Here, Kayla, here he is!"

Kayla swung around as Grebe lifted her into his arms. She planted gentle kisses on his cheeks and lips.

"Oh my god, you're okay! You're okay! But if you're okay, then who is in there?" She motioned towards the pulled curtain of stall 3.

"It's Thomas, lass. Thomas hit his head on a post and was knocked out."

"Aye, but Grebe was given a TKO because his cross knocked the boy down and he never got back up. Within five minutes it was over. He retires as the middleweight champ!" Ian was bursting with pride.

"Can we see him?" Grebe asked.

"We're not really family, Grebe, but you could say you are his dear friend and his family is tied up. We can't all go in there."

Grebe went to the desk and spoke to the receptionist who then called a nurse out to speak to him. After a few moments, they watched him go into the stall and pull the curtain shut. Fifteen minutes later he emerged, a slight smile across his face.

"He's awake, both his eyes are puffy from a few punches, but he knew who I was and where he was. He cursed me, you know. The nurse said they didn't see anything significant on the brain scan and that he would have a full recovery. He has a pretty good size lump on the back of his head, but with that thick skull it couldn't hurt him too much. I told him we would stay with him until his family arrived."

Ivan took Erika by the hand. "Let's go get something to drink and bring something back for these two. I have a feeling we're going to be here for a while."

Kayla watched as they got on the elevator then turned to Grebe. "I was so scared. I thought you had gotten hurt badly."

"No, not me. I have something to live for now. How could I miss our date this weekend? I would never forgive myself."

They kissed deeply for a few moments, then Grebe stepped back. "I love you, lass. And as I promised, this was my last fight. I am now retiring and going to be a landscaper. That way my worst injury would be pricking myself on a thorn or slipping in the mud. Of course, the smell of manure comes along with the package. Does that suit you?"

"That suits me just fine. Just fine indeed."

The two couples waited for nearly two hours when they heard the mountainous roar of Toby coming through the ER doors.

"Where's my brother? I demand to see my brother!"

Grebe met him at the receptionist desk, just as Henrique and Sandra trailed in behind him. Toby stood over Grebe for a moment, causing Kayla to think that there might be some kind of altercation.

"I'll deal with you after I see my brother, Grebe. Don't go anywhere."

"I have no intention of leaving, Toby."

Thomas' family was taken into the room by the nurse as Grebe waited outside the curtain. A few minutes later Sandra pulled the curtain back slightly and motioned for him to enter the room. Kayla waited with baited breath, clutching Ivan's hand.

Inside the stall, Thomas was sitting up, taking sips of water. He looked from his big brother to Grebe then back again. "So Toby, did ye win the fight. Are ye still the champion?"

"Yes, Ireland is still smiling tonight. They are proud. And we left the Welsh a little something to puff their chests out as well. So both countries win. And maybe now you'll listen to me when I tell you to watch for that damned cross from Hascall! I told you how many times about it. Did you even watch the films, boy?"

They all had a laugh and Thomas turned to Grebe. "I hear I won't get another shot at you, Hascall. Is that true?"

"Yes, it's true. I'm getting too old for this game. Now you can go on and be the champion, Thomas, following in Toby's footsteps. I'd even coach you if old Henrique gives up the ghost."

Henrique nodded and shook Grebe's hand. "Good fight, boy, good fight."

Several minutes passed before Grebe emerged from the stall. He rejoined his group and sat down next to Kayla. "It's going to be alright. I promise."

Toby came out shortly and joined them. "Grebe, you fought a clean fight. I know it wasn't your fault about the head injury. The shiners and sore jaw, yes, they are your fault, but not the bump on the head. I'm sure you good folks want to get on home but I appreciate you staying with him until we arrived. I promise if we come back to Wales we'll be visiting Anwylyd and its beautiful hostess."

Everyone shook hands before heading towards the door.

"And Hascall, if you mother ever gets tired of your ugly mug, tell her my invitations stands. She can come live the good life in Ireland."

CHAPTER **THIRTY**

On Saturday morning there was a huge family breakfast at Anwylyd to celebrate Grebe's win, his retirement and new career. There was also much ado about the big wedding plans, seating arrangements and the menu. Kayla and Grebe were eager to head off on their holiday, but didn't want to seem too anxious. Erika poured fresh cups of tea and coffee and placed them on the kitchen island.

"It's such a beautiful morning, why don't we take our beverages out on the back patio. Then I can envision the layout of the tents and choose just the right spot for us to take our vows."

Everyone rose from their chairs and began to shuffle out the back door. Kayla picked up her cup to join them but was cut off by Elizabeth, causing her to take a few steps backward.

"What is it Elizabeth? Is something wrong?"

"Kayla, I know you love my son, and I am very aware of how he feels about you. But I do hope you two are taking care when you are together."

"Just what do you mean by that?"

"Anwylyd has a long history of being owned by bastards, and I certainly don't want the two of you to continue the trend."

"And just what is that supposed to mean, Elizabeth? A long history of bastards?"

"Your grandfather, Ian Williams, was a bastard, the result of a tryst between Thelma Williams and his playboy father, who himself was a bastard as was his father before him. Your grandfather, Ian, courted your Aunt Becca for quite some time, as I was told, and she lost a baby when he left to go to the U.S. There he met and married Becca's sister, your grandmother. Becca was devastated. That is why she left Anwylyd to you, you know. You are the granddaughter of Ian Williams, the man she loved."

"Whoa there, Elizabeth! Why didn't you tell me all of this before now?"

"Because I thought you would fix up the place, sell it and leave before my son got too involved. But he is all in now. He is in love with you and would do anything for you. And I have accepted all that. I genuinely think you are a good person. But I don't want him to be part of the bastard legacy that is here."

"I assure you, Elizabeth, if and when Grebe and I decide to have a child, it will be the luckiest child in the world, surrounded by family, loved and adored. And if it were born out of wedlock, so be it. Neither I, nor Grebe, would abandon our child and I know that we will eventually be married. If you wish to be a part of the baby's life, that is your choice. If your reputation is so important to you that you would need to distance yourself from us, then that is also your choice. I know your son loves you, but he loves me, too. So you and I need to come to an understanding. I am in love with your son and he is in love with me. I will show you all the respect in the world, but I expect the same in return. Anwylyd is our home and you are welcome at any time. But if you think you can take him from me if I should become pregnant you are so wrong. I think this is what Aunt Becca wanted for me. To have the family that she never had the opportunity to have. I…"

Grebe peeked his head in the door. "Are you coming, love? There is a lot of wedding talk going on out here and only the barbaric men to listen to it. And mother, Erika is spouting a menu as if it were the gospel. You might want to participate."

The women looked at each other and, out of respect for Grebe, rose from their seats. Erika hooked her arm into Grebe's as they joined the others on the porch. Elizabeth followed behind them. The conversation was joyous and upbeat, putting smiles on all their faces. It was exhilarating to be planning for the future, the future of Anwylyd.

Erika dragged the men out onto the lawn, handing them measuring tapes and having them walk off distances for each of the tents. She and Kayla took cans of colored spray paint to mark off each one, as well as the locations of the flowers, podium, and any other stationary items that would be in place. She then went over the new landscaping that Grebe would be working on. Everything had to be just perfect for her wedding day. Ivan sat back and watched all the hullabaloo, grinning from ear to ear. Whatever Erika wanted, Erika was going to have.

Once the slave driver released her charges, everyone assembled back in the kitchen for a cold beverage and a crumpet. Looking around the place, they all knew how much work and dedication it had taken to bring Anwylyd back to its former glory. They had a lot to be proud of, especially since Kayla had been approached about putting the estate on the Historic Registry of Wales.

The women tidied up the kitchen while Ivan and Grebe did the same outside.
    Less than an hour later Grebe and Kayla were stuffing their overnight bags into the trunk of Kayla's new Mini Cooper, preparing to write their own chapter.

CHAPTER **THIRTY-ONE**

    Kayla was awakened by flickering rays of sunlight shining through the slats of her window blinds. The huge golden orb was peeking over the hillside directly in front of Anwylyd. She had come out of her exhausted sleep slowly. The work that had been accomplished over the past few days had taken its toll on her. But every task had been completed, every 'i' dotted, every 't' crossed.
    She heard the shower going and opened the door to a hot steam floating just above the floor. Padding across the room in her slippers, she stood in front of the sink, only to be absconded into the shower by her handsome husband. He rubbed soap on her shoulders and down her back, gently rinsing it down into the drain. He turned her to face him and kissed her passionately on the lips, taking hold of the gold and emerald ring that dangled from the chain on her neck.
    "Will you wear this properly today, Mrs. Hascall? Or shall it remain a secret forever?"
    "Aye, Mr. Hascall. Once the wedding is said and done, I promise to slip it on my finger along with its mate and leave them there until death do us part. And I expect that you will do the same?"

"My finger is itching and something else is twitching, Mrs. Hascall. But I shall keep them under wraps until you let me know it's acceptable. It hasn't been easy hiding the fact that I'm married to the most gorgeous woman in all of Wales, you know."

"Tonight, my darling. Tonight you can spill all of the beans if you wish. I'll let you take the lead on that."

He lifted her and swung her around, sending streams of water across the room. She pried herself from his arms and grabbed a towel, throwing one to him as well. They slid into their comfy clothes and headed downstairs.

Elizabeth was already cooking when they entered the kitchen. The smells of beef, onion and baking bread filled the air. She greeted them warmly and handed them each a cuppa.

"We couldn't have ordered more perfect weather for an outdoor wedding, do you think? And there is no wind to damage the tents nor send napkins flying across the yard. Where is Erika this morning?

"I think she was showering when we came downstairs. I heard water running in that vicinity."

"Aye, and I heard more than one voice coming from in there. Either her telly is on high volume or my rotten brother sneaked into her room last night. You young people, I don't understand. Isn't anything sacred anymore? You have relations out of wedlock and think nothing of it. You're all going to hell, you know."

"Yes, mum, we are all off to hell when we die. But at least we have enjoyed our life! You should go on one of those trips you have always been talking about. Fall is a perfect time to go on holiday. Go and enjoy yourself. Your menfolk have good women to care for them now. You can take care of yourself for a change. What do you think, Kayla, my love?"

"Yes, I think you deserve a vacation Elizabeth. Where would you like to go?"

"You kids are really something! I can't just be going off by myself to some strange place. I'd be petrified."

"Then take one of your friends, mum. We'll give you a trip as your Christmas gift. Just name the place and we'll set it all up for you!"

"I'll think about it, my son, but for now we have a big job to do today. You'd better get out there and mark off the parking spaces for the wedding guests and the ones for B&B guests. We have both coming in you know!"

Grebe nodded to his mother and backed out of the kitchen, bowing to the two women. Kayla couldn't stifle her laughter and Elizabeth joined in.

"I think, Kayla, for the first time in many years he is happy. And you, my girl, are the reason. I know I have been hard on you at times, but I think he is genuinely finding himself again and for that, I thank you."

"He is easy to love, Elizabeth. And although he will carry the guilt for Marlene's death forever in his heart, it is much deeper now, not so close to the surface. He is a very good man."

Erika bounded down the steps in her jogging suit, a smile so big it could light up all of Wales. "Today's the day!! I'm marrying the love of my life! Could the world be more perfect?"

"No, no it couldn't be. I am so happy for you, my friend."

"Now you're sure you want to take on the likes of my brother Ivan for the rest of your life? He's a handful, you know!"

"Yes, Elizabeth, I have never been more certain of anything in my life. I can handle Ivan as well as he can handle me. And I'm not exactly the sweetest woman on the planet."

"To him, you are. He talks about you day and night, girl. He was smitten from the day you met, I swear to you."

"Then it's meant to be, Erika. He is your soul mate, the one you were supposed to end up with all along. Just glad I was the catalyst to put you two together."

"And I will be forever grateful to you, Kayla, for the rest of my life. I love my future. Now give me something to eat that won't affect the fitting of my wedding dress. I'm starving!"

Elizabeth sat out a tray of scones and biscuits with butter and jam while the girls fixed their tea. A nervous energy filled the room as Erika went on and on about their plans for the future. Kayla felt a satisfaction deep inside. Yes, everything was going to work out and Aunt Becca was the reason why. She was the one who set all this in motion. Somehow she knew it was how things were meant to be.

By noon everything was in place. All the tents were up, all the chairs unfolded. Flower wreaths hung on the end of each row of chairs, large baskets of flowers stood likes soldiers at either side of the altar. An antique podium was in place for the clergy at the center. Tables with small bags of rose petals and bird seed were assembled at the rear of the 'church' for blessing the couple at the end of the ceremony.

Kayla and Erika were upstairs getting all of Erika's things organized. Something old, something new, something borrowed and something blue would all have their place in her ensemble. She removed the cover from her custom gown which was hanging on the back of her door to let it breathe. Kayla was in charge of hair and makeup and had pulled Erika's hair back and up into a sweeping curve, adding bits of baby's breath throughout. Erika was instructed to stay in her robe and not pull any item of clothing over her head. It was an hour and a half until the ceremony and she promised to behave.

Kayla headed downstairs to find Ivan in the kitchen finishing off the breakfast scones, much to Elizabeth's disapproval. He was looking dapper in his suit, his generally uncontrolled mane combed back into a ponytail. His face was clean shaven with no dark shadows across his chin. And his smile was so genuine, she knew how deeply this man loved her friend. It was a wonderful feeling.

"Where is Grebe? He does know what time to be ready, doesn't he?"

"Aye, lass, the boy is ready. Perhaps he is getting to like the idea of a wedding. Maybe he'll pop the question to you soon."

Kayla blushed, reaching for the chain around her neck which bore her secret. "You are so silly, Ivan. Where is he?"

"He's out front helping your hostess greet the guests. But the way you are looking right now, I doubt he will pay attention to that once he sees you."

"I'll be out front if anyone needs me."

"And if Erika needs something should I attend to her needs?"

"No! You are not to see her until the ceremony! Elizabeth, I expect you to hold him to that!"

"I'll try, Kayla, but he is as stubborn and strong as a bull."

Kayla turned, heading for the front door. When she opened the door she was delighted to see that Catherine Adamson was handling her new career as hostess with extreme prowess. Each guest, whether for the wedding or otherwise, was handled individually with style and grace. Grebe had set up a gift table covered with white lace and he was taking the gifts as Catherine showed each guest the map of the grounds and directed them to their room or the tents for the ceremony. Catherine was in her glory, dressed in a beautiful plum gown with matching pumps. Kayla stood back and watched them work in precision for a few moments before approaching them.

"You are doing a great job, Catherine. I am impressed!"

"I can't thank you enough for this, Kayla. I am having such a wonderful time. And what you have done with Anwylyd is amazing! I am so happy for you!"

"Remember that you brought me here, first, so you are the one who started it. I do love it here. It is the perfect place for me. Do you mind if I steal your assistant away for a moment?"

"Not at all. He has been a great help, though. Send him back when you get done with him, will you?"

Kayla nodded and took Grebe by the arm, directing him to the swing on the far end of the porch. She sat close to him and pressed her cheek against his shoulder. The scent of him soothed her. He put his arm around her, stroking her hair ever so gently.

"I love you lass, more than anything in this world. Are you ready to show everyone that a bastard child won't inherit Anwylyd?"

He gently lifted the chain over her head and slid her wedding band on her finger, then removed his from his pocket and put it on as well. He placed his hand over her stomach and rubbed it ever so delicately. Kayla felt the first stirrings of the new life responding to a father's touch.

"Not yet darling, we don't want to rain on Erika's parade. After the ceremony and all the guests are settled in or gone, we will tell the family the whole truth. But not until then. Are you sure we should wear our rings publicly now?"

"No one is going to notice, Kayla. They will all be so wrapped up in their chores and the wedding that it will be the last thing that anyone sees. I am not ashamed to be your husband. You have made me the happiest I ever recall being in my entire life. I want you to know that everything is going to work out right. It was meant to be."

Kayla smiled, knowing that Grebe was right. For once in her life, everything was right in her world.

THE END

Made in the USA
Charleston, SC
02 April 2014